TRUTH
DARE
KILL

GORDON
FERRIS

CORVUS

First published in Great Britain in 2007 by Crème de la Crime

This edition first published in the UK in 2012
by Corvus, an imprint of Atlantic Books Ltd.

9 8 7 6 5 4 3 2

A CIP catalogue record for this book is available from
the British Library.

Paperback ISBN: 978-0-85789-553-0
E-book ISBN: 978-0-85789-493-9

Printed in Great Britain by CPI Group (UK) Ltd, Croydon, CR0 4YY

Corvus
An imprint of Atlantic Books Ltd
Ormond House
26-27 Boswell Street
London WC1N 3JZ

www.corvus-books.co.uk

To my mother, Jenny Ferris [1929 – 2011] for the genes;
and to Sarah for never doubting.

Thanks to:

Sometimes you get a second chance; overdue thanks to Janet, Kathryn and Helen for putting up with my early scribbles and absence. Tina Betts, my loyal agent. Lynne Patrick for my first break. Team Corvus for breathing new life into Danny McRae. And to everyone dragooned into reviewing my first words: Ray Barker, Robert Cardinaux, Helen Ferris, James and Simon Hanley, Margaret Hill, Candace Imison, Hazel Rice, Tricia Sharpe, and by no means least, Sarah.

A dead man is the best fall guy in the world.
He never talks back.

Raymond Chandler, *The Long Goodbye*

ONE

I stopped typing and listened to the sound of high heels heading my way. They clipped up each rise on the toes, then clacked across the landings, heel first: Morse code for "this could be your lucky day". But who needed my services on New Year's Eve? I hoped they wouldn't stop at any of the two lower floors. There was a long moment's hesitation on the second; I thought I'd lost them to the chain-smoking old woman who lives below. Then they came on.

I stopped pretending I was busy. The only person I was fooling was me. For the past couple of hours I'd been stabbing the keys and banging the return as if I hated the battered Imperial. I'd twice reached into my drawer and fingered the neck of the bottle like a lover. I'd twice closed the drawer without taking a swig. If I started I'd never see midnight: a prospect that had grown more tempting by the minute.

The stairwell is visible through my open door. Her hat appeared first, then she climbed round out of sight and up to the top landing. The tap-dance continued until she stood in the doorway. Her slim shadow flung itself across the lino towards my desk. She was hesitant, as though she'd never done this sort of thing before. Few had; Finders Keepers had only been going for three months.

She could see me at my desk but not clearly enough to make out the details. Her veil wouldn't help, but nor would my lamp. I keep the light low because of my face, and because I don't like being silhouetted: a habit I got into in my previous line of work. But whether I was scared of being laughed at or shot at, it meant that visitors had to get right up close before they could see my expression. Especially on a winter's night with only the dim glow from the street lights drifting in through the window.

"Hello?" she said, not sure what this creature in the shadows would do.

It said, "Come in," in as inviting a voice as it could muster. I stood up, hoping she wasn't lost and looking for directions.

She gathered herself and strode forward like an amateur modelling clothes for the first time. It took her just five strides to arrive in my pool of light. With a practised sweep she pulled the veil up and on to her hat. She might have been a model, but she was no amateur.

I wouldn't have guessed the eyes. They were grey, as though the blue had leached away. Her lips were a perfect red, retouched on the stairs – *that* was the pause. With the pale eyes came the blonde hair, that special soft gold-white that no bleaching can ever mimic without turning the hair to straw. It was pulled back so tightly from her face it must have hurt. A small blue hat was skewered to her head at the angle of an airman's forage cap. I've known women take an hour in front of a mirror to get all those effects just so.

The rest of the outfit must have cost a year's ration coupons and twice my annual income. Though twice nothing is nothing, I reminded myself. And the suit bore the same relation to an off-the-peg Utility dress as men to apes. It was likely a pre-war ensemble cut short to the knee. Quality lasts. This woman was top drawer. And what was Philip Marlowe wearing? A worn cardigan with elbow patches.

"Mr McRae?" The vowels matched the classy outfit, soft but beautifully shaped. I wanted to hear her say it again.

"Danny McRae. Can I help you?"

"I hope you can, Mr McRae. I hope you can."

"Take a pew, Miss…?" I waved grandly, as if she had a choice of seating.

"Graveney. Kate Graveney. How do you do?" She lifted a languid hand towards me. I leaned over my fourth-hand typewriter and took it. It was sheathed in white leather so fine you could have sworn it was her own skin. The handshake was short, almost perfunctory, but it left a sensation, as if I'd been stroked. I imagined her bare fingers touching my face.

She sat down, parked her bag in her lap and crossed her legs. I realised how long it had been since I'd heard the sound of real silk sliding on silk. The everyday stuff rasps, like sandpaper on wood. A faint but distinct perfume reached me. I'm no connoisseur, but I know what I like. I liked this smell of warmth and undiluted femininity. It raised an echo in me, then drifted away tantalisingly, like so many memories since I got back.

I shoved the typewriter out of the way so we had clear space between us. I made a play of ripping out the report I'd been typing: another stray husband. I removed the carbon and slid the thin sheaf into my in-tray. My only tray. I straightened my new phone. Its shiny black curves said, I'm here for you, you just have to call. It said commitment, I'm here to stay – for as long as I can pay the rent. I was the pro, busy, tidy and ready for business in my model office.

"Now, what can I do for you? It's a funny time of year and I'm just closing up. Don't you have better things to do?"

"It *is* a funny time." She smiled, and that made the time perfect. "Do you mind?" She was already reaching into the bag and pulling out a silver cigarette case. She took one out and waited. I got the message and dug out my matches. She pulled off her gloves and leaned forward with the cigarette perched between those red lips. There was a ring, but on her right hand. She drew deeply and pursed her mouth and blew the smoke out in a steady stream. It unfurled and floated out of the cone of light, to add to the tidemarks on the ceiling.

"But I need help *now*." There was a petulance; she was used to getting her way. I bet her dainty little heel came off the floor just then, ready to stamp.

"This can't wait. Not even till tomorrow. I can't rest until I know I've at least got something going. A new year's resolution, if you like." She looked down, then up again. She knew how to gain attention. She smiled and gave me a look with her grey eyes that made me realise I hadn't given up hope of a woman smiling on me again without being paid for it. And how I'd never been with a woman like her.

"Well, I've got a party to get to this evening Miss Graveney." I hadn't, but I wasn't going to look any more desperate than I had to. "So why don't you tell me why you're here." I leaned back in my chair and tried to look nonchalant, as though classy women dropped into my hovel every day of the week, including New Year's Eve.

"May I ask you something first, Mr. McRae?"

"By all means, Miss Graveney." I realised I was beginning to raise my vocabulary and soften my Glasgow accent to stay level with her precise words and BBC tones.

"Your advertisement. It said you were discreet. That you were a professional and you respected client confidentiality. Is that right?"

She must have seen my ad on the front page of *The Times*, offering unique experience and guaranteed results. Who says advertising doesn't work? But it had cost me ten of the hundred and fifty quid the Government gave us heroes for setting up a new business.

"This sort of business depends on discretion."

What I didn't say was that she was the most stylish piece of business that had come my way. The others amounted to lost dogs or lost loves. Only the dogs seemed pleased to be found. What had *she* lost?

She nodded and took another deep pull on her cigarette. "What about the police?"

So it wasn't a poodle. "Do you mean do I work with the police or that you don't want whatever you say to be heard by the police?" I knew the answer, but I wanted to see how she responded.

She chose her words with care. "I may need to involve the police. But not yet. Not till things are... clear."

I thought about Inspector Herbert Wilson who'd paid me a courtesy call a few weeks back, and how he'd love to be a fly on this wall. And how I'd love to have a fly-swat. But that's another matter.

"You have my word. Everything you say to me tonight is privileged. It goes no further."

"Good. That's good. Because what I have to tell you is... unpleasant." She stubbed out her cigarette halfway through and lit another one – herself – using a silver lighter with the power of a flame-thrower. I could see her hand tremble a little

5

this time. Her eyes stopped meeting mine. *Unpleasant* didn't sound nearly enough.

"I think I've killed a man."

TWO

I t was a bad start to a new year. Not that I could say '45 had been much of a year either. Not for me. Or maybe that's being ungrateful. They gave me a medal and said I was a hero, that I nearly died for my country. I don't know; literally I don't know. All I want is a year of my life back. Some days I wake and don't hurt too much and then it doesn't matter. Like a scratch on a record. The needle jumps and I miss a word or a beat. Then I catch up with the song, and I'm back with the melody as if nothing has happened.

Other days, bad days, when the ache wakes me, and it takes till midday and a big shot of scotch to make it go, it feels like the song will never be right, not with that missing piece, and I can't bear it to go on. They've done all they can, but I'm left with just the bass line, not knowing if the singer has paused or gone.

In the meantime I have to live. Heroes don't get paid any more than cowards. And jobs don't come any easier if your trade is subterfuge and you can only ply it on good days. I'm a copper. *Was* a copper. Now I'm a thief. I steal people's cover from them. I pull them blinking into the light and nick their happiness, those libertine days and nights that the war permitted. I hand them back to their loved ones to exact their revenge in small cuts every day until they've had their pound of wayward flesh. Which explains why I was sitting here, flustered by a pretty girl's smile, on this night of all nights.

At least I was alive. Sort of. A lot of blokes like me didn't make it. I should have been out there rejoicing with the rest of the world. The war was over, it was New Year's Eve, and though London wasn't much more than a pile of rubble, there were enough pubs still standing to make for one helluva party. And like VE Day (I was otherwise engaged for that, but I'd seen the newspaper photos of folk hanging off lamp-posts) the streets would be jammed with hugging and kissing strangers.

There was a sense out there that the world had changed for ever. For the better, of course, was the official view. And in truth, it had to be an improvement over the Blitz. But we'd lost something too: an identity, a purpose. Like a really good party that had gone on too long and we were all creeping home in the cold daylight, embarrassed at how we'd let our hair down. Days of reckoning when we had to stomach the hangover and explain the inexplicable pregnancies and challenge the evasive eyes until our infidelities were soaked from us in great confessional homecomings.

Maybe tonight of all nights, I should have gone home after all. Caught the overnight sleeper back to Glasgow, then the branch line down to Kilpatrick. Tracked down my old pals and got blind roaring drunk like we used to. Three days of parties, everyone your friend. No doors closed. Maudlin tears for the old year and Celtic fear for the new one.

I remembered the last time, just as we turned into the year when our lives jumped the rails. Me and Archie and Big Tam rolling a barrel of beer down the Cowgate. We mowed down other drunks in high good humour. And we got to Kilpatrick

Cross and set up our barrel and tapped it and toasted 1939 in with a singing, dancing bedlam of new friends. I was twenty-four. I'd wangled leave for Ne'erday by doing the Christmas roster at Turnbull Street police station in Glasgow. The youngest detective sergeant in the force. On target for inspector and then who knew?

But I couldn't go back. Not yet. Have you ever wondered what it would be like to lose every recollection of a whole year of your life? To wake up and be told you were a year older, with nothing to show for it except some startling scars and blinding headaches?

It's not an unbroken gap; occasionally a flake of memory from the missing time floats to the surface. I grab at it, straining to hold on to it and lodge it in some mental archive, like portraits in a grisly art gallery. I feel if I can get enough pictures, and in the right order, then I have a story. Doc Thompson tells me not to expect too much. There's no saying where these images are coming from. They might even be false. That scares the shit out of me. I've got a loose enough grip on reality, thank you very much.

I came back from my own particular war in pretty bad shape. I'd lost every single reference point after leaving England for France in May 1944. All I remember is a round man called Gregor with a huge moustache, and his hard-handed compatriots. And how I briefly led these faction-riven amateurs and melded them into a fighting force. Then there was a huge hole in my head until the moment when I stuttered back into life in April this year, on a bunk bed in a small town called Dachau in southern Germany.

*

"Is this one dead?"

"Cain't hardly tell. Help me lift him."

Somewhere in my head I realised the voices were American. I thought that was nice. Americans always sounded hopeful. Heaven should have slow Southern accents. But I didn't want them to disturb me. I was quite happy being dead. It was... comfortable. And being alive recently hadn't been. Not for a while. So when I felt rough hands on me and my body being hauled out of my little wooden coffin I rebelled. That is, I did the only thing that my body was capable of: I groaned.

"He's alive. Get the medics. Christ, he smells!"

What did they expect? From somewhere a shard from my broken memory surfaced and I remembered being appalled at how my bunk mates stank when I first arrived. Then the smell went away. There were other things to worry about. Like the beatings. I can't recall much about the people doing it – they all looked like wolves - but I know it was me on the receiving end. I guess the Americans hurt me when they pulled me out because I don't remember any more of that bit either. Later, the pain came back, with the light.

I tried to explain this to my mother when she came to visit me in the hospital in Hatfield, four hundred miles from home and her first time south of the border. She looked old and bewildered when she came through the door of the ward. She'd always been small, but now her best coat sat too big and too long on her tiny frame. I hadn't noticed how white her hair had got and how lined her skin was, despite the make-up. She never wore make-up. It made her look like my Aunt Jeannie, last seen in her plush-lined box, victim of the undertaker's embalming arts.

Mum was rooted to the floor, twisting the handle off her handbag. She scanned the faces on the beds looking for mine. Her scared eyes slid over me, not once but twice. The bandage round my head didn't help, but neither did the sunken cheeks and rictus grin, my feeble effort to smile at her. Then she found me and through the greetin' – no English word has quite the sense of heartfelt sobbing – she told me about my pals and how lucky I was.

Big Tam hadn't made it. He died on Gold beach with half his regiment during the landings. And Archie was missing presumed dead according to the telegram to his mum. Somewhere over Germany. His plane falling out of the sky into the cauldron they'd stirred up. I wondered how he'd felt, the air shrieking over the fuselage and the tracers coming up, diving into their self-made funeral pyres. Was it like our boyhood suicide runs, free-wheeling and screaming like banshees down the forty-five-degree slope in Burns' Park? Archie and Tam and me on bone-shakers with no brakes? Death or glory? Seems I got the glory, but it didn't feel like it. Not with a steel plate in my head.

And now I'm scared to go home to Scotland. Scared of what I'd find and who I wouldn't find. Scared of how they'll look at me now, those glad girls from my boyhood. Scared that I'll see in their eyes what my own don't want to tell me. That the head wound goes deep. That I'm *no a' there*, as they'd put it. So, I'm here in London, prowling my last haunts, looking for clues to my lost time, asking the folks round about who I was. Seeing in their eyes the wariness of the sane for the demented.

"I think I've killed a man." The words sat between us like a newly dealt card in a game of poker. Call or raise. But the blonde had said it as though she was reporting a broken nail.

I did up the bottom button of my cardigan and sauntered over to the fireplace. I tapped the dying briquettes with my toe to encourage more heat and put another one on for show.

"You *think*?" I asked with a little sarcastic edge. "Let's take this step by step, shall we? Is he dead or not?"

"Probably."

I sighed. "Let's – for the sake of making progress – assume he is. My condolences, miss. But did *you* kill him?"

She wrinkled up her nose and smiled sweetly. "Well, that's the trouble. I'm not sure. That is, I can't remember. Not exactly. We were celebrating."

Christ, that's all I needed. The amnesiac leading the amnesiac. I adjusted my desk lamp to throw stronger light across the desk and across her face. Maybe it would have an illuminating effect on what she'd been telling me. So far, it wasn't clear at all.

I saw her glance at my face and her eyes widen a fraction. I knew what she was seeing. My thick red hair, combed now on the wrong side for me, hides most of the damage, but the main scar runs like a wide ribbon from the hairline to above my left eye. It looks as though someone took a steel bar and hit me with it full on, bending it round my skull, and then didn't bother to stitch the sides back together. Which is pretty well what happened.

The other wounds around my nose and right brow would have looked dashing on a duellist from Heidelberg. They made me look like a hard man from the Billy Boys, one of Glasgow's finest razor gangs. They help if you want elbow room at a bar, but not if you're hoping for a dance at the Palais.

"You may have to give me a wee bit more information than that so I can see if there's some way I can help, Miss Graveney."

I tried to keep the vinegar out of my voice but it was hard. "Excuse me asking, but just how much had you been celebrating?" I left it dangling. Pretty young things like her would have access to the best that the black market could offer: booze or cocaine.

She looked at me strangely, as though I'd overstepped the mark or said something she wasn't prepared for.

"We might have had a glass or two of bubbly, but I most certainly wasn't drunk. Or anything else for that matter," she admonished, reading my mind. "We were visiting a friend. In Pimlico." Her eyes shifted, then came back to mine. "Actually, we'd borrowed his flat." Her tightened mouth challenged me to find any fault. I didn't change my expression.

"We had a bit of a row. Oh, if you must know, it was over a woman. I'd just found out he was married. The swine." Quiet venom. I would not like to have been on the receiving end of her bit of a row. Beneath the perfect femininity was a wildcat. Just how much, I would learn later, but the hint of danger already hung in the air alongside her perfume.

"So I had it out with him. His wife was in the sticks somewhere. He operated from his club in Jermyn Street. He was a Major working in Whitehall; hush-hush, you know. We were introduced at a party." I noticed the past tense. "Anyway things got a bit het up, you see. I'm afraid when I get mad I get a bit demonstrative. And he was trying to deny it, you see. So I was throwing things at him and he was ducking and I think his foot tripped on the carpet because next thing he's down and he's moaning and groaning. He'd hit his head on something, I suspect. And then the wall is coming in and the curtains are flying at me and I hear the bang and that's it…"

"The bang? When was this? We haven't been bombed for…

a year now, is it?" I wasn't around – one way or the other – so couldn't be sure.

"That's the crazy thing. Just crazy." She shook her head. I wondered what it would be like to hold it steady between my hands and put my mouth on those red lips. "It was a month ago. Thirtieth of November, to be exact. I remember it precisely. It was supposed to be my birthday celebration. We had a table booked at the Carlton." Her grin was rueful.

"The bomb was a left-over. Unexploded. No one saw it land. Or had forgotten about it. They think it had a delayed fuse and during the clear up that day a bulldozer started it up again. Anyway, when I came to, I was wrapped in these huge curtains. Great black velvet jobs. All lined. I thought – it's silly, I know – for a moment I thought I was dead or buried alive. You know, in a velvet-lined coffin. I was in a perfect state. Couldn't move my arms or legs. The velvet was so heavy and it had wrapped itself around me. Like a shroud." She shuddered. I didn't tell her that I knew exactly how she'd felt.

"But I could shout. A bit. And I heard people talking and walking about, and they heard me and unwrapped me and I was completely all right you know. Not a mark. Though my shoes had gone. Funny, that. We never found them. They were good shoes too. Anyway, they took me off and it wasn't till we got to hospital that I remembered Phil – that's the chap I was with. And I asked them if they'd got him too, and they said they hadn't seen any other body but they would look under the rubble."

"Did they find him?"

"That's the silly thing. I don't know. So I'm just wondering – well – if I knocked him down and then the wall fell on him and he died and was… bulldozed away." She lit another cigarette. I let the silence settle to see what else she'd come out with.

"I was fine. I kept telling them that. A bit of a shock but otherwise absolutely fine. I stayed in hospital overnight. Called Mummy to tell her what had happened – well, some of it – and not to worry. Next day she came round and whisked me off to Surrey, and that's it. I left messages at his club telling them what had happened – not everything, you understand. And one time I called and they said someone had been in to collect his things from his locker. So…" She shrugged.

"Anyway, I keep thinking I'm going to hear from Phil any day now. You know, that he'll just ring up and say sorry, old girl, got hit on the head and wandered off or something. But nothing. Last week I even went back to the flat – the one we borrowed so we could meet. But it was cleared. I mean just a big hole where the house had been."

"Did you report this?"

"Just the bare bones… sorry… to his club. And not the bit about the fight and Phil falling. It didn't seem… relevant somehow. And I couldn't very well call his wife and ask if she'd retrieved the body of her husband from the flat, could I? Even if I knew where she lived. That's why I'm here. I want you to find out what's happened to him and let me know. Do you see?" She took a deep pull on her cigarette and eased back in her chair, uncrossing and re-crossing her legs.

"I mean, I wasn't in love with him. Especially when I found out about his domestic arrangements. But I do think I ought to find out. One way or the other. Don't you?"

I wasn't sure. It all sounded too unlikely and messy. But I gave myself a mental kick in the pants; mess was my business now. And I might just get a decent bit of cash out of this. God knew, I could do with it. I had no other clients; maybe they'd all made new year resolutions to be nice to each other. Thankfully it wouldn't last. Human nature guaranteed my business would pick up before January was out. But that left me a short-term cashflow problem and some difficult choices between eating, smoking and drinking. Good job I wasn't a big eater.

"My God!" she cried as the lights went out.

This never happened to Marlowe. "Sorry. Don't move." I scrambled to my feet, dug into my desk and found the tin. I took out a couple of bob, and walked smartly out the door to the meter on the wall. I stuffed a shilling in and then another, swearing all the time under my breath. The lights came back on and I strolled back to my desk as nonchalantly as was possible in the circumstances. I sat down and steepled my hands.

"Now, where were we?" I tried to smile even though the perspiration was beading my spine. I needed this work and here I was looking like a rank amateur down on his luck.

She looked shocked, as if I'd just asked her to take her clothes off. Then amusement filled her eyes. I preferred shock.

"Do you think you can help? I can pay you in advance," she said in the caring way of the rich for the poor. Her accent was beginning to wear down my very recent infatuation with her grey eyes. Though we Scots consider ourselves amused onlookers to the English class system, it doesn't mean we can't spot when we're being talked down to. But this was no time to stand on my dignity.

"My rates are twenty pounds a week plus expenses. And – as you suggest – I prefer in advance."

She didn't flinch, even at twice my normal rates. She wrinkled her fine forehead, reached into her bag and tugged out four large notes from a splendid fold of white fivers. She handed them over. I should have gone higher. But I had a client. A paying client. Maybe my luck was turning, a good omen for the new year. I tried not to grab the money, and coolly slid my drawer open and dropped the notes in it, as though fivers went in there every day. I decided she'd earned some professional attention.

"Let's start with some details." My hand went back in the drawer again and dug out a pad of paper and a pen; the good fountain pen the "office" had given me to mark my return, and my hasty departure.

"What's Phil's full name?"

She looked coolly at me for a second. "Philip Anthony Caldwell. Major."

My pen stopped, frozen over my pristine pad. "Did you say Caldwell? Philip *Anthony* Caldwell?" My scar was throbbing and hot.

"Yes. They *said* you might know him." She wanted to see my reaction.

"They?"

"Sixty-four Baker Street."

Head office of the Special Operations Executive. They'd told her more than they seemed ready to tell me. I played for time to get over my shock.

"Maybe. Can you describe Major Caldwell to me?"

She did, and in my mind's eye the sketchy figure took on three dimensions and emerged clearly as Major Tony Caldwell. I met him two years ago. Clever Tony, Tony with the affected smile, and the knowing eyes, who wouldn't take no for an answer. The man who might have the key to the locked door of my mind. The man I'd been searching for, ever since they let me out of the loony bin.

*

"Good morning, Sergeant McRae." The voice is bright and breezy.

I struggle fully awake and ease myself up on my elbows on the bed. At the foot is an officer, a Major sporting the winged Mercury badge of the Signals Regiment.

"Morning, sir. Sorry, didn't see you there."

"It's perfectly all right Sergeant. I should be apologising to you. I've disturbed you and you need your rest, nurse tells me."

"I'm sleeping too much. Catching up, they tell me." The hospital ship from Salerno took six days to get back to Portsmouth, and Biscay was bloody. I push myself back and up so that I'm sitting, a bit bleary-eyed, but receptive. I presume this is some sort of visiting rota he's on. To buck up the troops or something. I preferred the kip.

"Mind if I sit?"

"Of course not, sir."

"And, Sergeant, do you mind awfully if we drop the rank stuff for a bit? I'm Tony, Tony Caldwell. Can I call you Daniel?"

"Yes, of course, sir, I mean Tony. I'm Danny." He's not wearing padre duds, or doctor's insignia. What's he after?

"I 'spect you're wondering who I am and why I'm bothering you?" My eyebrows give him the answer.

"I'm actually doing a spot of recruiting. Not for my regiment." He points at his shoulder flash. "I'm on secondment to a unit in Whitehall and looking for more talent."

His accent is hard to place. To my untutored ears it's just posh English, the accent of officers, the natural enemy of the working class. I inspect the man more closely. About five feet ten, I guess, strong shoulders, open face. Blue eyes and gingery moustache under a nose with a bump in the middle. His hair is lighter than his moustache, more sand in it, and it falls across his forehead in flat lines from a severe side parting.

"How's the leg, by the way?" He points at the tent covering my lower body.

"Better, thanks. They think they've got all the shrapnel out, but I think they took some of me with it." I try to joke, but I know the bone got pretty smashed up and can't see how they managed to put it all back together again. Even with the steel pin I was likely to be lopsided. And I'd never play for Scotland now.

"Look, Danny. Fact is you've been shot up enough not to have to worry about the war any more. Find a nice desk for you somewhere, eh? Or go back to your old work in Glasgow. Policeman, weren't you?"

He knows that. But I play along till he tells me what he's here for. "A sergeant in civvy street and a sergeant in the army. Seems like I've found my level."

"No, you haven't. You stayed on at school. Passed the entrance exam for Glasgow University. Made Detective Sergeant by twenty three. And you've twice been recommended for officer training." There's a sudden toughness in his eyes.

"Officers lead from the front. And get shot first." It's my standard defence. I just feel more comfortable with the lads.

"You've got the wrong war." He smiles. "When you're fit, we could use a chap like you. With your sort of background. You've got pluck and intelligence. And you'd get paid as an officer. Lieutenant. Wartime commission obviously. Like mine."

"Why should I take a pay cut?" A top sergeant gets paid more than a first lieutenant.

"We might be able to swing Captain."

Captain Daniel McRae has a ring to it. But no doubt it comes at a price.

"Doing what, Tony?" I can use his name more freely now if we're to be brother officers. But I'm already feeling a con coming on. You don't get officer's pay for sitting behind a desk.

He leans closer. The ward is heaving with nurses and soldiers. "Heard of an outfit called Special Operations Executive? The SOE? Yes? Well, keep it simple, old chap, we train you and then send you to France or Greece or somewhere Jerry is. Then you link up with the local resistance and mess things up a bit. Blow up bridges, trains, give Jerry a hard time of it. We're building up a big operation for when we go back. SOE's role will be to cause havoc behind the lines until the rest of us get through. Absolutely vital stuff. And great fun."

Fun! This was his idea of fun? It wasn't mine, thank you very much. At least that had been my first reaction, and my second and third. But Tony Caldwell was a determined character and liked getting his own way. Insisted on it. And, as I was about to learn, to hell with the consequences for anyone else.

THREE

Kate Graveney walked out with head high and without a
backward glance, her uncertainty cast off like an out-of-
date ration book. She seemed to have got what she came
for. I wondered what it was. I listened to her all the way back
down, toes hitting every step. I got up and went round and
sat in her chair. It was still warm. I touched the arms where
her hands had rested and thought I could feel a faint slick.
Her scent hung about me as though her body had left a dent
in the air. I sniffed deeply, trying to hang on to her spoor and
in trying too hard, lost it, as though she was one of my
elusive memories.

Enough. I stood up, pulled my hat and coat off the rack
behind the door and made ready to go out into the night. I
kicked the new briquette back with my toe so that it would
die and I could use it to start the fire in the morning. A last
impulse pulled me to the window. I eased the bottom pane up
and looked out into the street. I was just in time. Kate
Graveney was being handed into the back seat of a big Riley
by a bloke with a flat cap. The car was standing with its
engine running, as though petrol rationing only applied to the
hoi polloi.

As she bent to enter she turned her head up and looked up at my window, as though expecting to see me. I didn't withdraw. We should have waved but we didn't know each other that well. She gave no sign, but got into the car, and I watched it drive off down the street. Its exhaust left a trail of grey smoke on the dank air. I thought I saw her face looking back at me from the rear window, and another head wearing a hat, but I couldn't be sure.

I closed the window and dug back into my desk drawer to check it hadn't been an illusion. Sometimes things get blurred. I see things that turn out to be flotsam from my memories. I folded the four very real, very crisp notes and tucked them into my breast pocket. As I was closing the drawer I saw the front page I'd torn from this morning's *Daily Sketch*. The rest I'd already quartered and hung in the shared lavatory on the floor below. I made sure I got a paper every day; it was one of the ways I could tell if I'd had a blackout.

The headlines were howling about the third body found in a flat in Soho. A prostitute again. But not a single clue, other than a man sighted going into the building around the time of the murder. Hardly noteworthy, given her occupation. No fingerprints that matched any found at the other sites, and lord knew how many prints they found.

The body was naked and brutalised. Words like gruesome and sadistic were bandied about. But the details were omitted from this family newspaper: just vague references to a knife wound to the lower body and the head. My detective sergeant's imagination translated this as genital mutilation and a killing stab through the base of the skull up into the brain. I hoped she got the skull thrust first.

I stuffed the page back in my drawer. I'd file it later. I've kept them all from the very first that merited only half a column on an inside page four months ago. Maybe it was getting to know Mama Mary and her girls. Maybe it was the way they'd died. Maybe it was the echo of a recurring dream. But these killings revolted and intrigued me at the same time.

I'd read and re-read the reports. I bought other papers to see if they said anything more, and kept picturing the dead women, naked and bloody, as though I'd been an eye witness. And I couldn't recall if my dreadful dreams began before or after the first killing. Doc Thompson told me that it was my way of coping with the violence I'd seen in the camp. Violence without reason. Violence for pleasure. Trying to understand how a so-called civilised world could co-exist with such wide-spread perversion and sadism.

That's what worried me. I used to think that most of us would rather cut off our right arm than beat a child to death with a rifle butt. That only a handful of warped bastards would set to with a will and enjoy the exercise.

But what if the devil were in all of us? Christ knows, they're still counting the corpses in the thousands of camps across Europe. They're talking of millions, but I can't believe that. Who would kill a million people just because they had bigger noses? And it wasn't just the poor bloody Jews that copped it – as I knew to my personal cost. Every phobia catered for: gypsies, homosexuals, communists, book readers, hunchbacks, noisy neighbours...

Neither could you point the finger at the Germans and say it's something in *their* blood. We know that Poles and French and Italians – half the Continent – sent women and kids to the camps knowing what would happen. And then there are the Russians. Just don't start me on the Russians. I even feel sorry for those bloody Berliners.

If our *allies* could do that, why couldn't we? Why couldn't I? Three dead prostitutes in London hardly figured in the scale of horror over there. But it showed that the sickness was here among us too.

Outside, the crowds were getting excited. They were heading to Westminster and Waterloo, and then on to Trafalgar and Piccadilly. I went the other way. I rammed my hat tighter on my head and pulled the coat collar up, as much against the mounting revelry as against the night air. It was just gone eleven by the clock on the tower in Camberwell Green. The cheerful crowds began to thin. I pressed on up Denmark Hill, enjoying the gradient and the need to put some effort into my stride.

I didn't know what I wanted; company or to be alone, a drink or just a walk. A bit of me – to be frank, a baser bit of me – would have liked to be meeting up with Sandra tonight and cosying up with her in front of a warm fire with a full bottle. But three months back, with my face as healed as it was going to get, I called at the King Billy, and Sandra told me to get lost. More precisely, she got Big Alec, the guv'nor, to tell me.

She was standing behind the bar as though a year hadn't happened, her hair piled up the way I loved. She saw me come in and her face went pink. Then she gave me a look that made me want to check the date of my last anti-tetanus jab. I know I'm not as pretty as I used to be, but a monster?

She walked straight over to Alec and spoke to him, quickly and quietly. Alec raised his brooding eyes and found me. He didn't hesitate; he lifted the bar flap and came over, full of intent. He was an old pug, with hams for hands and Plasticine for a nose.

"Piss off, Red. You've done enough damage round here."

"I just wanted a pint, Alec. What's the problem? Don't returning heroes get a beer?"

"Red, you're no fucking hero for Sandra. She don't want to know. So, save you, me, and all of us, some trouble and sling your 'ook."

I was aware of how quiet it had got. Sandra was standing as far away as she could from me, watching with hard eyes and sucking nervously on a fag. It had been the same eyes that had caused the barney the last time, over a year and a half ago. We'd been going out for a couple of months. I'd got digs round the corner in Peckham while I was getting trained up by the SOE. Sandra was fun, lively, beautiful and a champion cock-teaser. I never knew where I was with her; she could be dragging me into bed one night and sending me packing the next.

I guess I'm slow. It took me five weeks to realise I was one of a string. I don't like that; don't like being taken for a ride; don't like sharing. I told her so and she promised to be faithful. But I didn't trust her. And I was right; the night she should have been out with her mates – one of them was supposed to be getting married – I found her with her tongue down the throat of a right wee spiv round the back of the Streatham Locarno. He deserved the pasting I gave him, and she came back to me; she liked men fighting over her, I suppose. She was less happy when I gave her a clip, and from then on Sandra and I were fireworks. So I suppose Alec was right to get me out of his pub before we started some new slanging match.

"OK, Alec. Point taken. I suppose I'm not as gorgeous as I was."

His eyes softened, as did his voice. "S'nothing to do with your fizzog, Red. You're still prettier than me. She's not bleedin' worth it. She's a tart with big tits. Which is what my clientele pays for. Forget her."

I looked round at his clientele, over to Sandra, and nodded to Alec. I turned and walked out. I tried to put Sandra out of my head, but couldn't help wondering if I should have just done a Nelson and ignored what she was up to; enjoyed what she gave me. For when she gave, it was memorable. Jealousy is my curse.

I shook her from my thoughts by focusing on the conversation I'd just had with Kate Graveney. I tried to make sense of her words and how they connected with me. I didn't know whether to feel angry or relieved at being thwarted in my search for Major Tony Caldwell. It all seemed a wee bit too convenient for my liking. My short time as a detective in Glasgow convinced me that there was no such thing as a coincidence. But I'm also aware that I tend to get a shade paranoiac these days.

I stopped and looked back down the hill. I kneaded my leg with both hands where it was aching; the damp seeped into the bones where they knitted. I thought about the year ahead; it held little promise for me. New Year celebrations are sadder than glad affairs at the best of times. And these weren't. The skies were soaked with rain that could turn to snow any time. The wind was blowing straight off the North Sea and up the Thames with few enough buildings left to take the edge off. At least it was keeping the fog away.

There was hardly a line of houses untouched; great swathes cut through residential streets and factories; stumps left where buildings either side had been straddled on a bombing run.

Pipes hung out from nude walls like entrails, and wallpaper flapped in upstairs rooms open to the skies. Queues everywhere for everything. Half the city had no lights. London transport sent their buses and their trams out, but never enough, never on time to take the grey-faced folk off to their makeshift offices.

I laughed. If there was a god, sometimes you had to smile and shake your head at his bent sense of humour.

I came to Ruskin Park where I used to walk in the summer. It was cold and empty now. On impulse I climbed over the waist-high gate and walked in. I followed the path down to the pond in the middle. I smelt it before I saw it: that ripe stink of decay. It glistened like oil in the dark. Bare trees hung over the water. I didn't see the girl on the bench till I was nearly on her. It was the white of her hands that caught my eye.

I coughed to warn her. "Hello. Are we too early for the party?"

She didn't jump; must have heard me coming. She lifted her face. It was wet. She sniffed and took a hand to her cheeks. She looked about my age, though it was hard to tell through the long dark hair that hung like pondweed over her face. She sniffed again and pushed the hair back to show a trembling lip and stricken eyes. She looked familiar, probably one of the shop girls from down at the Green.

"I hate crowds," she said, meaning get lost, mate.

"Two's not a crowd, is it?"

Normally I'm the first to take a hint, but I suddenly wanted company. Still missing Sandra, I suppose. There was room on the bench for me without getting too close. I didn't want her to run away. We sat gazing at the pond, not looking at each other. There was no moon but enough light to let the shrubs and trees and pathway show up clearly. I could see her legs stretched out in front of her. They were slim, with good ankles. She had to be daft, sitting alone in a park at midnight with a madman around.

"I just wanted some peace, you know?" Her voice had lost its edge. "Stuff to remember."

Of course. A city full of tragedies. New Year's Eve, and all you can think of is the family you lost in the Blitz or the boy who never came back from the front. I began to get up. "Sorry. I didn't mean to…"

She was quick. "It's all right. Really. Shouldn't dwell on things. Been here long enough. Go before I catch my death." Her words were wreathed in vapour.

"I'm sorry…"

"Not your fault, was it?"

I turned properly and looked at her. She was crying again, and it grew to a sobbing and she didn't cover up her face. She let her hands lie by her sides and let her chest shudder and fall in helpless anguish. I was scared to touch her but wanted to reach over and squeeze her arm. She turned her head towards me and the sobbing began to slow. The last time I'd seen such hopeless eyes was in the mirror.

"Come on. You're frozen. I know a bar. I'll buy you a whisky. It's good for cold hands; helps you forget too." Not that I needed help, I almost added.

"I'm not a pick-up, you know!"

"Course not! But there are enough nutters around."

Her glistening eyes sized me up. I tried to look like I was wearing a dog-collar. She smiled gamely and nodded.

"I'm Danny. Danny McRae. What's yours?"

"Valerie Brown. Val."

We got up and we walked back out of the park and up the hill till we cut over to Grove Lane. She was the right height to fit under my arm if we ever got that far. The George Canning still had its blackout curtains up; handy if you wanted to let your best customers go on drinking after hours. We had about ten minutes to go before midnight. Just before we went in and the lights hit us, I stopped and turned to face her.

"Val, I need to say something. I'm a wee bit war damaged too." I took off my hat and made her see the white lines that I knew would be gleaming silver in the moonlight like a snail trail.

"You trying to impress me?"

"I didn't want you to faint. Or drop your whisky."

"You haven't bought me one yet, have you?" She gazed with interest at the scars, then lifted her finger and stroked each one, so lightly all I could feel was a line of chill. She smiled and we went in.

We were clouted by light and noise and the smell of folk who've been wearing the same clothes for too long through too much. A few turned their heads to see who it was then went back to shouting at each other. Their faces were red and sweaty. I cut a channel for us through the smoke and the crowd and found a tiny bit of corner space with a shelf.

"Whisky, Jock?" mouthed Terry, the bald barman. I raised two fingers twice. He got the drift and two double scotches hit my hands. He whistled when I handed him the big new fiver and checked it against the light. He nodded and rang me up the change. I fought my way back to her and perched the glasses on the shelf.

In the heavy air her pale skin was already going pink under the eyes. The hair was gypsy black, like the Catholic girls I used to know in Glasgow. Her eyes were dark brown, not washed out like Kate Graveney's. Two pretty women cross my path in one evening. Maybe the new year wasn't going to be all bad?

"Cheers!" I clacked my glass against hers. She smiled and toasted me back. She took a swig and choked and spluttered but held it down. This time the colour spread across her face and down her white neck. Someone called for quiet and several others joined in and suddenly there was still. Terry was twisting at the dial of the radio. The sound of Big Ben's midnight chimes bonged through the waiting bar. As the last one fell, a cheer went up. Happy New Year!

I raised my glass and shouted, "Here's to you, Tam and Archie!" as I promised I'd do every Ne'erday till I joined them – wherever they were.

People started embracing and kissing and weeping. Val didn't seem to be too put off by what she'd seen of me in the light, so I leaned in to give her a quick kiss. She smiled, but like a flash, got her finger across her lips. Too hasty, that's me. I saw her eyes brim and turned away so she couldn't see my own tears welling. A maudlin Scot at Hogmanay. Silently I sent word to my mother, and hoped the neighbours were looking after her.

We had another drink and tried to talk but it was like shouting into a Hampden roar. So we gave up and just smiled at each other and at all the daft folk around us and I shook hands with strangers and for a moment I seemed to lose her to drunks. Then she returned to me flushed and flustered. They started singing, all those Vera Lynn songs, trying to recapture the best bits of the war, when we were all in the same boat rowing the same way. But I'd heard "Tipperary" and "White

Cliffs" murdered once too often. I sank my scotch and nodded towards the door.

We walked back to my place without saying anything, without agreeing anything. I lit a fire and we sat gazing into it, supping more Scotch. We saw our own past in the flames and hoped... well, all I was hoping was to wake up beside her. But she made it clear there would be no hanky-panky. She stayed with me anyway, dancing out of her top clothes in front of the sparking fire. She kept on her slip and slid shivering between my cold sheets. We lay like orphans, the folds between us, spooned but passion-free, just glad to share a bed against the dark. Her thin limbs shook until our bodies made a bubble of warmth under the heavy blankets.

I smelt the fag smoke on her hair and the cheap scent on the skin of her neck and gladly relinquished the memory of Kate's costly perfume. We began to drowse. A big spark would shake us and make her twitch. I'd shush her like a pony and she'd subside again. The fire dwindled and the shadows deepened. Her trembling eased and stopped, and sleep took us both.

The morning light woke me. But Valerie was gone.

FOUR

The first day of the year. The wireless was being deter-minedly cheerful: *bells of liberty ringing across Europe... first year without war since 1939,* and other such breath-less stuff. I switched it off. Here in liberated south London the streets were quieter than normal as the good citizens grappled with a massive hangover. But the buses were running and I could hear the steady rise in volume as folk battled into work. The Blitz couldn't stop them. Why would a sore head? But I knew full well that in Scotland it would be graveyard quiet; New Year's Day was a holiday, an essential respite for recovery and in some cases, resurrection.

I seemed to have drunk more than I thought last night. My cure is fresh air, so I decided to take a walk. As I stepped out the door, the cold hit me. The wireless had warned that the temperature would drop, but the frigid air stung my lungs and set me into a coughing fit. I went back up for a scarf and gloves and set out again. I like walking, even though it makes my leg hurt. When your world is defined by barbed wire and machine gun towers, the sense of exhilaration at being able to stroll without being shouted at or fired at runs deep. It was only slowly that I realised that in a haphazard way I was looking for *her*. I'd known her only one night. I'd slept beside her, but not made love to her. But already I missed her. I didn't know I was missing *somebody*. I didn't know where she lived or how to get in touch. So much for my detective skills. I'm an idiot. I didn't know if I'd ever see her again. Was I just a warm bed at a bad time for her? A new year flirt?

This was stupid, a kid's game. And I was in no state – mental or physical – to be thinking about acquiring a girl-friend. I had other ways of dealing with my basic needs. I could do nothing, so I decided to turn my walk into something with a purpose. I'd visit Kate Graveney's scene of crime, *if* there was a crime.

The arctic wind burgled its way inside my coat. I adjusted the scarf and pushed my hat on more firmly. At least the sky was clearing. There was even some blue to the west. I willed it my way.

I put in some zigzags round the back streets, aiming to pick up Kennington Lane. Away from the main arteries that fed the City and the West End, the streets were quieter. When I met another walker we touched hats and wished each other a happy new year. I passed boarded windows on bomb-damaged streets, and one huge crater that they hadn't got around to filling in. Surprising really, given the amount of material lying around. I crossed the river at Vauxhall, heading into Pimlico. There didn't seem to be as much damage here: no factories or docks to blitz. Though lord knows how they missed the twin legs of Battersea Power Station. They say they'll build another pair alongside, but I'll believe it when I see it. It would look funny, like a table on its back. The streets were busier now, shoppers queuing for mean lumps of cheese or slivers of meat, cars rumbling along chased by their own exhaust clouds.

I was getting good and warm now and could open my coat collar a bit. I thought about the two women I'd met last night. The contrast. The accident of birth and where it leads you. I could guess how growing up was for Val, but I had absolutely no idea how it was for Kate. Money and position make everything possible. I wasn't jealous, just curious, as you would be about another species. Even that little blink of fear I'd seen in Kate's eyes when she saw my scar had been quickly controlled – mustn't show emotions in front of the servants.

But at least I knew how to contact Kate Graveney. I had her phone number, somewhere in Chelsea – of course. I was to call her the moment I heard anything. With Val – Valerie Brown; I rolled the syllables in my mouth – I had nothing, and the thought of not seeing her again filled my day with a shadow that had nothing to do with the weather.

I came into Lupus Street and began looking for my number. I didn't have to do much counting. I could see the gap from the corner. I walked closer but stayed on the other side of the street, sizing it up. It was as though a giant bread knife had taken out a clean slice, leaving the buildings either side untouched. I guess all the terrace buildings had been constructed one by one. I walked over. There was still some rubble in the back garden. Bare trees stood at the end, and an old shed. What was I looking for? A pair of feet sticking out of the debris? I walked into the garden. The grass was sodden and studded with bricks. There was that depressing smell of burnt wood and plasterboard soaked by persistent rain.

I kicked a brick sticking up on the edge of the pile and saw something lying to my left. I bent and picked up a shoe. High heeled, navy blue, good leather and size 4. I didn't need to be a Prince Charming to know whose foot this would fit. And she was no Cinderella. I brushed it clean and stuck it in my coat pocket. I looked but I didn't find the other one.

"Hoi! No looting here, laddy!"

I turned to see an old man in a big cardigan and knotted scarf waving his walking stick at me. His breath ballooned about his head. I put on my best smile and walked over to him.

"It's all right, sir. I know the lady who used to visit here. She asked me to see if I could find her shoes." I dug out the shoe and showed it to him. He still looked suspicious.

"What lady would that be? I live across the road, you know. I see what's going on here."

"She was using the house. It belonged to a friend."

"The Jamesons. Been abroad, they have," he said triumphantly. Then his wrinkled eyes narrowed. "She a blonde?"

I nodded. I bet this nosy old bugger watched every passer-by and all the goings-on.

"She might be."

"Her and her fancy man?"

"Could be."

His suspicious look had turned into a secretive know-it-all one. He was dying to tell me more.

"You her husband?"

I laughed. "No."

"A private dick, then."

So, not so daft. "This isn't about infidelity, sir. Did you see the explosion?"

His face fell and crumpled with annoyance. "I was asleep, wasn't I. Near threw me out of my bed. Thought it was Jerry starting all over again."

"Did you see the ambulances?"

"Oh, yes. But I couldn't see what they were doing. Fire engines and everything."

I could see I'd get nothing else from him and finally had to be rude to get away from him. Lonely old bugger. I walked back towards the river and struck north towards Parliament, and to Soho beyond. I was thinking about those poor lasses that had been killed there, the last just four days ago. The trade of the victims, and the way they'd been butchered drew a pattern, but I couldn't read it yet.

Because of their precarious line of business the first murder had barely been given a mention among all the other news. Though for my own quaint reasons I had picked up on it and began my cuttings collection. But the second jolted the city, and the third began to set up a clamour. Now it was front page with headlines talking gleefully of the new Soho Ripper and "Jack's back!"

It was as though something wicked had followed me from the camp. I had a *sense* of their deaths, as though I'd known them or shared their terror. Maybe it was this that drew me towards their killing ground. Or my copper's training. One day it would kill me.

I walked straight up Whitehall, still marvelling at how so many of those grand buildings had survived. Parliament had taken a stick or two but they'd just moved to another part of Westminster Palace. Funny, the bombs couldn't silence old Winston but we, the grateful voters, did. It wasn't personal, he was just leading the wrong party. But it must have hurt.

Nelson was still on his column. And pigeons had never left Trafalgar Square except to take a breather from the incendiaries. There was a lot of rubbish around. It had been a good night for some. The dustbin men were getting stuck in. I pressed on up by the Windmill with its signs claiming they never closed during the Blitz. They were promising a New Year's Day special: half price for the first twenty customers. I slowed to take in the photos of the girls, splendid with their feathers and smiles and impossible legs.

I walked along Rupert Street. It looked different from the other times I'd come here; daylight versus dark anonymity. I entered the little hallway and knocked on Mary's door. Silence, but it was still only late morning: time for rest, especially if there had been some new year celebrations. I knocked again, harder.

"Wat you want? We no open yet. Come back later!" Mary's high thin voice cut through the door like a dentist drill.

"Mary, it's me, Danny. It's business."

I heard nothing for a minute then grumbling and catches being taken off and bolts sliding. Mary's little round face showed round the crack of the door. She wasn't wearing make-up. She had no eyebrows. It was a shock to see how old she was. Blessed night-time.

"Wat you want, Danny? Girls not up. They need beauty sleep. Like me."

She did.

"It's about these murders, Mary. I need some information." I was calling in a favour I'd done her a couple of months back. There had been a spate of stealing from the girls' rooms. Mary thought one of them was the culprit but didn't want the boys in blue rampaging through her house. I caught the thief on the fire escape round the back: he was the neighbour's kid. Justice was meted out according to local custom: the kid was given a good hiding and cash changed hands in reparation. The problem stopped.

She opened the door a little wider. She was in a blue silk

dressing gown that fell to her tiny feet. Her hair was tightly held in a net. She looked even shorter today, shrunken. I thought of my mother. "Why you interested, Danny? You private dick, not real Bobby."

I smiled at Mary's sing-song cackle; we suffered the same degree of incomprehension by the English at times.

"Call it professional curiosity, Mary. Can I come in for a minute."

Her eyes narrowed even further, then she stood back and let me in. She glanced outside to see who might have spotted me – the neighbours, and hence the police, didn't like callers much at any time, far less during the day.

The familiar smell of incense and cheap perfume hit me like a shovel. I would catch a whiff on my clothes for days after one of my visits. I didn't come here often, and when I first knocked on Mary's door it wasn't so much about the act itself as proving something to myself. They beat the shit out of me in the camp; I wondered what else they might have knocked out.

Mary was a psychologist. She'd give Doc Thompson a run for his money. She took my measure that first time like a chef inspecting fruit at Covent Garden. She gave me green tea and talked to me, drew out a little of the story, a little of the need. Then she introduced me to Colette, a lippy dyed blonde with a happy heart. A natural at her profession. She told Colette to take her time, no rush. I guess it worked as I've come back a couple of times since. Mary runs a clean house and it's only for a wee while, till I can face up to the rejections on the dance floor.

Besides, I'd also dropped in on Mary on business, my business. I'm new to London, and it's important in my line to know who the bad guys are and what they're up to. You don't want to be crossing anyone important when you're on the scent. I learned that the hard way when I got mixed up in the affairs of a certain Annie MacGuire whose old man turned out to be making hay with the lady wife of a rival mob leader in the East End.

Annie was a brazen-haired, big-breasted girl who laughed a lot and wore more jewellery than Hatton Garden. She stormed into my office, bangles clashing like cymbals, demanding that I tail Mr Stanley MacGuire. Stanley seemed to be spending too many nights at the office. Which was tricky; Stanley's line of work – putting the arm on late payers of the loan shark he worked for – placed his office in the back seat of a big Humber Hawk.

So I spent a couple of weeks and a lot of shoe leather finding out that Stanley was not so much putting the arm on people as putting it round a certain Laura Dayton, who had the edge on Annie by about ten years and twenty pounds. I didn't know Miss Dayton was a Mrs and also fooling around. Or that Mr Dayton was well known for his trademark habit of breaking people's shins with the iron bar he kept up his very big sleeve. It was an effective deterrent to folk who thought they might like a cut of his fag and booze racket.

I made my report, Annie threw a fit, but instead of – or maybe as well as; I never heard – taking it out on Stanley, she tracked down Laura Dayton to the Brickie's Arms in the Old Kent Road and took a slice out of her rival's younger face with Stanley's clasp razor. Poetic justice, she must have thought. Gang war broke out, two pubs got wrecked, five people ended up in hospital, some with bits missing that would never grow again. And I began vetting my clients a little more carefully.

*

Mary's ears were tuned to the jungle drums and she was happy to gossip except when it came to clients, for whom she would undergo torture to avoid naming or shaming. I followed her through to her tiny living room, and remembered to duck as we came in through the door to avoid the huge wind chimes that dangled from the ceiling. As ever, I was mildly shocked at the amount of junk on every flat surface and every wall. And, apart from the enormous pile of old newspapers in one corner, the overwhelming preference for *red* junk. I think the colour of my hair was the other factor in her being helpful to me.

I pushed aside an avalanche of red satin cushions and perched on the edge of her couch. Tea appeared to lubricate the conversation. "You sure you no wanna girl? Can get one up, lazy cows sleep all day and night too if can."

I grinned and shook my head. "What's the story on the streets, Mary, about these killings?"

She turned her mouth down. "Very bad, very bad. Bad for girls bad for business. Men stay away 'cos they scared of bobbies."

I bet. "Does anyone *know* anything, though? Anyone see anything?"

"Dead girls all work for one man. Big-time pimp. No like my place. You safe here. I kill anyone who hurt my girls!" She raised her little arm and dropped it in a swift chopping motion. It was a threat not to be dismissed lightly. I doubted if Mary herself had the strength to squash a bug but she had good connections in China Town where the Tongs held sway. I also knew that Mary's concern for the half-dozen girls who worked here was more than just business or posturing; the girls themselves talked of her kindness to them. Mama Mary they called her.

"Do you know the name of the man? This pimp?"

"I know, I know all right. He Jonny Crane. Hard man. Don't you cross him, Danny. He chop you into chow mein. Eat you up for dinner!"

I stored the name away. "What else? Any sightings? Any disturbance?"

She shook her head. "Only bobbies. Big chief, big fat bastard. He come round, throw everything up in air. Make questions. Scare customers. Scare girls."

A thought struck me. "What's his name?"

"Wislen. Somet'ing like that."

"Wilson? You mean, Inspector Wilson?"

"That him." She nodded hard. "Stinky bad man. Always round here. He like girls, but no pay for them."

"Wait, wait, Mary. Are you saying that Wilson comes round here and uses the girls? And that he doesn't pay for it?"

"That right. He pig! But not here. Other houses. He know not come China Town house. Chop, chop!" She stabbed the air. "They say he hit girls and make 'em do bad stuff." She shrugged. "That OK if girls say OK and he pay. But not for no money."

A businesswoman to the roots of her dyed-black hair. I thought of Wilson and shuddered at what he might demand of a girl. Fat bastard indeed. I remember the first time I met Detective Inspector Herbert Wilson of the Yard. I'd been going for about six weeks and was starting to make some headway; a few clients, enough to pay the rent anyway.

Did I mention the cat? There's a thin moggy with half a tail that comes by most days. It creeps up the stairs, pauses at the second top step and checks out the lie of the land. If it sees me at my desk and I don't make shooing noises it comes up on to the landing and rubs itself against my door. It meows as it rubs. I've taken to leaving a saucer of Carnation milk for it. That seems to work. It doesn't come near me, doesn't demand stroking or – God forbid – a lap, just recognition and milk, then it goes on its way, its stumpy tail the last thing I see as it glides off down the stairs.

Wilson scared the cat the day he paid me a visit. Its thin head shot up, its ears twitched, and it was away before I'd even heard the first steps. I heard his big feet clumping up the stairs. They even sounded like copper's feet, relentless, heavy, full of their own importance. A hat sailed into view, then the shoulders of a big coat. The man wearing them was sucking for air. He held the top rail for a second or two till he got his breath. Then he came in through my open door. No knock. He just stood there wheezing, eyeing me and my place. I waited.

"McRae?" His chest still heaved.

"That's me. Sorry, the lift's out."

He ignored my humour. "You a so-called private dick, then?" He made it sound sinful.

I still didn't know he was police, but he had that look. In his first five seconds he'd itemised my office, memorised my face, and noticed the door to my bedroom.

"At your service. Can I help? Need a debt collected? Lost a wife?"

I watched his mouth twist. "I'm Inspector Wilson. *Detective* Inspector, CID. You're on my patch. Wanted to see you, what you were up to. I don't like what you do."

What the hell was a DI doing making house calls?

"I'm honoured, Inspector, and it's really nice to be made welcome. But I'm a bit puzzled; we haven't met, and yet already you're pissed off with me. Isn't that a wee bit unfair?

And before we continue this nice chat, can I see your warrant card, please? Can't be too careful these days."

I could see his jaw muscles tighten. We were getting on famously. He hated me and I loathed him. I'd seen too many of his kind; they'd been in the force too long, got too used to throwing their weight around. Wilson let his fell gaze roast me for the obligatory five seconds, then he reached into his great overcoat and pulled out a card. He strode over to my desk and rammed it under my nose. DI Herbert Wilson. I wondered if he'd let me call him Bertie?

"Satisfied?"

"Thank you, Inspector. Now, shall we start again? What can I do for you?"

"You can tell me who you are, where you come from, and what you're doing here."

"I thought we'd established who I was and what I'm doing? And my accent's a bit of a clue, is it no'? I needed a job after getting demobbed. This – palace – is it."

"You could have got your old job back. What was it?" He settled his great bulk into my chair. He seemed to take up the whole view from my desk. I sighed. He wasn't going to let this go until he found out.

"I was in the force. In Glasgow. Thought I'd try the private sector. More money." Potentially, I thought, potentially. I thought it smart not to tell him I'd been a detective sergeant.

He didn't look surprised, which was surprising. He chewed on the end of his moustache for a bit, then wiped it dry with a big paw.

"OK, McRae. Here's my warning. I don't like *private* investigators. Especially don't like former coppers doing private investigations. Only one who investigates around these parts is me. I can't stop you. Not until you do something illegal or get in my way." He leaned over my desk, and his bloodshot eyes held mine. "Just – don't – get – in – my – fucking – way." His breath would have stripped paint.

I didn't blink. I'd been through worse sessions with real bullies. Much worse. They hadn't made threats, just carried them out.

"I'm sure there's room for both of us on these gold-paved streets, Inspector. And I'm prepared to give you a big discount if you ever need help looking for Mrs Wilson."

I thought my poor visitor's chair would explode under the pressure. Wilson wrenched himself clear and lowered over the desk at me, leaning on his knuckles. He singed my eyebrows with his blast.

"I also don't like a smart arse, McRae! You're on my list, boy. I'm looking out for you. You hear me? One foot wrong and you're visiting my nice nick. The lads will enjoy you. They don't like smart arses either."

I decided I'd done enough goading and kept my mouth shut – about five minutes too late – until he'd stomped off down the stairs. A little later the cat's head appeared round the corner. She meowed angrily. She hadn't been impressed by Wilson either.

"Just one more question, Mary. Did you know the name of the last girl who was killed? Know where she worked?"

"Name was Jasmine. Round corner. Marsh Street. Forty-three. Only single girls work there. They all gone now." Her brows knitted as though she worried what became of that flock of flushed birds.

"Thanks, Mary. And thanks for the tea." I stood to go.

"You sure, Danny? Wake Colette? She like you."

Ah, Colette; real name Betty; aspiring actress and Windmill girl, but her curvy legs were too short. It was tempting, so tempting to take some comfort from skin on skin, but I declined. Not while I was working. Even in my dirty line of business I try to have some professional standards. Mary closed the door on me with a last admonishment. "You come round soon, you hear. And keep your head away from Jonny Crane and big fat bastard!"

I should have listened harder to Mama Mary.

FIVE

arsh Street paraded its usual collection of street artists.
A man in a doorway sleeping it off, his empty bottle by
his side. A publican with his braces round his knees and
a fag stuck to his lip opening up to let out the fetid air. A pair
of spivs with darting eyes, oiling each other's business with
cash and information. And a couple of big women tottering
along in party frocks and last night's make-up, clinging to each
other for dear life. If one fell, they'd both go, and would probably die there on their backs, limbs flailing uselessly like
upturned turtles.

I looked for number 43. It was three stories high and had a
block of six bells each with a name on it, except for the top one.
There was just a blank where I guess Jasmine's nom-de-guerre
had been. I walked in and began to climb the stairs. I had no
idea what I would do at the top. I had no idea what I was doing
here in the first place. The stairs had a rough carpet for the
first three flights and then bare boards the rest of the way.
They creaked and groaned as I made my way.

It had been four days since they'd found her. Jasmine.
Probably christened Jean. Wee Jeanie. Jeanie with the light
brown hair. Somebody's daughter. The door was closed. I

knocked and got no answer. I turned the handle and it opened. I stepped inside. There was a short hall. A bathroom to the left and ahead a bedsit area. They'd cleared every-thing, bedding, carpet – I could see the tidemark of dirt where it had lain – and all the drawers were hanging open, empty. A mattress stood against the wall. There were two huge brown stains on it, one where a head might lie and the other in the middle.

I'd seen a few murders in Glasgow. Though each was different in detail and context, I'd begun to find a dreadful familiarity. Same here. On the surface this was just a sad, empty room with dirty windows and red net curtains. Jasmine/Jean had left no mark on the world except the head-lines in the papers for a few days. But as I stood there, absorbing impressions, picturing where he stood and where she lay, my imagination detected a spoor, an afterimage hanging in the air. An aura of violence and death.

They share a cigarette while she tells him how much it costs. He puts the money on the dresser. He takes off his coat and then his jacket. It's going to be warm work; warmer than she knows. She stubs her fag.

She sheds her floral dressing gown and her pants and bra. She lays herself back on the bed and offers herself. He unzips and tells her to turn over on to her stomach. She smiles and tells him he's naughty. Maybe he smacks her bum a little, to see the flesh colour and tremble under his stinging hand. She is being paid to be used so there are no screams at first, just the thought that the client is being a bit rough, something he'd have to pay more for.

There's a pause and she hears him move to his coat. She turns her head and sees the knife and knows this is way

*beyond naughtiness. He shoves her face into the mattress
to stifle her screams. He squats on her back, feeling for the
spot on her neck where the skull starts, and drives the weapon
up and into her brain. He mounts her as her body spasms.
He...*

"And just what the hell are you doing here, McRae?"

I whirled round, feeling my guts flip. His bulk filled the door.
I hadn't heard his big feet.

"I'm waiting."

Wilson was indeed waiting. I was in the flat of a murdered
prostitute on New Year 's Day, and here was an inspector of
police asking me what I was doing here. It was a fair question.
I didn't have a fair answer. So I tried the truth.

"I was just curious, Inspector. I was out for a walk and found
myself wondering what happened here. The old law enforcer
in me, eh?" I tried to smile in camaraderie. He'd understand,
policeman to policeman.

"I warned you. I fucking warned you not to get in my way.
And here you are. In – my – fucking – way!" His moustache
quivered with the violence of his last words.

"I'll get out of your way. Right now, if you'll excuse me?" I
made to go round his bulk but he blocked out the entire
doorway and much of the room. I could smell tobacco and stale
drink on him, and old cloth. I didn't expect the punch. It caught
me full in the mouth and I went backwards on to the floor. My
hat rolled away from me and I tasted iron. I wondered if he'd
ever had an exchange posting with Glasgow; this was their
style. I clambered to my feet, my fists clenched ready to have
a go at the evil bastard. He was smiling.

"Come on, Jock. Take a swing. And it'll be the last thing you
do before you hit the floor of my nick. Assaulting a police officer.

Disturbing the scene of a murder. Obstructing justice. And anything else I can think of. Come on. Here it is." He stuck his fat jaw out and pointed at it.

I stood wiping the blood from my mouth, swaying with anger. He knew he had me. I picked up my hat and straightened my clothes.

"My mistake, Inspector." I could already feel my lip thickening.

His smile dropped. "Your second. The first was setting up on my patch. Now beat it, Jock. Before I really lose my temper. It's just as well I'm still full of new year spirit, or I might have taken you in as a suspect."

I looked at him blankly. He continued. "I still don't have a proper answer to what you're doing here. That makes me wonder. And when I wonder, I start delving. Do you want me to do some delving on you, sonny Jim?"

It sounded rhetorical; my wants were irrelevant to Wilson. "Can I go now, Inspector?"

He stood aside slowly and I sidled past him, feeling his malodorous breath on me and waiting for a second blow. It didn't come, and I escaped down the stairs and into the outside air, angry at Wilson and angrier at myself. What a shitty start to the new year. You lose the girl and get beat up by the police. What next?

Next, my head began to hurt, displaying all the early signs of one of my episodes. Wilson's punch had set something off. It was getting dark by the time I got home, and my neck was rigid with the pain that flowed from behind my eyes, back along my skull and into the top of my spine. I've seen iron hoops with screws in them that the Inquisition used to encourage heretics. I wore mine inside my head and wondered what I'd done wrong and who was tightening the screw.

Light from my office pooled down the stairs as I slowly climbed, gripping the banister like a blind man. A visitor, or maybe my eyes; they're usually the second sign. Everything goes bright and then pitch dark. I slowed and tried to walk quietly on my toes. Friend or foe, or maybe old Mrs White from downstairs. She does my laundry but wouldn't leave the light on. She hates extravagance.

I stood swaying at the doorway and saw there was no one in my office, but the door to my bedroom was open. There was no light on, but a fire threw guttering shadows against the wall. I slid softly over to the door and pushed it wide.

She was sitting on my bed. There were few alternatives; it was that or the sagging old armchair that the landlord should have burned to curb the fleas. She'd made the fire. The room was warm and welcoming.

"Hello. You're back, then?" I said, stating the glaringly obvious, and feeling stupidly pleased to see her.

Val smiled. "Am I welcome?"

"Seems you've made yourself welcome." I nodded at the fire. A couple of briquettes were half-eaten.

"Do you mind?" She frowned.

I shook my head, then clutched it as the pain ripped through the base of my skull. I took a deep breath. "Depends how long you stay and why you're here."

I wasn't going to give in so easily to a woman's warmth. There were things I hadn't noticed last night: her hair wasn't just black, it had chestnut depths; her eyelashes were the longest I'd seen; and though she was as skinny as a ferret, she had nice legs. I didn't want her to vanish again.

"I'm here, now. Isn't that enough?" She should have known it was enough. Women usually have a true sense of their worth to men. "What's wrong?" she asked.

"Head. Got a bit of a headache." I could hear the words slurring.

"Any aspirin?"

"They don't work. Not on these."

I struggled off my coat and tried to hang it up behind the door. It fell in a heap, like I would any second. My words sounded a long way off. "Want some tea? Don't have much food. Couple of sausages, maybe. Wasn't expecting company."

"Tea's smashing. I don't want to eat all your rations."

I fumbled in the little shelf above my two ring stove and found the little package. "Three. One and a half links each. Let's shove them on. There's some bread. Brown sauce too."

I smiled as encouragingly as my head would let me and she got up. I took my jacket and tie off and wrestled with the collar stud until I wrenched it off and dropped it on the chest of drawers. We found the dripping and dropped the bangers in the pan. The rich smell of hot fat quickly filled the little room. There are few finer sounds than sausages sizzling. I lit two fags and gave her one.

"Ta. What happened?" She pointed at my lip.

"Ran into a fat policeman."

I brewed the tea and filled two mugs. "Milk? Sugar?" I asked. She gave Churchill's salute.

We sat there on the bed, supping like a couple of old marrieds, not speaking, just enjoying the sight of each other and the sounds from the frying pan. Despite my head, and for the first time in a long time, I felt a bit of hope gather. I even felt the black weight lift a little from behind my eyes and wondered if she was some magic talisman against the pain that would normally have begun to incapacitate me.

The bread was a bit stale so we put four slices under the grill. Made two rounds each out of the toast and sausages. Made a bit of a mess with the marge, and the sauce ran down our fingers. Didn't mind licking it off. Not something I could have done with Kate Graveney. Those white gloves. Not sure I'd want to. The pain was steady now, but bearable. The food helped. Sometimes it does, sometimes it just makes me throw up.

I said between bites, "You should have stayed. This morning, I mean."

She cocked her head to one side, like a budgie. "I shouldn't have stayed last *night*. Give you the wrong idea 'bout me. I'm not that sort. I was cold and a bit fed up. And I'm not used to whisky. God, my head! As bad as yours now, I expect."

I doubted that.

She looked down. "Look… I needed a pal. Can we be pals? Nothing else – for a bit anyhow. See how it goes? There was a bloke. Bit of a mess. You know."

I needed a pal too. Needed more than that, but given what I had until yesterday, this was a step up. Was the other bloke still around somewhere?

"Fine by me." Was it? At least she hadn't closed out other options.

She brightened. "I just want to come and go. As I fancy. Is that all right?"

Shades of Sandra again? Well, I'd learnt; I wasn't going to get jealous this time. I'd take Val for what she was and what she offered. Friendship and sausages.

"Help yourself, Val." Then something struck me. "Look, if

we're going to be pals, you'd better know a wee bit more about this." I indicated the scar.

"Does it hurt?" She reached out. I let her. Her finger was like a mother's touch.

"Not the scar. Underneath. I was in France. Got caught. They gave me a right belting. The doctors here found a bit of my skull was pushing against the brain. I can't remember much since May '44, and I still have blackouts. I can feel one beginning now. Starts with a headache, then the vision goes… it's a bit like a migraine, only worse. So don't be scared if you pop in and find me, you know, lying down…"

She was nodding in sympathy. I could see the curve of her breast every time her arm moved. I felt something well up in me. Not sex. Deeper than that. I had to blink and rub my eyes. A woman's finger had more power than Wilson's fist.

"Next time, when I come again, you can tell me all about it. You're tired. Have a sleep."

I lay back as I was told. I was wrong about the pain; it wasn't going away. I felt the now familiar slide begin. The pressure behind my eyes was building up like water trapped in a hose. I wanted to be sick but knew I wouldn't. That would come when I woke. The panic rose in me as I began to lose all control. I couldn't stop myself falling over the edge. Vertigo overwhelmed me.

I woke a long while later, alone on the bed, and cold, even though I was wrapped in the quilt. It was daylight. I was in my pyjamas. The fire was out and had been cleared up. New kindling and rolled up newspapers sat under fragments of half-burned briquettes, ready to be lit. Just the way I liked. My head felt like it had been ripped open above my temple. I made it to the sink before I threw up. I felt helpless, like a rag doll, hanging over the bowl.

Slowly I dragged myself back up out of the hole. I looked round. Two plates washed and neatly stacked on the draining board alongside two mugs. How had I got into my pyjamas? That must have been a treat for her. I had a pal. Which was all the relationship I could handle at the moment.

I walked over to the bed and sat down, before my legs gave way. I slumped over into my hands waiting for the kettle to boil. I glanced at the clock on the mantelpiece. It was light outside and the clock read 11.30. I assumed it was the morning of the second of January, but I've been known to miss a complete twenty-four hours.

On the bedside table was the notebook I kept during my episodes. Sometimes I write in it, trying to talk to my future self, my "normal" self, to give me some clues about what I'd been doing and saying and thinking during my *fugue* – as Doc Thompson would say. It was always a bad moment. I picked up the notebook – a school jotter – and found my pencil wedged at a point halfway in. A new entry. The kettle whistled and I levered myself up and over to make the tea. I didn't want to look at what my alter ego had written.

I slunged some cold water on my face, dried it and took a sip of my tea. I felt life slowly creep into my bones. I settled back on my bed and opened the jotter.

SIX

The writing was big and jagged, like a child's. It was new all right. I'd carved out 1 Jan at the top, like a kid leaving his initials on a tree trunk. But my eyes were pulled past my own scribbles to an uneven line of capital letters at the foot of the page. I could see her with clenched fist and jutting tongue.

DON'T WORRY, DANNY. EVERYTHING WILL BE ALL RIGHT. YOU'RE A GOOD MAN. YOU MUST BELIEVE THAT. NO MATTER WHAT.

VALERIE.

I wondered what was so bad that Val had to try so hard to make me feel better. And what the hell had she thought of my other jottings? I turned back to my own writing.

abandon all hope arbeiters – this isnt freedom – its a lie I know its a lie – cold and hunger and arbeit makes you dead – the dead are free

they sent the dogs into the hut today – hot breath slevers cold nose sniffing me wanting to make me run and then hunt me down – you had to lie – he maketh me to lie down in green pastures – yet will I fear evil

not moshe – moshe didnt lie – was always afraid we were all afraid but moshe wore it like a coat – the dogs love that – they love fear it drives them mad

I chucked the notebook down on the floor and stumbled into my office. I pulled out my bottle from my desk drawer and poured a big shot into my tumbler. Then I sat down on my visitor's chair in my pyjamas and rocked and rocked. In my mind's eye was a day, two days, all the days in the camp. A double row of wooden huts inside a high barbed wire fence. On the edge of a sleepy little village, a thousand years old, not far from Munich. I often wondered why the villagers stayed there. Afterwards. Why would you want to live in a suburb of hell? The name Dachau tainted for evermore?

I saw Moshe's chubby face. One of the world's helpless types. Couldn't do anything for himself. His mother had cootered him all his days. A big baby. The Nazis loved hurting him. Bullies always picked on the weakest. They kept him alive – just – so that they could go on hurting him. He was so good to hurt.

They would take him away and bring him back blubbering and howling, his pants wet, tears soaking his bruised face. At least he had a face, until they sent in the dogs. All you could do was bury yourself into the wooden bunks – two of you to a bunk. Hide your head and your hands, anything that the dogs could get their fangs into. You didn't try to escape. Moshe did. Terror overcoming sense. Moshe ran and we watched him from our safe bunks get almost to the door before they brought him down and went at him. Like they'd found a rat and were going to worry it to bits. Moshe stopped screaming when they tore his throat out. His heels went on kicking on the wood floor a while longer, but finally stopped.

They pulled the dogs off. They didn't want them sated. They made us clean the mess up and take it to the big pile by the ovens. For three days Moshe's skull grinned at us from the rotting heap of human remains. The skin had blackened and puffed up and the crows had his eyes before they found room for him in a batch, and consigned him and us to something like rest.

I sank the whisky and poured another. It stung my lip and I cursed Wilson again. But at least the pain was real. Sometimes when I went out into the London crowds – for the solace of watching folk doing normal things – the gap seemed to be between two worlds.

When I was a kid, everything was in colour like some of the latest *Pathé News*. Then there was now, and it was monochrome. I sometimes wondered how far back my amnesia really went and if my early recollections were really mine. I have a sense of me that doesn't fit with the earlier images. I wander the crowds and go out hunting for people and places I knew before the gap, to see if they can make the bridge.

Doc Thompson told me it might be like this, but he was really guessing; none of them really knew the effect of the damage to my brain. They took off the bandages one day but whatever they'd done inside my head wasn't working. I was in constant pain. In fact, I *was* pain. It was the centre and reason for my existence. Morphine worked until it became a problem; that is, I couldn't get enough.

"We're going to try something," he said.

I was barely listening, could barely hear him, for the pain. "Anything. Try anything. Try cutting my head off, Doc, if that would help." I was feeling pretty bloody sorry for myself, lying pinned to my bed by the huge rock on my forehead.

"We're going to give you some EST."

"Fine."

"Electric shock therapy. A new treatment from Italy. We'll put some mild current through you to see if that alleviates the pain."

I screwed open my eyelids. "Are you just guessing?"

"The results have been very good. It's worked for other head injuries. And people with trauma."

"But you don't know?"

"We can't give you any more medication. As it is, you're at the limit. Look, there's no harm trying this. It's perfectly safe. Been used scores of times to good effect."

I'd heard. My mother told me of a neighbour who went doolally at times and had to go in for some wee shocks, as she put it. I remember the neighbour, always drooling. But, hell, she seemed happy in her own wee world. What choice was there?

They wheeled me into the room and helped me climb on to the bed. There were three people tending me – stopping me running away – all in white coats and – conspicuously and bizarrely – wearing Wellingtons. The bed was covered in a thick rubber sheet. It felt icy and silky and smelled of old petrol.

They fastened my arms and legs with thick straps and I began to think I preferred the headaches. I felt the helplessness overwhelm me. The same feeling I had just before the guards hit me. I started to struggle.

"It's all right, Danny. You'll be all right." The Doc made it all right by sticking a needle in my arm and filling it with happy juice. I settled down and let them wheel the machine over next to my bed. I let them wet my forehead with jelly of some sort – it was chilly and greasy. Then they clamped two metal pads on the same patches and put what looked like a scrum cap on my head to hold them in place. The Doc held up a rubber mouth-piece, like you get when you go to the dentist to keep your teeth open. I hated dentists.

"Stops you biting your tongue," he explained.

He prised my jaw open and jammed it in. It tasted of cold rubber and meths. I thought I would choke and fought back the panic. My chest was heaving. Doc smiled at me to make me brave. It didn't work.

"We'll start with some low-level current to see how it affects you, Danny. All right?"

Even if I could speak, what could I say? He didn't really care anyway.

"Stand well clear, please."

So they didn't want to get electrocuted as well. I heard a click and felt a tickle, then a jolt. My head and body twitched like a frog's leg in the science lab. That's what I'd become. They did more, lots more, and increased the level. I don't remember going back to the ward after that. In fact I don't remember much about the next few days. The pain was less but so was everything else. Just a kind of numbness, as though they'd cut something out of my head.

They gave me four more sessions over the next two weeks. Then they let me vegetate. Most days when it was fine, they'd wheel me into the sun and park me under a tree. I'd sit there and gaze at the early summer flowers. Or maybe the flowers were gazing at me; we seemed to share the same level of sentience. I didn't have many visitors. Couple of army types. I even think Caldwell showed up once but I couldn't be sure.

I know my mother came. She came every day for a week. She'd got lodgings nearby in Warwick and got a bus over to the hospital every day. Once she got past the crying stage she just sat and held my hand. We didn't talk much. We were never great talkers. But on the second day she brought out a book from her shopping bag – *Ivanhoe,* one of my favourites – and began reading it to me. Reading till I fell asleep in the sun listening to her quiet Ayrshire burr recounting tales of glory and struggle. I suppose she was trying to tell me something.

I missed her when she went. But already I was feeling better. The pain would come down like a tempest a couple of times a week, but mostly I was free of it. The dreams started, and the memories began to erupt, like waking up with a jolt in a cinema just as the hero is getting a pasting.

I was there through that glorious summer, growing stronger – outwardly – every day. I began to do my own reading; this was the second time in my life my mother had got me going. We'd been the only family in the street of red sandstone tenements that borrowed library books from the big Victorian pile across the other side of town. And my folks kept me on at the Academy with the unheard-of goal of university, not apprenticed to a good trade like my pals. It caused pursed lips from the gossips hanging over the fences, their Friday hair in curlers and their fat arms folded. "An' him only a miner. An' as for her, wi' her airs and graces…"

But the simple reason was that my mother – whose only air was worry and whose only grace was kindness – clenched her jaw and wouldn't let me follow my dad down the pits, like his dad and his dad's dad. I was to be educated, become a teacher or a lawyer. Anything rather than ride the cage down to die in the dark. When my mother's worst fears were realised, she and I fought for a while until we found a compromise between my dead father's academic aspirations for me and my need to prove myself by doing a man's job. I began a rapid rise up the ranks of Glasgow's finest, earning plaudits from the Chief Constable himself. Then a bloody wee Austrian with a silly moustache and big ideas decided to screw up my life – and here I was.

I began doing exercises, the ones they'd taught me at SOE. They came damned hard at first and left me breathless and dizzy. But they worked; I left the hospital, on my own two legs, freckled and fit in late August. The Doc said he could have got me fixed up as partially disabled and I'd get 11 bob a week. I declined. At that rate, with ciggies in civvy street at two and fourpence a packet, and a bottle of Johnnie Walker at twenty-five bob, I could have got drunk maybe once a year.

Besides, I'd found Raymond Chandler in the library, and his books had pointed the way to fame and fortune. I had the training, did I not? I was ready to face the world and raring to go. All I needed were some juicy cases. And the right hat.

SEVEN

I picked up the bottle, examined it and pushed the cork in firmly. It would be too easy. But then I'd lose another day. I touched the lines Val wrote and took heart. Someone cared. I shook myself, shaved, and washed as best I could in the basin – I have a little gas immerser that gives me enough hot water to keep myself decent. Once a week I go down to the slipper baths at Camberwell and soak until my fingers and toes wrinkle and my skin turns the colour of boiled prawns.

I was still shaky but hungry now, with a great empty place inside my body and head. I made some toast and jam. It filled my stomach but made no impression on my head. But at least I'd added another couple of memories. They were rotten ones but I could cope better knowing than not knowing. Assuming they were real, of course.

I put on the wireless. I like the Home Service in the afternoon. I was in time for *Music While You Work*. Jimmy Dorsey's big band filled the room, then Dinah Shore sang Cole Porter. Music lifts me. I'm a great reader but I don't understand classical music. I reckon I could if someone explained it to me; it can't be that far from something like *Moonlight Serenade*. I mean they're all tunes, aren't they, though they seem to use more violins than Dorsey.

I stepped out the building humming "Star Dust", filled with new determination. I had one lead. Kate mentioned a club that Caldwell belonged to over in Jermyn Street. Truth is, I'd thought of that, too. But there were simply so many in London that I hadn't had the heart to trek round them all. To be even more truthful, I don't like them. I don't feel comfortable in their plush entrance halls, trying to get past the flunky. I'd been made an officer but I was a long way from feeling like a gentleman.

I hopped on a bus up to the Elephant and then caught another over the new bridge at Waterloo and down the Strand. I watched the young ticket collector swinging from the pole and jumping up and down the stairs. He seemed happy in his work, chatting to the old girls who cheeked him back. Chatting up the young birds who flushed and stammered. Maybe I should try a different profession?

I got off at Trafalgar Square and walked through Admiralty Arch and down the Mall. The Palace was flying the Union flag and looked as if it would be there till Doomsday. God knows how they got away with only one bomb. Unkind folk say it's because they're all Germans. You have to admit it's suspicious. It's an easy bombing run: follow the Thames upriver until the Houses of Parliament, a smart right, skim over the lake in St James's Park, and bingo.

The Parthenon looked like every other club in the West End: ponderous, heavy columns and high windows. The doorway was reached up a short flight of steps. Some lights were on inside and, sure enough, there was a flunky waiting to pounce. This time I had my story ready.

"Good afternoon, sir. Can I help?"

He was way too old for the last war but looked like he'd done his part in the Great one. There's something about an NCO that you can tell a mile off, especially if you've been one. Maybe it's the suspicious eyes and the slight rocking motion on the balls of the feet.

"I hope so. My name's McRae, Captain Daniel McRae." His head went a bit higher and I swore his arm twitched in the reflex of a salute. "I'm an old friend of Major Anthony Caldwell. He may sign himself Major Philip Caldwell. Is he in?"

I could see the flunky's eyes narrow a fraction. But he was good, very good.

"Caldwell, you say, sir? Major Caldwell? I'll just check our members' list. We had so many new members, many of them temporary during the war." He walked behind his desk and picked up a big book, which he carefully shielded from me. He was lying, of course. These chaps know all their members by sight, by name and by inside leg measurement. He continued with the pantomime. I continued to smile. At last he looked up. He adopted a carefully placed frown of concentration, suggesting he had some delicate information to impart and wasn't sure how to do it.

"It would seem, sir, that we *did* have a Major Caldwell with us. But there is an entry here saying that we can't divulge details."

He savoured *divulge*, as though he'd only just learned it. "Not even to an old friend? We served together. SOE."

It cut no ice. A sympathetic smile grew on his face. "I understand, sir. But I think it's possibly because you *were* both with SOE that we have this instruction. If you see?"

I smiled my "I-quite-understand-but-you-don't" smile. "Can

you even tell me if he's alive or dead? I know this sounds silly. But it's been a while."

"I'm sorry, sir." He shook his head sorrowfully. "The instructions are clear. We can't say anything at all about the Major." He closed the book and the conversation.

"Can I leave a message?"

"By all means, sir. But I can't say if it will be answered or not. If you see?"

"May I borrow some paper and a pen, please?"

I kept it short, just asking Caldwell or his relative or friend to get in touch with me. I left my telephone number. I walked out of the club fully expecting never to hear from anyone, and wondering what other leads I could trace that would earn me Kate Graveney's up-front fee.

Three months ago I'd tried his old regiment – the Royal Signals – to see if they had an address. It was my first stop after being stonewalled by the document guardians at the SOE. I spent a whole day on the phone being sent from office to office, clerk to clerk. I finally found a corporal in the Signals records unit who was very helpful but ultimately useless.

He explained that one or two officers had been commissioned into this regiment simply as a holding arrangement while they went off and did some skulduggery in occupied Europe or at Bletchley Park. These officers never saw the inside of the mess at their nominal regiment, but it gave them a unit against which they could be paid and draw a uniform. There had been a Major Philip Anthony Caldwell associated with the Signals but he'd been demobbed. They had no forwarding address; why didn't I try SOE?

I decided to check the hospital, St Thomas's, just across Lambeth Bridge from Pimlico. That's where Kate said she'd been taken. I explained my situation at the desk – a version of it anyway: the old pal act. The receptionist was a bit reluctant at first but when I took off my hat and she saw my scars in all their glory, she became more sympathetic. Maybe I should only make passes at nurses?

The girl got up and sifted through the drawers of a filing cabinet. "There's no record of a Major Caldwell or even a Mister Caldwell around that date, sir. But there's lots of hospitals around this area. They could have taken him anywhere."

"Do you have a record for Miss Kate Graveney, then?"

She searched again and paused at one file. She turned and looked at me queerly. "Did you say the lady was brought in here with injuries from a bomb explosion?"

"That's right."

She became cagey. "We do have a patient coming around that time. But it doesn't mention that sort of injury."

Around that time? Maybe Kate got her dates muddled. But wasn't it her birthday? "What *does* it say?"

The girl shoved the folder back in the cabinet and shut the drawer firmly. "I'm sorry. We can't talk about patient's conditions with non-medical staff." She put her professional shutters up and I could see I'd get nowhere on this tack.

"Maybe it's just a misfiling."

"Perhaps. These things happen." Her smile was as bright and diamond-hard as her determination to say nothing more. My scars were getting no more sympathy. I put my hat on and left.

One thing I learned in Glasgow was never take anything for granted. Check everything. If you can't see it, smell it or hear it for yourself, it doesn't exist. It took me two days and a lot of shoe leather to get round the rest of the hospitals in the centre. I began with the Royal and the Brompton in Chelsea. I then did a circular sweep that took in King's in Camberwell, Guy's at Southwark, over the river to St Bart's and a big swing round to St Mary's. Nothing. Their records weren't all they might be and there was a bit of reluctance to tell me anyway.

Then I decided to change tack. I'd been looking for two hospital admissions, one unhurt, one probably dead. Dead people get recorded at Somerset House. My heart sank at the prospect; there had been a lot business coming their way in the last few years. Nevertheless I slogged my way back up the Strand and joined the queue for a day to get in front of a harassed clerk. I could see the hysteria in his eyes when I asked if I could track down a certain Mr Caldwell thought to have died about a month ago.

"We're a bit behind with the filing." He tugged at his greasy tie. The knot looked like a Boy Scout had been practising his sheepshanks on a bit of string. Knotted once two years ago, slackened off every night and tightened each morning.

"How far?"

"You mean how deep?" Definitely a glint of mania.

"Like that, is it?"

"We've caught up to June," he said promisingly.

"I hope you mean June 1945? So, you've got a backlog of six or seven months?"

"We're in October with births, though, and marriages are November."

"So if the man I'm trying to trace had been born three months ago you could have found him?"

He just grinned. I left him to finger his tie. I wondered how long before he'd use it to hang himself. Soon, I hoped. Post-war, and nothing worked. The machine we'd put together to win it had been broken up. All the soldiers back from the front had been offered their old jobs back, but I guess the better ones had lost some of their enthusiasm for the filing department now they'd had a taste of Paris and Rome; red wine and grateful girls.

This was keeping me fit but getting me nowhere. I holed up in my office and began to wait for either inspiration to strike or the phone to ring with an answer to my message at Caldwell's club. I made a promise to myself if I heard nothing by the end of the week, I'd phone Kate Graveney and offer her the advance back. Maybe half of it.

It was day two and I was like a squirrel in a cage. I paced the floor and nibbled everything I could find: mouldy cheese, fish paste on toast, and fritters I made from the shavings of gangrenous spuds. I didn't dare go out in case I missed a call. I checked my phone five times in case it was broken, until the operator began to get cranky. On top of everything, Valerie hadn't shown again and I didn't know how to find her. As a detective I was a joke. But I kept that thought to myself during discussions with a prospective client.

She must have been 60 or so. My mother's age. But she didn't have my mother's neat white hair and carefully cleaned and pressed clothes. Mrs Warner was on the grubby side of careless; her hat was bashed on to her head and nailed there with a huge bobby pin as though she slept with it on. Instead of an overcoat she wore a worn Paisley-pattern housecoat over a thick calf-length skirt and misbuttoned cardigan. I was surprised not to see old slippers on her feet, but she'd managed to find a pair of scuffed boots with ankle-high laces. Her ensemble was completed with a sorry string bag containing papers of some sort. She sat quivering in my chair while I made her a cup of tea.

"So, tell me, Mrs Warner, what can I do for you?" I was treating her as a potential paying customer but knew from looking at her she hadn't a bean. Still, age deserves respect. And some of these old dears can hardly get to sleep for the lumps of cash under their mattress.

She fixed me with her watery eyes, both yellow with cataracts.

"I want you to find my son, Charlie."

I pulled my pad closer and poised my pen. "When did you last see him?"

She thought for a moment then reached into her string bag and pulled out a thin sheaf of blue letters held together with three elastic bands. She rummaged again and came up with a spec case and put on some glasses. She gazed at the envelopes for a bit, trying different distances to find a focus that worked.

"Here. That's the one." She handed me a well-thumbed forces air mail envelope. I knew what was coming. "Go on, open it," she said.

"Are you sure, Mrs Warner?"

She waved her hand, and I unfolded the single sheet of thin blue paper. It was dated 12 June 1943. The hand was big and childlike. I could almost see Charlie's tongue gripped between his teeth as his pencil sprawled across the page. It read:

Dear Mum,
never felt so hot in my life. But they give us plenty of water
and tucker so dont you worry none. Cant tell you nothing
really but just wanted to let you know I was ok. Hope you
and Deke are ok too.
Love Charlie. Xxx

"Deke?" I asked, stalling for time.

"His dog. Charlie loved that dog. It's got fat. I can't walk it much like I used to. Me legs." She pulled up her thick skirt and

I could see the ridges of varicose veins all round her calf and ankles.

"Mrs Warner, this is the last letter you got from Charlie. But didn't you get a telegram or a letter from the Army?"

"Oh, yes. Yes, I did," she said eagerly, as though I was on to something. "Said he was missing. That's why I'm here. I wants you to find him." She stared at me defiantly. "I can pay, you know. I always pays my way." She rumbled in her string bag again and pulled out a worn purse.

I didn't know what to say to her. Couldn't tell her that I'd seen blokes like her Charlie blown into so many pieces there was nothing to put in a coffin. I was as gentle as I could be. But she needed a padre.

"Mrs Warner, I suspect your son was killed in action somewhere in the desert. See, he says how hot it was. I know where we were then. If he'd been taken prisoner then he'd have come back by now. You see?"

She saw all right. But she wasn't going to believe it. She was shaking her old head. "Charlie's dad died in the last one. He never saw Charlie. They can't take him too. It's not fair, you see. It's not fair." It was a simple statement of faith, as if fairness had a role in deciding who got shot and who didn't.

No, it wasn't; it wasn't bloody fair. I gave her more tea and listened to her stories of Charlie as a boy. Then I helped her out and down the stairs and went back to my desk and took a long drink even though it was only mid-afternoon. A little later, I went out for a walk to clear my head.

So I was more than a little pleased to get back just as the phone was ringing. I galloped up the last flight and skidded across the lino in time to take a call from a woman calling herself Mrs Caldwell, Mrs Liza Caldwell, Tony's wife.

EIGHT

Next day I made an early start. Too early, as it turned out. The straight run up the Northern Line from Kennington to Hampstead took just 35 minutes. But for all that, I popped up in a different world. It didn't feel like London. It seemed like I'd jumped down a rabbit hole and emerged in a country town from another century. Hampstead village runs up and down a steep hill. The houses are red brick and three or four storeys high with elaborate peaks and windows. I'm hazy about architecture, but think I can spot the Victorians' hand when I see it. These looked older. Who would that be? George? Edward? But which? Why couldn't they invent a new name for a new king? Good King Danny had a ring to it.

I wandered down the High Street, window shopping and enjoying the outing. I had an hour to kill before my meeting with Mrs Caldwell. A weak sun broke through the clouds and I saw faces lift and turn towards it like daisies. I treated myself to a *Times* and read it over a pot of Tetley's in a little tea-shop. I scoured the front page in case there was a job for an ex-cop, ex-soldier, ex-SOE agent with a hole in his head. Nothing sprang out. I then got into the meat of it; it made the *Sketch* look like a comic. There was talk of the first meeting of the new

United Nations Organisation in five days' time. The big guys who ran the place were flying into London with high hopes for a new and better world order. The scale of their dreams threw me for a bit. Almost sounded hopeful.

I sat up and looked around me. Nice folk were doing ordinary things, like eating jammy doughnuts and talking about the weather. And here I was, ensconced in a cosy café with a couple of quid in my pocket and most of my faculties in working order. Life wasn't so bad, was it? How had I let it get so narrow? I should just kiss the past goodbye and get on with the present. As my dad used to say, the future never comes. I resolved there and then that whether Caldwell was alive or dead, I'd let it all go. There were a thousand stories more tragic than mine out there. Maybe I'd go back to Glasgow. Why should I be afraid to go home? Or maybe I'd stay in London. It was ten degrees warmer down here.

But first I had some business to finish. I stuffed the paper in my pocket and walked back up the hill with my raincoat slung over my shoulder and my hat tipped back like Sinatra's sailor cap in *Anchors Aweigh*. I was whistling "I Fall in Love too Easily" as I turned down Willoughby Road, but the trees and tall houses and solemn gentility soon shut me up. I turned right into Willow Road. More quiet elegance. It wasn't the sort of area I would have picked for Caldwell. Too neat and placid somehow. Caldwell was a city bloke, a clubbish sort of chap who liked to be at the heart of things.

Willow Road runs at an acute angle from Willoughby and gently downhill. For the first 50 yards the tall terraces face off against each other. Then suddenly there is only the one side, the right side, as the street runs into a broader road coming in from the left. Then the heath starts and rolls up a grassy slope and into dense thickets of shrub and trees. I carefully noted the lines of sight.

The Caldwell house was one of the first batch. It was tall enough – four storeys – for four Kilpatrick families. A short path and a little flight of steps led up to the front door, which was capped by a wooden porch painted green. I saw a curtain flick in the first level window as the gate swung closed behind me and thwacked into its socket.

A guarded middle-aged woman answered my knock. She fitted the house, but not my idea of the wife of Major Tony Caldwell. She seemed too reserved, sullen almost. On the other hand, you usually find the extrovert needs someone to lord it over. Caldwell wasn't quite a bully, but he certainly liked getting his own way. Unless her appearance belied her strength of character, Mrs Caldwell would have been no match for our Tone. Which probably explains Kate Graveney. Which reminded me, I would have to watch what I was saying here.

"Mrs Caldwell? Sorry if I'm a little early…" I took my hat off.

"No, no, it's quite all right. You must be Mr McRae. Or is it Captain? It was in your message." Her voice was tight with nerves. She held the open door for me and tried not to stare too hard at my face, at my scars. She hung my coat in the hall.

"The rank was handed back with the uniform. It's just plain Mister. Danny, if you're OK with that?"

"Mister it is, then. Go in." She pointed into a room off the hall. "Please take a seat. I'll make us some tea." She kept touching her mouth and avoiding my eyes. What did she have to feel guilty about? She wore a good dark frock and her brown hair was carefully combed back and pinned up in a style she probably hadn't changed since she was sixteen.

As she went to the kitchen I looked around. It was a good-sized room in a tall thin house, but a bit stark and smelling of polish and stale air. It was clearly the "best" room, with an outlook on to a back garden with high hedges to keep out the neighbours. The antimacassars sat in perfect regimen on the backs of two brown armchairs and a couch. There was a heavy wood table and chairs, and an upright piano squatting on a plain brown rug. On the piano were photos. I got to my feet and walked over smartly. Sure enough, it was Tony Caldwell, in all his army finery, smiling out at me. There was a black ribbon edging the frame. Another photo showed Tony and Liza – Mrs Caldwell to me, obviously – smiling and looking several years younger.

"I see you recognise him." Mrs Caldwell had materialised silently. She was bearing a tray with all the tea accoutrements on it.

"Yes, of course. As I explained…"

"… you used to work together in the SOE." She began clattering cups around.

"Right. And I was trying to look him up. Someone said… well, that he was…"

"Dead?" Her eyes looked accusingly at me, as though I might have something to do with it. Then she was dabbing away at them.

"I'm sorry. That was very clumsy. I…"

She was shaking her head. "No. It's all right. I still can't believe it. To go through the whole war and then… a bit ironic, don't you think, Mr McRae?" She was pouring tea as she spoke.

"So Major Caldwell *is* dead? I'm very sorry."

"He died, as you may have heard, in a friend's flat. An unexploded bomb. Which finally did. Explode, I mean. There's a lot still lying around, they say. But that doesn't seem to make it any less stupid. Do you believe in fate, Mr McRae?" She went on without waiting for a reply. "I used not to. Now I'm not so sure. Sugar?"

"Two, please. I'm afraid there's been a lot of fateful events these last few years. We've all lost something."

"What did *you* lose, Mr McRae?" Her voice was sharper suddenly, and I caught a glimpse of steel beneath the softness. Her eyes seemed brighter, more penetrating.

"My memory." I pointed to the scar. She'd already noticed it and only glanced briefly at my forehead. "I lost the best part of a year of my life. Only some snatches come back to me. And it's hard to know what's memory and what's imagination."

"Does it matter? It's sometimes better not to remember." Her lips pinched tighter. This woman needed more sugar in her tea.

"You may be right, but if it's all the same to you, I'd like the chance of choosing what I want to forget. That's why I wanted to find Tony. He recruited me to SOE and briefed me for my mission. I wondered what other gaps he might have been able to fill in for me."

"That's all you remember? Tony sending you off?" She was quite still now, as though this was the most important bit of our conversation. I assumed she was hungry to hear about him, to rub his memory. I thought I should oblige.

Tony organised three months of training at stations, as we called the several country houses scattered around England. I expanded my repertoire of unarmed combat. The Scots Guards had kept it simple: head first, then the boot. Glasgow rules. Not cricket, but then we weren't big on cricket. I learned explosive handling and radio communication, and buffed up my schoolboy French to a level that might fool a deaf German but would be ridiculed by a native speaker. Despite my protestations about the number of red-haired Frenchmen, they made me dye my hair black to look less conspicuous. At the end of my training Tony met me in Baker Street.

He took personal charge of the last session, which went on all day, repeating and repeating our instructions and our communications plans till he was satisfied. He had quite a temper if you got it wrong; his handsome face would go red, his eyes would pinch up, and his voice would rise a few notches till he got control again.

We shook hands and smiled at the end of it, and I set off down Baker Street in the car that was taking me to the airfield and France. My last sight of him was him standing in the doorway, stroking and twisting his moustache with both hands.

"That's Tony," Liza was saying. "I kept telling him not to play with his moustache. It looked affected. Like biting your nails. And you can't remember anything else about him?"

I shook my head. I could have told her that in some of my nightmares I could see his face leering down at me. But I guessed that wasn't what she wanted to hear.

"Mrs Caldwell, I'm sorry about your loss and I'm sorry that I found you too late. The office wouldn't tell me anything about Tony. As though they were shielding him from me."

She sized me up for a moment. "I suppose I should tell you." She took a breath. "Tony mentioned you. Said you'd been brought home and were in hospital. He said that you had *problems* and that it might get a bit difficult when you were let out."

I felt my face colouring. I didn't ask what sort of problems. "Difficult for whom?"

She studied me. "For him. For us. For the people you worked with."

"That I might become a nuisance? Is that it?"

She shrugged and said nothing more.

"So your husband told SOE not to talk to me about him? Is that it?"

"I have no idea, Mr McRae," she lied. "More tea, or do you have to be going?"

As I pulled on my coat, Liza Caldwell watched me as though she had something else to say but wasn't sure how I'd take it. I gave her a second or two after buttoning my coat to see if the silence would draw her out.

"Did you know he was with a woman the night he died, Mr McRae?"

Now, *that* was unexpected. My face must have given it away.

She was nodding. "I suppose everyone knows about it." It wasn't said as a question. "You can always tell with a man. They can't help themselves. They have needs that seem to override all sense. Tony was like that."

She seemed to be summing him up. I stared at her, not knowing what to say. She was talking in a flat, calm voice. As though she had been resigned to his ways. It might explain why she didn't seem quite as distraught as a woman should be who'd lost her husband barely a month ago. I wondered if she knew Kate.

As I walked back towards the tube I thought about how SOE had blocked me. A word or two planted by Tony would have been all it took, so that when I showed up, I'd be treated like a leper. With my scar it was like walking around with a label saying *warning – madman*.

The sun had gone in and the afternoon had turned colder.

Much colder for me. I caught the tube in the favoured village of Hampstead and surfaced again in dreary London. I looked at the faces and saw the new year celebrations were over. We were back in the real world, and it was colourless and impoverished. One egg a week and all our clothes like uniforms.

I started walking home along the Walworth Road, watching their faces. No one complained much. We all knew we should be grateful. Even for our ration cards. I turned up my collar against the cutting wind, strangely depressed by what I'd found, depressed by the rubble and grubby houses around me. London was like my mind: a broken landscape with tantalisingly familiar patterns that slipped from my grasp the tighter I gripped. Maybe my eyes had changed. Maybe I had a different vantage point now. But this new year was more than ever like a death than a birth.

NINE

I got in, half expecting, half hoping Val would be there. She wasn't. So I called Kate Graveney to report. She sounded busy. She cut me short and fixed to meet at my office the next evening. I didn't know why that should raise my spirits, but it did. Then for one daft moment I felt guilty, as though I was being disloyal to Val. We were just *pals*, for God's sake, and Kate was business. But it was a surprise that Kate wanted to wait to get the news face to face. Fine by me, given her face. But why hadn't she wanted to get the gist of my findings on the phone? Why didn't she just ask me if Caldwell was dead?

And then she was late. It was twenty past six when I recognised the sound of those elegant heels picking their way up the stairs. This time I was on my feet in front of my desk to greet her, jacket on and cardigan well out of sight. I sat nonchalantly on the edge of my desk and let one leg swing free to show how well creased my trousers were. I'd damped down my hair with Brylcreem and a hard brush. The fire was in good shape in the grate. I'd queued for two hours today to get a stone of coal, mainly dross as usual. Half a dollar it cost me. And I had to queue twice. They only let you have seven pounds at a time, but they didn't mind how often you came back. It was easier if you had a big family or knew someone.

She looked preened and pampered. I wondered what they'd made of the fur stole out on the Walworth Road? I don't know mink from sable, but whatever it was stood out from the coney coats I see down the pub. I pulled the chair out and pushed it behind her, only just stopping myself from stroking the fur. I took the other side of my desk. She had a cigarette ready and I lit it for her, then one for me. I reached into my bottom drawer and pulled out a bottle of Scotch, a bottle of soda and two glasses.

"Drink?"

She looked thoughtfully at me and sucked in her cheeks. "Why not? It's past six. Half and half, please."

I poured us two big ones. She sipped.

"Well, Mr McRae?" She had lost all her first-night nerves. This was the upper class in full sail, unflappable and in control.

I'd rehearsed a dozen different ways of telling it, most of them involving a steady build-up to the punch line after some impressive detective work. "In a nutshell, Miss Graveney, I regret to tell you that Mr Caldwell is dead."

She blew out a plume of smoke. She didn't seem surprised or much upset for that matter. How would *you* feel if you learned your lover – albeit a deceitful one – had been blown to bits in the explosion that you survived? Which reminded me. I reached into my desk drawer.

"Recognise this?" I placed a lady's blue leather shoe on my desk. I'd given it a clean and brush-up. A fine shoe. She cocked her head.

"Do you have the other one? They were a good pair." She took another drink, a bigger one. Did nothing get through to this iceberg?

"Sorry. I thought I was looking for one heel, not two."

Her eyes flickered in surprise. "Most amusing, McRae."

I thought so. "Do you want to hear the story?"

She nodded but it was nearer a shrug, almost as though she was being polite. But I didn't want this over in a hurry. And I wanted her to feel I'd earned her advance. I told her of my hospital trek and the Somerset House fiasco. Finally I explained how simple it had turned out, once the message got picked up by his wife from his club.

"What's she like?" She meant what did she look like. That's women for you. Always squaring up to the competition.

"Quiet, but tough underneath. Took it surprisingly well." I didn't tell her that neither of them was finding his death over-traumatic. But then I couldn't rustle up much of a wake either for Tony Caldwell.

"Did she say anything about how, or rather where, he died?"

"She knew about you, if that's what you mean. Maybe not *who* you are."

"But *what* am I, eh, Mr McRae?" She stubbed out her cigarette. "Well, that seems to be that." She was pulling on her gloves. "You've been most efficient and thorough. I think we can all move on now, don't you?"

She uncrossed those trim legs of hers and stood up to go. I stood up too.

"He was cremated, his wife said. So there's no stone or anything."

She blinked, as though startled at the thought. Why hadn't she asked about that? It would have been normal to have wanted to pay your respects, wouldn't it? There had been something between them, hadn't there?

"Right. Thank you. That really does close the case, doesn't

it?" She must have misinterpreted my waiting expression. "Do I owe you any more money?"

"No. Not at all. In fact it didn't take me a full week. I owe you…"

She was waving it off. "Goodbye, Mr McRae. I hope your business does well. Good hunting and all that."

We shook fingers and I watched her disappear down the stairs, clacking musically all the way. I went back to my desk, put my feet up and pulled her glass over. It was barely touched. There was lipstick round the edge. I covered her impression with mine and knocked back the remains. I could taste her through the Scotch.

I topped up my own glass and sipped and wondered why I was being lied to. This didn't smell right. Her act was wrong. There was no grief; there are stiff upper lips and then there are people who just don't care. It could be that I was simply confirming what she'd known all along; she had already come to terms with it. But the natural reaction would have been to want to don the black rags and the veil, visit the grave, shed a few last tears, put it all behind you. Women never miss a chance to act a part. Even when they're lying, they make a better job of it than this. A dab of the eyes, a downward glance, a question or two about the funeral was all it would have taken.

It was also a bit too bloody convenient for my liking. The man I most wanted to talk to in all the world about my missing moments gets killed by an old bomb. His lover doesn't go to one of the big detective agencies; she asks *me* to do the checking. And there's no body, not even a headstone. Bloody convenient.

TEN

I woke in the early hours, roasting on the spit of my troubled dreams, and overwhelmed with the familiar image. The woman is lying face down. Blood oozing from the back of her head and gathering in a pool below it. There's another pool under her hips. I'm holding a bayonet. Red drips from it and from my hands. The blood feels hot and slick. I'm pleading with her not to lie in the blood. That she'll get cold. And then I hear the running feet…

I got up and made some tea and had a fag to calm me down. It was nearly light anyway. So I sat and watched the winter sun edge up over the rooftops. It didn't warm me. I shouldn't follow the stuff in the newspapers. I certainly shouldn't go on a sodding tour of inspection. Serves me right for being a ghoul. With a brain as precarious as mine, I need to avoid inflammatory situations.

I decided to cook some porridge, a comfort food that reminded me of home and my mother. It was also cheap. I was on the point of excavating the grey lava from the bottom of the pot when a little voice took me unawares and banished my night-time blues.

"Knock, knock. Is there enough for two?" Val said.

I was inexplicably happy to see her beaming face, and grinned at her. "Only if you have it with salt. I'm not letting you English put sugar on my porridge."

She screwed up her face and came into my room. Her hair was pulled back in a ponytail. Its end curled round her neck. She looked just fine.

"I'll try it. Why not? We eat anything now, don't we? Horses, yum, yum. Powdered eggs, goody, goody."

I laughed. "I'll get my mum to send us some haggis."

"That's where I draw the line."

"One of my guys caught a snake in the desert and ate it."

"Yuk! Was he sick?"

"Violently. I think he ate the wrong end."

I lifted up the top of the fold-down table and sat out two bowls on the red Formica. When I make porridge I always make too much, so it stretched easily. I spooned the steaming sludge into the bowls.

"Watch, mind. There's nothing hotter." She flicked her ponytail back. "It's nice like that," I said, staring appreciatively.

She blushed and tugged at it. "It's too long. Drives me mad. I'm thinking of having it all hacked off. Like those magazines."

"Don't do that! You've got lovely hair."

She smiled. "OK. I'll keep it. For you."

I took a chance. "There's an old Scottish custom that says if you share porridge with someone, you must share a secret."

She looked wary. "A likely story."

I pressed on. "I've met you twice now and I don't know anything about you, except your name. I don't even know where you live."

She shook her head and laid a scalding spoon of porridge back down. "Don't make it hard, Danny. I told you, I don't want to get involved. I just want to be able to drop in and have a natter. I don't want the third degree." Her eyes were determined. I was scared she'd up and leave. And what did it matter where she lived or what she did?

"OK, *pal*. Just curious." I smiled.

She sighed. "Look, there's this bloke. He hurt me real bad. I'm trying to sort things out. Maybe then I'll tell you the whole thing, OK?"

I knew it. We're all bastards. Was she living with him? Would she leave him? Not if I pushed her. I changed the subject. I told her about Kate Graveney and the strange coincidence of Tony Caldwell. Val seemed rapt and let her porridge go cold. Or maybe it was the salt. She had her elbows on the table and her hands under her fine jaw. Her eyes were big and dark, weighing everything.

"Why did she need *you* to find Mrs Caldwell? She could have got anybody to ask at his club. Women like her know lots of men. It wouldn't have been hard."

I noticed the little bit of spite in her voice as she spoke of *women like her*.

"It worried me too. Like it's all being done for my benefit. To keep me away."

I told Val about Liza Caldwell's comments, how Caldwell had probably told SOE not to divulge his whereabouts. Especially to me.

It was then that Val came up with the mad idea, and I felt it take root in my brain like the seeds of a fever.

"Won't SOE have files on you and Tony Caldwell?"

"Yes...?"

Her eyes were gleaming. "Why don't you get in and see for yourself?"

"You mean break in?!"

"Would it be hard?" she asked, all innocence. She lit a fag.

I thought about the layout of Baker Street. It had grown like a rabbit warren to take up virtually the whole street. But I knew the records on agents were kept centrally at number 64. I also knew they were closing the whole shebang down. They didn't need our kind of talents any more. So security might not be as tight as it used to be. If I could get past the guards at the door and then hide till...

"This is daft! Completely daft! You're a madwoman, so you are, Valerie Brown. And you're turning me as mad as you."

"I'm crazy," she agreed, and blew a smoke ring. "But I'm not mad. Come on, eat up. I'm taking you to feed the ducks. Got any old bread? Better not take any of this stuff, or they'll sink!"

She didn't finish her porridge. I dunked the two bowls in water so they wouldn't set like concrete. Then she dragged me out. The weather was kinder: broken clouds and a southwesterly. We chased a bus and leapt on as it slowly eased away from the stop. We landed breathless on the platform, faces aflame and laughing. I saw nothing but kind eyes from the passengers. We must have looked like lovers.

We got off at Hyde Park Corner and ambled into the park. The rolling slopes were winter drab, and the green seemed to have leeched into the Serpentine. Bare-armed trees stood around the flat water as though they'd been stuck in the ground upside down. There were ducks marshalling by the landing stages and hoovering up the soggy bread thrown at them by squealing kids. Val joined in and I stood and watched her and felt something turn over inside. She was so fragile. She came back to me, smiling. "What? What you looking at, then?"

"You, you daft thing. Like a big kid."

"That's me. Come on. Let's run." And she was off. I could have caught her in ten steps but I let her run till she was shrieking and breathless. There were dozens of folk around, but all in our distance. I caught up with her and collapsed on a bench beside her. Her cheeks were glowing. I would have kissed her then. I should have. We watched the water shimmer and the ducks take off in a panic of wings.

"What happened to your dad?" she asked suddenly. She knew my mother was still in Scotland.

I realised I'd never talked about it. I could talk about it now. I remembered the day like it happened last week. I was sixteen. It marked the end of my university pipe dream.

"My mum always waited by the window every evening. Darning socks or polishing the brass. But she'd keep looking at the clock. To make sure he came home. One night he didn't. You know what happens when a pit collapses? And when they finally get the bodies out?" I didn't expect or wait for an answer. "They lay all the men out in rows on open carts at the pithead. Then the women walk along and pick out their men."

I felt her tense beside me. "They were all wearing shawls and sobbing and holding on to each other. I walked with my mum. She was clinging to me as if I could stop her from drowning."

I paused and watched the wind whip up ripples on the water.

"She used to kneel at his feet and take his boots off every night when he came in from the pit. He never asked her to do it; it was just something she did. To thank him for putting food on the table, a roof over our heads. He'd stick his feet in the grate. I can still see the steam rising and smell his socks."

Val said nothing, just looked at me with the same anguish she'd shown at midnight in the park.

"This time, she knelt by the cart and held on to his boots. As though she could stop him. As though she could haul him back from his journey. She kept them for me."

I didn't tell Val that I still carried the guilt of not being down there with him, like the other sons. Maybe I could have done something. I was young and strong and quick. Instead, I was poncing around in a school blazer, talking about university when there was real life and real death going on all round me. Six months later, I put the blazer away for good and signed up for the police force.

Val got me up and walking again. Right round the lake. We were quieter now, closer. It was the best day I could remember. I would have stopped time. No, that's not true. I felt this was the start of something and that the best would come if I had the patience. To crown it all, we got off the bus near my flat and the newspaper seller was calling out, "Read all about it, read all about it. Ripper caught! The Soho Ripper caught!" I bought a copy. They were going fast. I greedily scanned the text.

"Look at this, Val. They've caught the bugger."

"Oh, that would be fine, Danny!"

She wouldn't come in, not even for a cup of tea. I said I wanted to see her again, go on a date, a flick or dancing even. Not that I'm much of a dancer. But she wouldn't say when or if we'd see each other again. I watched her waltz off into the night. I wished the day could begin again. I climbed the stairs whistling and nursing all the flavours of the afternoon, making sure I wouldn't forget a single moment.

I propped the paper on my table and dug out my folder with the other clippings. I sat down and read the news in detail. I read it again and turned to some of the earlier reports. I began to rub my scar. This didn't feel right. On my third reading I became convinced: they'd got the wrong man. They were quoting my old friend Detective Inspector Wilson of the Yard.

A suspect has confessed to the murder of all three unfortunate women. The suspect was apprehended yesterday evening after a tip-off from a vigilant member of the public. The suspect is an army deserter who was apprehended in the act of burning a blood-stained army greatcoat in the back yard of the block of flats. The constables were attacked with a bayonet which may be the murder weapon. A search of his flat revealed other stained items of clothes. All items have been sent for analysis.

The journalist hadn't let it rest there. He went on to quote neighbours. They described the man as drunk and violent. He frequently had women round to his flat. Often these sessions would end up in fights, verbal and physical. There were reports of disturbing smells coming from the flat and late-night screams.

Great, but it didn't fit with my view of the murderer. Whoever had been doing these killings went about his business quietly and discreetly. He wouldn't make a song and dance about it and draw attention to himself. He wouldn't be so stupid as to wear an army greatcoat on his murderous outings. Neither would he stand in the back yard of his flats and try to burn the evidence. The real murderer was wicked, not stupid; evil, not careless. He wasn't a loudmouth with a penchant for drunken parties.

So why did he have a bayonet? There are thousands of war souvenirs out there. I hear of one bloke who came home with a German motorbike and sidecar still fitted with a machine gun. But why did he confess? Did Herbert Wilson and his merry men beat it out of him? Was he drunk or delusional? I've seen other confessions that turned out to be false; from lost men, men on the fringes, wanting attention, any attention, including infamy; or so addled with booze or drugs that they'd say yes to being the Pope. It was a favourite test of mine.

The real killer was still out there, reading this and laughing at us. How long would it be before he proved it? I ringed Wilson's quote with my thick black pencil and scrawled *Ha bloody ha!* across it. I cut it out and put it with the rest.

I turned to the bottle to see if I could hang on to the best part of the day, but it was already fading and I could feel another damned headache creeping up on me. As though the false hope had soured things. It wasn't fair. But then I wasn't expecting it to be. It's a bitter thought that on sunny days Scots say to each other: *fine day, enjoy it, it'll no' last*.

I fought against the tide of pain that was gathering behind my eyes. But finally I surrendered and crawled into my bed. The pressure built and I pleaded for it to stop. But I was crushed and drowned and sent off into my personal dark...

It was a beauty. It came and went over two days. A high price for half a day's simple pleasure. I emerged shaking and thirsty and unshaven. The mirror told me of my suffering. The sink stank of my vomit and the porridge had grown a fine culture. My clothes looked like they'd been borrowed by a tramp for a month. When I had half my vision again, I saw my jotter had been used. I couldn't face it, not yet.

I scraped my beard until my chin was covered in bloodied bits of paper, then took myself down to the slipper baths at Camberwell, towel under my arm. My head had an anvil pressing down on it and my stomach rumbled and ached as the bus jolted over the potholes. I lay for the full hour in the hot bath soaking the pain away, and then made my way home. I was clean. Washed out more like. But I was beginning to think I'd live.

I stopped at the Co-op for a fresh loaf, and waited while the girl stabbed and chopped with her two wooden spatulas at a slab of butter. She finished off the pat by pressing on the shape of a sheaf of corn. It weighed in at exactly my weekly allowance of four ounces. She smiled in pride. I bought a can of sardines and a packet of fags and handed over my coupons. I picked up the paper to check the date and saw it was Monday the seventh. Two days lost. Then the headlines jumped out. "Ripper suspect released!" Forty-eight hours was all it had taken. I glanced down at the smaller print, trying to get my eyes to focus.

The suspect had indeed been trying to destroy the evidence – but of a very different crime. The blood on the coat had been a pig's. The man had been pinching meat from butchers all round Borough Market. He'd been boiling the carcasses in his flat and flogging the boiled meat to housewives who didn't ask where he'd got it or how many stamps he needed. He was also making his own hooch. Stuff that would make you go blind. Between boiling the pigs and running the still, it was hardly surprising the neighbours had reported funny smells.

He'd retracted his confession when he'd sobered up and the police had to let him go for the murders. To show there were no hard feelings, they nicked him again for pinching the meat and making the booze. There were no comments this time from Inspector Wilson of the Yard.

I went up to my flat and opened the sardines. The loaf had a good black crust, just as I'd asked for, and the butter smelled of rich pastures and warm hide. I wolfed down the sandwich and began to feel better. Then I remembered the jotter. Or to be honest, I hadn't forgotten, I just wasn't ready. I sat down with a cigarette and drew it to me. I already had faint impressions of what I'd been recalling. It wasn't good. It was never good. I read my words…

Don't go down in the woods today – teddy bears waiting – behind the furnace into the woods – wetting yourself

bring you back with arms funny and legs funny and head funny – and naked and screaming dead face screaming dead and throw you on to the pile for burning – pork burning

I held my head in both hands to stop it splitting in two. I was made to bring them back from the woods one day. They picked me and two others to wheel the cart out the gates and into a little piece of woodland behind the camp. It was pretty: birds, grass and the smell of green. But you knew you weren't there to pick bluebells.

We followed a track and found two guards stripped to the waist, their white skin gleaming, contrasting with their tanned faces. One was sitting on a fallen tree, smoking. The other stood behind him, massaging his shoulders in a leisurely way. Around them was the evidence of their morning exercise. Three naked, nameless men hung from the branches of a chestnut tree. It was a fine tree with fruit forming all over it.

The hanging men had their arms tied behind their backs. A rope was round their wrists and they'd been pulled up in the air so that their own weight dragged their bodies down and tore out their shoulder muscles and joints. The guards had been inventive. They'd tied stones to the swinging men's ankles to add a little to the pain. Their bodies were covered with welts and bloody lines where they'd been whipped till their flesh disintegrated. Finally they'd been used as target practice for the guards' Lugers. It must have been hot work.

We hauled them down and laid them gently on the cart and prayed to the god none of us believed in any more to spare us from being the centrepiece of the next picnic. As we shoved our laden little cart back out of the clearing I looked behind. The seated guard had his head arched back into the stomach of his friend and had his arms stretched behind him, round the other's legs, pulling him to him.

I closed the notebook. There were other scribbles and other memories. The gaps were closing, but there was nothing good worth remembering. Days of blood and hunger. Wills bent wholly towards surviving the next hour. You couldn't plan beyond that. To last a day was a triumph. To last a week or a month was so unlikely as to be not worth thinking about.

But it still left me with time unaccounted for. Time when I wasn't in the camp. Time when I was taken *to* the camp. Time when I was dropped into France. The only man who could have helped me fill in some of the missing pieces was dead. So it left one option. Val's crazy option. I'd have to be just as crazy to even think of trying it.

So I began planning.

ELEVEN

could think of two ways of cracking the SOE records department. I could be a sneak-thief and break in through a window in the dead of night. Baker Street comprised a number of blank-faced buildings with back entrances for deliveries and despatch riders. So I could probably find my way round and in. The problem would be the noise of breaking glass and alerting the security guards.

The other approach was to brazen it out and march in though the front door during daylight hours. I'd find a hiding hole and wait till everyone had gone home. Pretty chancy and completely dependent on the doorman being dozy. And I'd still have to get out again. Unless I waited till the next day and slipped out through the crowds.

I took a morning stroll along Baker Street to remind myself of the layout and to see how well manned the entrance was. It gave me a funny feeling walking past. I could see the younger version of me bounding in for the final briefing sessions. Then nothing, until time restarted in an English hospital, like coming round from anaesthetic. I was half expecting my younger self to appear at any moment; I could call out to him, tell him to watch out... but for what?

I was last here in September. The dark brown three-piece demob suit felt very new and rough on my skin. It even smelled new. From at least six feet away it looked smart enough. And to be fair, nobody looked any better dressed. With my new trench-coat and hat, and a good pair of shoes, I felt life could restart. All I wanted was some information about the last year. I thought the chaps in SOE would be able to help.

I'd phoned ahead from the hospital and arranged to see Major Cassells who ran agent selection and training. I recognised the security man at the door.

"Hello, Stan. How are you, then? Still got back problems?"

"It's this weather. It always... why, Captain McRae, isn't it? Good to see you back, sir. I trust you're well?" He squinted at my face sympathetically.

"Better than I was, Stan, and that's for sure. I'm here to see Major Cassells. Can you bell him?"

"Certainly, sir. Why don't you take a seat and I'll send a lad along to his office?"

I sat down and waited. The hallway and little reception area were unchanged: grey lino and camouflage-green walls. The chairs were government issue wooden jobs with slippery seats and a right-angled back. There was no position that was comfortable except ramrod straight and hands in lap. Designed by drill sergeants. I leafed through some well-pawed *Reader's Digest*s. None was more recent than June '44. I suppose they thought they wouldn't need any more after D Day and could economise.

About twenty minutes later I heard army shoes chewing up the lino and saw the Major heading my way. Cassells was immediately familiar to me, though he was greyer and more lined. He looked harassed. He was in civvies apart from the shoes. His hand was outstretched from about ten paces out.

"Hello, old chap. You look well. Better than I expected, actually, from the hospital reports." He laughed.

"I'm still a bit shaky, sir, but coming along. Good of you to see me."

"No, no. It's all right. And the name's Gerald. We can drop all that rank stuff now. Glad to do what I can for our agents. Lost enough of them. Good to see the ones who got back, don't you know."

We walked back along the hall to his office. It was piled high with boxes. His desk was under inches of paper. He lifted a couple of crates off his spare chair and got me to sit down. He sat back in his own and steepled his hands under his chin. He looked pensive.

"Sorry about the state of things here, Daniel. We're closing up shop in a few months. Disbanding. Pity, really. We were getting quite good at this. But who needs chaps like us in peace time, eh? So, what can we do for you?"

"You know about my memory loss?" He nodded. "Well, I'm trying to fill in some of the gaps. Like how I ended up in Dachau."

Cassells was nodding his head off. "Absolutely, dear boy. Quite understand. Do the same myself." He reached over to his packed in-tray and dug out a thick pink folder. "Got your file, here. Took a quick squiz the other day, eh?" He opened it and held it up like a book so I couldn't read it upside down. He stopped on one of the first pages. He read it and glanced at me, then flicked on. There seemed to be a couple of envelopes as well as carbons and other documents. I had the impression he was already pretty familiar with it; the dumb show was for my benefit. He closed the file and sat back.

"You had a rough time of it, no mistake. A rough time. Don't remember a thing, eh? No bad thing. Lot of jolly nasty stuff went on in these camps. Best to forget, eh?"

"I'm sure you're right, Gerald. It's just…"

"Course. Course. Not very complicated. May '44, it says. Picked up by Gestapo. Probably some local did it for money. Happened a lot. Sent you to Dachau. Bad show, that." He frowned, as though someone had tossed a low ball at cricket. That was it?

"I'd thought I'd hear a little more detail than that, Gerald. I don't particularly want to relive my camp experiences, but I do want to know what happened in France. What about my old boss, Major Caldwell?"

Cassells looked even more uncomfortable. He began tapping my folder with his index finger. I noticed how stained it was with nicotine. I always use a pumice.

"Demobbed, d'you see?"

"Is there a way of contacting him? Where does he live? I'd just like to have a chat with him."

He was shaking his head. "'Fraid not, old chap. No forwarding address. Once chaps are out, they're out. And we're closing up shop," he reminded me.

This wasn't what I expected. "But surely you have to be able to contact everyone? Sort out things like pensions? I can't believe there isn't a forwarding address. Can we get hold of his file?"

Cassells was beginning to look edgy and irritated. I didn't care. This was my life. He leaned into his desk and placed his elbows on my file.

"Even if we had such details we wouldn't give 'em out. Security, you know. The war's over and our chaps and gels need to get on with their lives. In private. I suggest so do you. Some things are best left forgotten. Sleeping dogs and all that, eh?" With that he was standing. The interview was over.

I stood on the other side of the street, examining the building, looking for entry points. They were due to wind up by the end of this month, the papers said. Surely they wouldn't be quite so hot on security? A sudden fear struck me; if they were winding up, what would they do with the files? Burn them? Keep them, but move them? What if they'd already been shifted? How would I find them? That chilling thought convinced me; I'd try the front entrance today. What could I lose? At worst they'd just throw me out before I got past the front door. But I'd be better waiting till five. That's when everyone shot out, heading for home. With luck I'd be able to slip through the crowds without raising an alarm.

I went home, rustled up some grub using the last of my spuds and a bit of stewing steak. After chewing through the best of it, I put aside the gristle for the moggy; her teeth were sharper. Then I went into my top drawer, pulled out a pair of old wool socks and unwrapped them. I took out my pride and joy, which was a funny way for an ex-copper to talk about the tools of a thief.

Part of our SOE training was in picking locks. The expert who spent a frustrating fortnight with me and five other rank amateurs had been let out of Dartmoor for the duration. His message was simple, if daunting: anyone could become a good lockpick with the right tools and 20 years' practice. In the absence of such a Fagin apprenticeship the best he could do was provide us with the equipment and the rudiments of the trade and tell us to practise as much as possible. And if all else failed, carry a good jemmy.

A lock is made up of pins that sit at different heights inside a rotating plug. The trick is to push up the pins to let the plug rotate and open the lock. A key has a variable profile – think of the Alps – which pushes up the individual pins in the right order. A pick mimics a key by pushing up the pins one by one and getting them to stick.

We started with bicycle spokes, a pair of strong pliers and a clamp. A pick has three parts: a handle, the body – or tang, to the professional – and the business end or tip. A bent angle will do for the handle, but the tang needs to be thin enough to get under the pins without being too pliant or you lose the feel. The tip is the vital bit and its shape and angles are crucial in dealing with the wide variety of pins. You need a handful of picks with different shaped tips if you want to get past most locks.

I made five, each with different angles on the front face of the tip and the rear face. For a Yale, I have a nicely bent and filed half diamond tip like a triangle pointing upwards. Its front face slopes gently, its rear sharply.

I added a pair of pliers and a screwdriver to my precious picks and rolled them together in a piece of cloth. My torch battery was in good shape; a layer of tape over most of the lens left only a small centre hole. With toolkit and torch in opposite pockets of my coat, I waited till it was getting dark, and headed back up to Baker Street.

It was a quarter to five when I walked past the building. Some people were already making for home. I guess there was little enough to do nowadays. I stopped at the corner and lit a fag, looking as though I was waiting for someone. I wished I was. Where was Val? The doors swung open and one or two secretaries bustled out, laughing and glad to be heading home to husband or family, or to hang round till the pubs opened at six.

Ten more minutes and the doors were flapping like sheets in a gale. It was now or never. I walked smartly over the road, waited till a new bunch of workers erupted, grabbed the door from them and shouted goodnight after them. The lobby was crowded with folk putting on their coats and nattering and shouting goodnights. My luck was in, old Stan was behind the counter.

I took my hat off so he could see my face and walked past him, putting some girls between me and him, but not trying to hide myself.

"Night, ladies," I said. "Evening, Stan. I'm just having a word with Major Cassells, OK?"

I headed through the internal swing doors and turned right as if I were heading to Cassells' office. My heart was hammering. I don't know what I would have done if Cassells had been out today. And now, of course, the last thing I wanted was to bump into the man himself and have him ask me what I was up to. It also wouldn't do if Cassells left on time this evening. Stan would notice and ask him if he'd met me all right. Then there'd be a hue and cry. If Cassells hung around as the senior staff used to, till seven or after, the chances were old Stan would have forgotten about me.

It was a lot of ifs.

People were still hurrying past me and I thought it was time to get off the main corridor. I pushed through the fire doors and found myself in the stairwell that runs from the ground floor up to the top. Some folk used it as a short cut between floors, so I couldn't simply hang around here. I had to find somewhere to lie up. On every other floor were gents toilets. Possible, but still too risky. I was looking for a broom cupboard or the like. Or even an office that wasn't in use, but that would mean venturing back into the main corridors again.

I took a peek through the fire doors on each floor. On every one of the levels there were boxes floor to ceiling against the walls. But most offices had lights on and people wandering about. I needed to buy time. I ducked into the gents on the third floor and took the end cubicle. I sat there and waited, feeling silly. Five minutes later the toilet door crashed open and two men walked in, laughing.

"Quick, man, we can still catch them if you hurry up."

"You can't rush a pee, Freddy. And the bints'll keep. You seen that Brenda, the way she was looking? I reckon we're in there."

"Shhh," said the first one. I think they spotted the closed cubicle door and my feet and trousers. They were silent apart from a suppressed guffaw. I could have been a senior officer for all they knew.

They ran the water in the sink and crashed out. I heard their laughter and wild talk as they dived down the stairs. If only I could be that carefree. I waited, and waited. At six o'clock I edged out of the toilet, listening for doors and footsteps. It had quieted down. Through the glass panel nobody was to be seen down either side of the corridor. There was one light on in an office halfway down on the right. I had to risk it.

I opened the door, gritting my teeth as it creaked, and took a good look right and left. I eased the door closed and began to tiptoe to the left. The first office was locked. Same with the next. Suddenly there were voices behind me as the door of the lit office opened and two people began to emerge. I flattened myself between two head-high piles of boxes and stopped breathing. The voices – a man and a woman – were walking this way.

"Stairs or lift, Miss Beacontree?"

"Exercise will do us good, sir."

"It certainly keeps you trim, Juliette."

"Shh, Cecil. Not here…" The fire door creaked open and their voices tailed away as they descended. I breathed again. I started my search again. Up ahead I saw it. An open door to a darkened room. I pulled out my torch and switched it on. The slim beam picked out boxes on one side and a stack of chairs on the other. Perfect. I shut the door behind me, lifted down a chair and switched off my torch. I made myself as comfortable as I could for the long wait that lay ahead.

TWELVE

I must have dozed. An old soldier trick. Grab a nap anywhere you can. I carefully switched on my torch. My watch said twenty to eight. The place should be deserted apart from the patrolling security guards. I began to pick my way down through the now quiet building, trying not to use the torch in case even its slender beam was detected. Moonlight came in through some of the windows that faced into the inner courtyard. I took a good look down into the well to see if I could spot an alternative escape route. There looked to be a wooden double door, about twelve feet high and scalable.

If memory served me right – not something I would have taken short odds on recently – the registry section occupied the whole basement area. I crept down and down until I was at the right level and began looking for the doors. Bingo! A sign declared the room the Registry and that only registry staff were allowed inside. The dragon lady in charge enforced that rule with an iron stare and a leather tongue. A little window was cut in the wall alongside the door. This was where the rest of the world accessed the documents. You put your slip through and a registry clerk would deliver the file to your office and pick it up at day's end. Tough work.

The heavy double doors were, of course, locked. So I took out my little packet of tools to see if my SOE training had been a waste of time. I shone my torch into the keyhole and squinted into it to see the make-up of the levers.

There are two basic techniques to opening locks: picking and scrubbing. Picking is more subtle and lets you probe and feel each pin and then apply force on the driver pin that's giving the most fight. When you feel the plug give a little, the driver gets trapped and the lock opens. Scrubbing is for speed and when you don't care if you leave evidence of your visit. I was a natural scrubber.

I selected a sinuous snake-tipped pick and slipped its double curves into the lock. I eased it backwards and forwards, feeling pins move and displace. As I scrubbed, I twisted, hoping to feel movement. I'd forgotten how hard this was. And I was rusty. I was sweating good and proper now. I put my hat down, took off my coat and jacket and started again. I put on more pressure, hoping I wouldn't bend or break the pick. My fingers were slipping and I took out my hanky and wrapped it round the handle. Suddenly the driver pin went, the others followed and the key turned. I gripped the wood handle, twisted and the door creaked open. I stood panting with nerves before picking up my clothes, slipping in and closing the door gently behind me.

I swung the torch round the long low room. There were floor-to-ceiling shelves stretching for yards in both directions. A large chunk of them were empty. Damn! I should have done this weeks ago!

With ebbing hope I started walking down the shelving. Halfway along they began to be full again. I began checking what the files contained. It wasn't till I'd inspected a dozen stacks of shelves that I ran into the personal files, the agent files.

Come on, please! I found the M series and then the Mc set. Nothing. Wait, wait. Try Mac. Plenty, but no McRaes. I was panicking now. Cassells hadn't put it back! It was somewhere in the mounds of loose papers in his chaotic office! Calm, calm. Think.

A last long shot, the MR set. Thank God. There were three McRae files sandwiched between McRennies and McRackens. I pulled the first one down. Nope. The second was mine. I felt relief then nerves. I wasn't sure I wanted to see what was in here. People should never see what other folk think of them, despite what Rabbie Burns says. But I'd come all this way for the truth.

I sank down on the floor, on top of my coat and jacket and opened the folder. There was a stack of papers, each with a neat hole punched in the top left corner through which a string tab ran to hold them in place. There was a covering sheet with the sparse details of my background and next of kin. My mum was shown, with her address. Then I got to the second page. It was simple and clear and was probably as far as Cassells got the other day.

Secret
The sealed reports in this personal folder are
for Executive Head Eyes Only
Do not open without express authority.
Under no circumstances is any aspect
of the work of the SOE
or the personal details
of the officers of the SOE
to be communicated
to Capt. Daniel McRae

That set my heart going. What the hell was going on? What the hell was in this file? Maybe Cassells was right; there's stuff better left forgotten. I turned to the next sheets; just some copies of my discharge papers and pension calculations. The numbers didn't add up to a comfortable retirement. Then came the sealed envelopes, two of them, with holes in their corners to take the tags. I carefully removed the sheets above them and examined the first envelope. It was gummed down and bore a blob of sealing wax on the join. But it had been re-sealed. I could see where the earlier wax had been eased off. It was initialled and dated 28 May 1944 in the bottom right corner. It had a big red stamp across the front classifying it Top Secret/Executive Head S.O.E Eyes Only. I took a little knife from my toolkit, slid it into a corner and sliced along the top fold. I pulled out a single sheet:

Memorandum   Staff in Strictest Confidence

To: Colonel Sir Collin Gubbins, Executive Head SOE
From: Major P A Caldwell
Date: 14 May 1944
Subject: Captain Daniel McRae / Avignon incident

Sir,
It is my unwelcome duty to inform you that Captain Daniel McRae, our operative in Avignon, was captured by the Gestapo on 24 May. We have not seen or heard of him since, and it is believed, as with all captured agents, that he has been taken to Gestapo / Vichy headquarters in Rue Saline, Avignon. He will be interrogated there and executed or sent on to one of the concentration camps as happened to agents Hastings and Temple.

However, unfortunate though this is, there is another matter which I must bring to your attention. A young female resistance fighter has been found murdered in one of our safe houses. She had been raped and stabbed in the head and body. McRae was known to have consorted with the woman in question though

*she is believed to have spurned his advances. He had an assig-
nation with her on the day of the murder and was seen to leave
the safe house shortly before the woman's body was found.*

*I was notified of this at midnight on the same evening by the
Maquis member who found the girl and who claimed to have
seen McRae slipping away. Understandably the Maquis member
was outraged and demanded immediate action. I went to
McRae's lodgings and confronted him. I found him sitting in his
room drinking brandy. Clothes were drying in front of the fire. It
had not been raining. I accused him of the murder and he
denied it. He claimed he had fallen and got his clothes muddy.
He had washed them off. I had no further proof against his
denial and resolved to leave the matter till the morning when I
could interrogate the witness again.*

*Unfortunately – or perhaps fortunately in some respects –
during the night, the Gestapo raided his house and McRae
was rounded up. My suspicions are that the Maquis informed
on McRae as an easy way of achieving swift justice. In subsequent days, though the anger among the Maquis has been
considerable there is an acceptance that McRae has paid for
his crimes. Given what we still have to achieve here, I am
letting the matter rest.*

*In the circumstances I am recommending no further action
from SOE in this matter. It could tarnish the image of SOE
and divert us from the main job. We do not have conclusive
proof, and the main suspect, Captain Daniel McRae is captive,
presumed dead.*

*Signed
Major Philip Anthony Caldwell*

There was a scrawled note: *Recommendation accepted. No
further action.* It was signed Colonel Gubbins.

I read and re-read the memo in a daze. Suddenly all my foul

dreams crystallised into the one terrible truth. I had killed a woman. It was why I couldn't remember, *wouldn't* remember. It was why I was obsessed by the murders here in London. It was why they wouldn't let me have Caldwell's address. I wanted to scream. I toyed with my screwdriver and wondered if I could kill myself by driving it into my heart. Or open my veins and let them find me drained and dead clutching the evidence of my guilt. I switched off the torch and there, in the darkened filing room, I let great sobs shake me apart.

Slowly I got control. I dried my face on my shirtsleeve. I hadn't realised I'd been keeping so much locked up inside. The image that haunted my worst nightmares – me standing with bloody hands and bloody weapon – must be a memory. But *why*? What had brought out the beast in me? Anger, jealousy, betrayal? I tried to recapture the days running up to this dark one, but nothing came. Just some vague shots of leafy gardens and a path running through it, and drinking in a café with a round man called Gregor. I could see his beaming face and huge moustache. It was clear too that Caldwell had been in France with me, but I couldn't "see" him. He must have been doing the rounds of his agents. Tantalising shreds of memory floated by; was that his face?

I picked up the second envelope and hefted it. The news couldn't get worse. I ripped it open. It was another memo from Caldwell, about a year further on:

Memorandum   Staff in Confidence

To: Colonel Sir Collin Gubbins, Executive Head SOE
From: Major PA Caldwell
Date: 14 July 1945
Subject: Captain Daniel McRae

Sir,

At your request, following the surprising news of the survival and return to England of Captain Daniel McRae, I have visited Moresley Hospital to establish his condition and to consider what action if any to take.

I saw both McRae and the senior psychiatrist, Doctor Richard Thompson. The latter's report is attached separately but the gist of it is as follows.

First, McRae was in very poor health when he was brought to the hospital in May. He was suffering from malnutrition and multiple injuries, the most significant of which was to his head. Either at the time of his capture or in subsequent captivity, McRae's head was struck with great force. His skull was fractured in three places and a piece of bone was dislodged and penetrated his brain.

He has undergone various operations and now has a metal plate in his skull. There is a large scar running across his head and down half his face. He is nevertheless in surprisingly good physical health. His body has healed and he is taking exercise.

However I found McRae in poor mental condition. He is undergoing Electro-convulsive Shock Therapy (EST), a ghastly business. He did not recognise me and it appears he has no recollection of events for most of the last year. His last clear memories are just before being sent to France.

The prognosis from Doctor Thompson is poor. Such a major injury may have serious and long term personality effects. As well as memory lapses which may or may not be permanent, McRae is likely to suffer from personality disorders including delusions and paranoia. He is due to be released next month as there is little more that can be done physically. However Doctor Thompson will bring him in for monthly reviews and possible further EST to make sure McRae is coping with his infirmity.

Once more my recommendation is that we let lie the
accusation of murder in Avignon. There is no evidence and
it would only serve to rake matters up. It would only
damage the fine record and high public regard for the SOE
if this matter were made public.

There is however a possibility that McRae will come
calling at SOE offices. He is already asking about his
missing months. I would therefore further recommend that
our stance should be to tell McRae nothing. We should not
feed his delusions or paranoia. Specifically, there should be
no information given out that enables him to pester former
colleagues such as myself. There is every likelihood,
according to his doctor, that McRae may blame me and his
former colleagues for what happened to him.

Signed
Major P.A. Caldwell

The memo had the Colonel's signature and comments
approving both recommendations.

Words blazed out at me; *delusions, paranoia, infirmity*!
How would I know what was real and what wasn't? How was
I to live with myself knowing I was a murderer? I looked at
my hands in the faint light from my torch. They were
shaking. Were they capable of killing? What does it feel like
to have innocent blood on them? I've always liked women:
too much? Would I have killed one just to get my way? I'd
given Sandra a slap but she'd deserved it; I think she even
liked it. Some women do. Was it an accident, a bit of rough
stuff that got out of hand? What would happen if I did
remember the killing?

I was a wreck and the people who sent me down this path

were treating me like a pariah, a mad dog. Or was this the paranoia talking? If you're mad, how do you know? Caldwell seemed to have saved my skin, though. I could hardly blame him for wanting to steer clear of me.

I suddenly felt the walls of this cellar pressing in on me. I needed air, light. I needed to run. Needed to talk to Valerie. Could I confess this to her? What the hell would she say? Should I go to the police and tell all? What should I do?!

I got to my feet, feeling hollow and sick. I put the file back. Should I take the reports out or leave them? Destroy the evidence? Who else would ever know? Caldwell was dead and the Colonel would never talk. What about Major Cassells; did he read these, or stop at the warning note? I pulled the file out again and tore out the two envelopes and stuffed them in my pocket.

I began heading to the door when I passed the C files. A thought struck me. I looked for his file and found it. I held Major Tony Caldwell's personal papers in my hands. I tucked it on to my left forearm, opened to the first page and shone my torch on it. I just had time to read the first few lines when the Registry door bashed open and lights flooded the basement.

"All right, Mr McRae, come on out! We know you're in here!"

Shit! Old Stan wasn't so slow after all. He must have waited for me to leave, or spoken to Major Cassells, for the next voice was his.

"Daniel? Daniel McRae? We know what you're doing here. It's no good. Come on out, man."

I dug into my pocket and pulled out the two envelopes. I slid them into Caldwell's file and put it back in its place, then tiptoed down the aisle away from the door. I turned left and headed further in. I didn't want them to find me next to Caldwell's papers.

"Daniel, we have the police with us and I am armed. It will go easier with you if you give up now."

I was far enough away. I stepped out of the alley of files, my eyes screwed up against the lights. Stan and Cassells were standing at the door. Cassells held a service revolver aimed directly at my chest. A policeman stood behind them.

"Seems like you were well trained, Captain," said Cassells.

"Not well enough," I replied. I didn't put my hands up. It seemed silly, and I didn't expect Cassells to shoot me. I didn't care much either. I walked towards them. Stan looked uncomfortable when I got close.

"Sorry, Stan. Hope I haven't got you into trouble?"

He averted his eyes.

"Far from it, Daniel," said Cassells. "Stan here alerted me an hour ago that you'd come in and hadn't come out."

"What now, Gerald?" I asked. He didn't like the first name this time.

"'Fraid we've got the police involved. Still a very secure area, this. You'll have to go with the constable here. I believe there's a car waiting outside."

The copper nodded and stood forward. "I'm sorry, sir, I have to put these on." He held out a pair of handcuffs. I could feel the weight of the law piling above my head, ready to crush me. Why shouldn't it? I held out my hands and felt the cold steel settle round my wrists.

The squad car took me round to the station in Marylebone. They booked me, fingerprinted me, took away my coat, jacket, tie, belt and shoelaces and led me to a cell. It was a routine I was familiar with, God help me. So were the cells. About eight by six, with one bed and a sink. The window was sealed shut. The door was a block of green-painted metal with a window hatch and a thinner food hatch like a letter box.

I sat on the hard bunk and pulled my knees up. Justice seemed to have caught up with me. I kept thinking about my dad and what he would have said to see me like this. If he'd known what I'd done. I corrected myself; what I'd been *accused* of. Innocent till proven. It's amazing how the mind works in self-preservation. I was already in denial, angry even, at not being able to defend myself. There were many possible answers to what had taken place in France. Why blame me? Could I live with the doubt? Why not? I was living with holes and visions and dislocations from reality every day.

More than ever, I regretted not talking to Tony Caldwell. I wanted to question him about that night. Find out exactly what he'd seen and what had been said. Then I remembered his file, his personal file. I'd only had time to scan the cover page, the page with name, rank, unit, next of kin details and such like. It was very peculiar. I expected to see Mrs Liza Caldwell of Willow Road, Hampstead as next of kin. No matter what you were getting up to on the side, you'd put your wife down as next of kin, wouldn't you?

Then why had he given an address in Chelsea and a next of kin by the name of Mrs Catriona Caldwell?

THIRTEEN

M y mind cantered round all the new information trying to make sense of it, put it in order. But there *was* no sense to it. The only reality was that the cell was cold and the bed hard. I pulled the coarse blanket round me but blessed sleep wouldn't come. I tossed and writhed and kept waiting for the headache to begin; all the ingredients were there for falling into one of my episodes. Mercifully I must have dozed, because I was startled from wild dreams when the metal window slid open and an all too familiar voice boomed into the cell.

"Well, well. What do we have here? Mister private detective, former policeman, Daniel McRae, Esquire. There's nothing worse than a bent copper. A copper who's gone bad. Well, Danny boy, I knew it was only a matter of time before you ended up in one of our nicks."

I sat up, fear clenching my guts. What the hell was Wilson doing here? This wasn't his business. He was CID, a Yard man. The window slid shut and I heard the bolts being drawn. The door opened. Detective Inspector Wilson loomed large against the outside light. He stepped in. He had taken off his coat and jacket. His braces swelled out in a great curve over his chest and stomach. He was holding something in his hand. I pulled myself into the corner of my bunk, my back against the wall. This wasn't good, not good at all. I found a voice; it didn't sound like mine.

"This is a bit off your patch Inspector, isn't it? I was caught doing some filing, not murdering anybody." I tried to make it light, keep it from slipping off into something serious.

Wilson turned round. I could see a uniformed officer holding the door. "Bring me a chair and then you can close the door." The officer came back quickly with a metal chair and placed it just in front of me. He looked at me nervously and raised his eyebrows as if to say there was nothing he could do. But he tried.

"Want me to stay, Inspector?"

"No, you fool. I'm not at risk from this one. Bugger off."

The door closed and Wilson and I were alone under the bare light bulb. I determined to do nothing, *nothing* to upset him. Give him no excuse. But I knew from Glasgow that some of these boys needed no excuse.

Wilson dropped into the chair and examined me. He laid something on the concrete floor and I saw that it was my makeshift toolkit. He crossed his big arms. He was one of those men whose body had a thick layer of fat over hard muscle. You see it in Irish navvies; beer bellies and double chins, but capable of pulverising kerb-stones with their bare knuckles. Or a man's head.

"You're right, Danny boy. This wouldn't be any of my business. Not normally. But I've made you my business. I put the word out that if you were ever picked up, for anything – blowing your nose the wrong way, overdue library book, anything – they were to call me. They did."

"Very efficient, Inspector." Easy, Danny, easy. Don't shoot your mouth off.

Wilson reached down. He picked up my toolkit. He unwrapped it and placed the items one by one on the edge of the bunk. The torch, screwdriver, penknife, pliers and various bent pins lay there accusingly.

"A bit of filing, eh? More like a regular little burglar's bag, if you ask me. Is that what you are, McRae? A little tea-leaf? A copper who's switched sides? Turns my stomach, that does."

"You've got it wrong, Inspector. This is how I was trained in the SOE. I needed to see my personal file. I was trying to find out what happened to me. How I got this." I pointed at my scar, hoping for some sympathy. Like a cow in a slaughterhouse.

"Got it wrong, have I? Calling me a liar, are you?"

Wilson's face had clouded. Shit. No matter what I said he was going to turn it against me. I wasn't going to win.

"That's not what I meant, Inspector. I'm just trying to explain these. That's all." I tried smiling.

"You're going to be difficult, are you? You're going to make this effing difficult for me?" He suddenly reached out and scooped all the tools on to the floor in a clatter of metal and glass. I heard the torch lens smash.

Terror gripped my bowels. I'd been here before. A concrete cell, pitiless light, helpless in front of a remorseless, vindictive thug. I shook my head desperately. "No. Not all. I'm telling you the truth. I just wanted to know what happened. That's all." I could hear my voice rising and breaking. I hated my terror, my cowardice. I could feel the first faint pangs of pain behind my eyes. Not now, please not now.

"On your feet, McRae!" Wilson had kicked back his chair and was standing above me, his fists clenched.

I cowered in my corner waiting for the jackboots to come in, the metal rods to strike. "I'm fine here, Inspector. I know my rights. You can't do this. All I've done is hang around my old office and look at my own file. I didn't even break in."

"No? Then what's all that then?" He pointed at the sorry pile of tools on the floor.

I had the pillow in front of me. A pathetic shield. He reached out and grabbed my left arm and yanked me up. He tore the pillow from my grip and tossed it behind me. I stood rigid, knowing what was coming and trying to brazen it out. I held his malignant eyes and kept my arms by my side so that he'd have to hit a defenceless man.

His big right hook hit me in the guts and I went down on the bed in wheezing agony. I couldn't call out. He pulled me up again. I was retching and coughing, fighting for air. This time I held my hands in front of my face, my elbows tucked in. They didn't help much. He was going for the body mainly. Not wanting to leave too many marks. A real pro. I tried to protect my kidneys and stomach. His fists broke through or smashed numbingly on my arms.

I felt a rib go and in that moment, felt something else snap. I found my lungs and began a scream that was anger, pain, hate all rolled into one. It made him draw back. Wilson was the school bully that I'd taken enough from. I hit him with my right and he was so surprised that he fell back. I flung myself at him. My arms were flailing, striking at his head and big chest, pummelling away so that he stumbled back against the door.

I could see blood from his mouth. Then a great roar erupted from him and he let loose. I stood no chance. I went down and he began kicking me. I tried to shield my face. I rolled into a ball. The jackboots smashed into me, into my head, my back my legs, my balls. I was screaming and screaming. Like before... like before...

I heard the door clang and voices a long way off. There was a lot of shouting. I couldn't hear. My ears were filled with blood...

"Thank Christ, he's moving. I thought the big prick had killed him."

"He will one day. He's a bloody animal. He's gone too bleeding far this time."

"It wasn't all one way. Did you see the corker he got?"

I felt hands lifting me, hauling me on to the bed. I hurt everywhere. And then I felt the familiar sickness rising in me, the pain in my head splitting it wide open, and blessed oblivion sweeping down on me...

"Are you awake?" It was a woman's voice. Irish. I wasn't sure it was aimed at me. And if it was, I wasn't sure if I was awake or not. I shifted and found pain shooting through my ribs and head. The rest of me seemed to be in spasm as well. Then I felt the nausea well up. I opened my eyes, couldn't see where I was, it was just bright light, too bright.

"Sick, going to be sick," I got out. Hands got under my head and back and lifted me up and to one side. The pain made me groan. I felt a steel bowl against my cheek and threw up into it. The action drove a knife into my chest and twisted it. I threw up again and fell back on the bed to get away from the pain. There was no escape.

"Sorry, sorry, sorry..."

"It's all right. You're gonna be all right. You've got three broken ribs. That's why it's hurting so much." There's something soothing about an Irish accent even when they're giving bad news.

I was bathed in sweat and felt a cold cloth placed on my brow. A blessing. I opened my eyes. A round freckled face adorned by a crisp white cap smiled down at me.

"Hospital?"

"In your state, that would be the best place, would you not say?"

My state? I wondered how bad I must look. Every inch, from my head to my toes, was hurting. I couldn't lift an arm without pain erupting in a dozen unconnected places. Those Nazi bastards had really done me over. And then memory hit me. I didn't need any scribbles in my jotter to jog this scene to mind.

"Raus! Raus Englander!"

They were in shirt sleeves and braces, their boots shining up to mid-calf. They hit me even as I began to sit up. They dragged me on to the floor and gave me a couple of kicks to make sure I got the message about who was boss.

I tried to keep up the bluff. I gasped out *why* in French and tried to use my small vocabulary to maintain the pretence. It didn't work. I knew they were Gestapo, but I couldn't recall how I knew or how I'd got here, wherever here was. I was already bloody and sore. But I soon found that they hadn't had their first team do me over.

I saw Wilson's fleshy face in grey uniform. I heard him shouting at me in German. I don't know how long they held me or how many times they hauled me out of my cell for a beating or a drowning. It was funny how quickly you dropped the pretence of being tough; they can make you scream like a child. But one day the routine changed. I think it was after they'd gone further than even they intended; a goon got over-excited with his lead pipe. I suppose that's when they fractured my skull. I was unconscious off and on for a while. No idea how long. They dragged me from my cell and threw me in the back of a truck. I hoped they were simply taking me out to be shot. I just wanted it over with.

But it was only the start. I saw the great metal arches of a railway station and a big clock, painted green and with cherubs chasing each other round the dial. I smelled the metallic steam before they flung me into a cattle truck. There were others in the smelly box. Too many others. The doors were closed and locked. The one high-up window had barbed wire round it. We had nowhere to shit except one corner. There was no food, no water. We stank, and I felt life ebbing out of me through every wound and bruise in my wrecked body. Though there was little enough room, the men gave me space to lie, curled up in a corner. They were kind, but remote, in the way of men waiting for someone to die and knowing they could do nothing.

Except for one man: Joseph the tailor. He had a couple of needles pinned behind his lapels. He tore the bottom of my shirt and loosened some threads. Then he stitched me as best he could. I was surprised how much the scalp hurt. I guess the skin had separated and he really had to tug at it to pull it together. Joseph worked on me with great love and attention as though I were a piece of his finest cloth. His round face kept shifting between a beam and a frown for what they'd done to me.

He did well enough, so that a couple of days later I survived the changeover at Paris. The men held me up as we were herded across the platforms. I saw people, ordinary French people, watching us from behind a line of Germans, and doing nothing. The journey began again. If anything the cattle box was smaller. We stopped and started a dozen times. They sprayed the train with water from hoses so that we were left soaking and shivering and still thirsty. I drew into myself. I guess I was unconscious for most of the journey.

Finally we halted in the leafy suburbs of a small German town. We could see the pretty roofs over the watch towers as we were shovelled out of our boxes. The welcoming committee had guns and dogs. Those of us who could walk were made to march to the parade ground in front of the rows of barracks. Those that couldn't walk were dragged aside and shot. It was a powerful incentive. I got to my feet in a daze and the men half carried, half jostled me forward. I suppose Joseph had an investment in me and he got the others involved. In the coming days, when I was given a little food and rest, I began to heal.

None of the guards paid me much attention; there was no interest in roughing me up when I'd been so patently done over by professionals. And half the time – as much as I could recall through the delirium – I was a joke to them. They had weekly fitness tests to cull the numbers – the penalty for failure was a bullet, if you were lucky. You had to run 25 yards. Run for your life. Every time, I forced a terror-filled sprint from my body. But I can remember the guards laughing at me as I kept veering into the walls of the hut. They thought it was hilarious.

I survived too – as I learned later – because Dachau was one of the oldest concentration camps; the Nazis had opened it before the war and filled it with political dissidents. Then they started adding Poles and Russians. It wasn't yet a factory for slaughtering Jews or gypsies. Though the guards did well enough in their casual way. I met little fat smiley Joseph at some point, though by then he wasn't fat and he wasn't smiling much. I don't know if he made it or not.

Full circle. I was back in an English hospital after a mangling by sadists in uniform. But this time it had been by a good old British bobby. Were we all rotten, deep inside? I was beginning to think I really was capable of murder. That we all were. I heard voices at the foot of my bed. One was familiar.

"Is he awake, nurse? How is he?" Cassells come to gloat?

"He's not to be disturbed. I told that policeman the same t'ing," said my guardian Irish angel.

"The police have gone. It's all right. I won't disturb him. Just wanted to see how the man is doing. He was one of my chaps, you see."

"Well, maybe you should take better care of him then."

I opened my eyes and tried to raise my head. It hurt like hell.

"There you are, Daniel, old chap! You all right?" He came to stand beside me so that with a little tilt of my head, I could look up at him.

I tried to speak and managed a cough, which was a big mistake. The sweat broke out all over as the pain fired across my chest.

I finally got out, "Super, Gerald. Just super."

He had the grace to look embarrassed. "Sorry this happened, old chap."

"What did they tell you, Gerald? That I fell down the stairs?"

His face reddened. "Actually, they said you'd been resisting arrest."

I smiled, though my lips were so split it may not have been obvious. "Does that seem likely, *old chap*?" I asked.

He had the grace to look ashamed. "Had no idea. Wouldn't have got the boys in blue involved, if I'd known. That's a fact. You've been through enough, for God's sake."

Amen to that, I thought. "So are they waiting till I'm better before they take me back for round two?"

"No, no! Look, the office has dropped all charges. And I

pointed out that they might just find themselves on the spot for being, shall we say, a little over-zealous? Anyway, they aren't taking things further."

"Can you lift me up?" The nurse and Cassells helped me sit up so that I was propped up at forty-five degrees. The process was excruciating, but it felt better than having to talk horizontally.

I gasped out, "What's the damage, nurse? You mentioned ribs?"

She was about my age, and round-faced. We shared the red hair, though hers was more ginger. A cheery lady, just the sort you need in a hospital.

"Now, don't you go fussing yoursel'. Whatever's wrong wit' you, you'll mend." She saw my look. "All right, all right. Starting at the top. You've got bruising and cuts – none as fancy as the old one, mind. But they're nicer stitched and we'll have the sutures out in a few days. Arms and hands bruised. Three ribs broken on the left side and multiple contusions on your back and front. Your testicles may be a bit uncomfortable for a day or two till the swelling goes down. And your legs are black and blue."

I lifted my arms and saw the swollen fingers and the purple and green discolouration.

Cassells looked distraught. "This is too bad, too damn bad! Look, Daniel, I'm not having this. I'm going to press charges on your behalf, even if you did put up a bit of resistance, eh? No need for this level of response. Dammit." He was genuinely angry. I was almost touched.

"It's a waste of time, Gerald. My word against theirs. But just to make it clear: I didn't resist arrest. I got beat up. There's a certain evil sod who's got it in for me. In fact, it's probably not just me. He's just plain rotten."

He looked at me intently. "Wilson the name? Detective Inspector Wilson? Big chap?"

"That's the man."

Cassells smiled. "Nasty bit of work. Wanted to see your file. Told him not a chance. Security and all that. But tell you what, you might not have been resisting arrest, but someone gave him a super black eye and bloody nose. Good for you, old man."

I wondered if my wee bit of retaliation had been worth it, and whether I'd still have intact ribs if I hadn't had a go. But then I was certain... I was *bloody* glad I'd fought back, no matter how feebly. There was no chance before, in that other cell. It had left me feeling ashamed. That I'd become someone who lets folk do what they like to me. So it was a small grim satisfaction to have landed a couple on Wilson, no matter the cost.

They let me out in a couple of days. I was stiff and sore and looked like an early piece of work by Frankenstein, but I could walk and move about pretty well. Bending or lifting was hard, even with my ribs tightly bandaged. I had to stop a couple of times on the way up my stairs. It was on the last landing below mine that I heard her call out from above me.

"Thank God! Oh, Danny, where have you been? What have they done to you?" Val sailed down the stairs to me, her spindly limbs flying, and would have hugged me, I'm sure, if I hadn't warned her back, pointing to my chest.

"I'm fine. Just a bit bruised round the ribs. So no jiving for a while." I grinned at her flushed cheeks and her wayward hair.

"Your poor face! Look at your poor face!"

"You mean I've lost my good looks?"

She led the way to my room as if she was clearing a mine-field; opening doors, moving a chair. She made me sit in the broken old chair while she fussed and made tea and put the fire on. Now I knew how my dad felt after a day down the pit. Val sat on the rug in front of the fire and tucked her legs under her in an impossible contortion.

"Right. I'm listening. You tell me every little thing that's happened. And none of your manly keeping it all to yourself, mind. I want all the details."

I told her. I told her nearly everything. But I didn't, couldn't, tell her about the accusation of murder in my files. I didn't want her to fear me, or loathe me. I was managing that pretty well myself.

She asked questions at first but grew silent as I told her of Wilson and how it had brought back the memories of the Gestapo. She drew her knees up under her chin and hugged them to her, and gradually she buried her face in her knees, as though she couldn't bear to hear any more. All I could see was the mass of her hair tumbling over her bony knees. I stopped and let the quiet envelop us. Outside it was getting dark, but already I noticed that the light was fading later each day as the year edged forward. But there was a long winter still ahead. I stopped. She raised her face and looked at me seriously.

"What's wrong, Danny? What did you find in your file?"

Her dark eyes knifed through me. How in God's name could I tell her? But her frank gaze held mine and wouldn't let go until I did.

"I need a Scotch." I retrieved it from my desk and poured a couple of fingers. After a big slug I looked into the fire and told her the rest. She kept her gaze on me until I ran out of words. I didn't try to fudge it. No point protesting my innocence. I didn't feel innocent. The silence hung for a while. I was scared to look at her.

"Do *you* think you did it?" she asked matter-of-factly.

I turned my face to her. "I don't know, Val. I just don't know. That's God's honest truth."

"Do you think you're capable of it?"

That made me pause. "No. I like girls. Always have." I smiled ruefully. "But I don't like being messed around…"

"Do you hit women who mess you around?"

"No! Once. I'm not proud of it. But a slap in anger is a long way from sticking a blade in someone. Isn't it?"

Was it? *Always, always there's the naked body with the hole punched in the back of her head and a red pool around her like a bloody halo. And I'm standing holding a bloody blade…* I cut off the image, scared what else I might see.

"Do *I* mess you around?"

"God, no! Don't even think it! You're different. Not like other girls. But I don't mind that. I like seeing you. I'm happy that we're pals. I'd like it if we were something… more. But we know where we stand, don't we? Or where we *stood*," I added with a hint of desperation.

"Nothing's changed. 'Cos I don't believe it," she said defiantly.

A wave of relief swept over me, but it was only temporary. I shook my head. "I can't prove it. Not with Caldwell dead. I can't very well go back to France and poke around, can I?"

She shook her head. "You can and maybe you should. But shouldn't you see your trick cyclist first?

"My…? Oh right. I'm due for my monthly session anyway in a couple of days." Then I stopped.

"What is it?" she asked.

"I'm scared, Val. Really scared. What if I tell him and he thinks I might have done it?"

She was quite firm. "You didn't. That's all. So go see him. And in the meantime, I'm going to look after you till you're properly on your feet. And then…"

"Then?"

"Then I think you need to ask Miss Kate Toffee-nose for an explanation. What were Caldwell and her up to, that's what I want to know."

"Me too, Valerie. Me too."

FOURTEEN

Val came and went. I was mobile but stiff and it was good to have company. Apart from her and the cat, I only had visits from Mrs White, who muttered and mumbled to herself as she took my dirty clothes away and returned them clean and pressed within an inch of their lives. She affected not to see Val, having on more than occasion voiced her thoughts on post-war morality and boys and girls *living up* with each other without the blessing of a minister on their union.

We just talked, Val and me. I told her how my mother used to read to me and my dad some evenings, her soft low voice making pictures in my head, and how it had started me off. That was it; Val wouldn't rest till she had me reading to her. We raided the Camberwell Green library. I gave her stories of Africa from Rider Haggard and tales of spies and British bravery from John Buchan. And I sent her mind flying high with notions of time travel from H. G. Wells. Sitting there, in front of a flickering fire, with her curled up on the rug, big-eyed like a child, I felt a contentment so rare that at times my voice caught and I had to hide behind a swig of whisky.

She came with me to the hospital to get the stitches out of my face, and lied when she told me how much better I looked.

She left me each night and came back each morning for four days, until the day of my monthly trip to see Doctor Thompson.

The peace and calm Val had induced in me lasted for most of the train journey to the hospital. I'd begun to enjoy these trips when the Doc told me they wouldn't be doing any more shock therapy. Now they seemed like wee holidays and Doc Thompson usually helped me see things better, get things in perspective. But by the time I got to Didcot, Caldwell's written accusations were haunting me. I was in a blue funk and thinking seriously about catching the next train straight back. But the taxi was waiting, so I climbed in and sat jolting in the back as we made our way into the cold grey hills around Cirencester.

"I can't answer that, Danny, other than to say that we are all *capable* of doing bad things. But in normal circumstances, for a person brought up within the constraints of civilised society, we *choose* not to."

He was sitting in a chair just to my right and behind me. It was the way he operated; he explained it was to avoid making this debate between him and me. It should be between me and the other me; my journey. He didn't know I was a bad traveller. Doc Thompson said he only provided the vehicle and greased the wheels. I think he laid the tracks too.

"But if the circumstances are abnormal?" I asked.

"Then we lose many of the markers, the touchstones for our behaviour. And we sometimes do things that may seem alien to us. But let's be clear: we don't fundamentally go against the grain of our character. It's like hypnotism; I can't tell you to do something that is ninety degrees away from your essential personality."

"How about forty-five degrees?"

"Under certain circumstances, we are capable of surprising acts. Bravery, for example. Men giving up their lives for others in the heat of battle…"

"Murder?" I'd told him everything.

"Perhaps. But, Danny, please remember that we are dealing here with hearsay. The only evidence…" I could hear the quotation marks in his voice. "… for this so-called murder is Major Caldwell's report. We don't know – a, if there was one; b, whether it was an accident; c, if you had anything to do with it, and d, if a woman *was* killed and you did it, whether you had been provoked in some way."

I turned to him. He was sitting forward in the hard chair, his big eagle nose jutting out over his notepad that he clutched in both hands. His fair hair hung over his forehead at the best of times but one slice of it was falling into his right eye. He sat up straight and pushed it back.

"What about the memories I have? Holding the bloody bayonet? How do you explain that away?

"An image in your mind doesn't have to be a memory. It could be a composite of several memories. You're a soldier. You used a bayonet? In earnest?"

"Once. Near Tobruk. We had to go into the trenches after the Italians. I blew it, thank God. The man dodged me and I only hit his arm. It was enough."

"That would do. You could be feeling guilty about *not* killing him. It was your duty, after all."

That made me think. It made me think these quacks always had an answer for everything. How did you ever get to the truth?

"Doc, you said there might have been a provocation. Is there any provocation that would justify murder?"

"That wasn't what I meant. Nothing justifies murder. But aren't there different shades? Premeditated, an act of revenge, say? Crime of passion, as the French have? Cold-blooded, sadistic…" he began to tick them off on his fingers.

"What about these murders of prostitutes in London?"

He sat forward again. His face took on an eagerness, as though filled with professional fascination for the slaughters. "Ah. We are clearly dealing with a psychopath, someone who has no human compassion, does not empathise with the rest of us. Doesn't have the same moral code. Freud would see a sexual motivation here too. Perhaps someone getting revenge on a woman: a cruel mother or a woman who rejected his advances."

"He?"

"It's usually a *he*. Men are by nature more violent."

My silence stopped his flow. I gathered myself to ask the big question, the one that was making me sick. "Doctor, do you think – from what you know of me – that I am capable of murdering this woman in France?"

His face took on a guarded look, and he rubbed his pointed chin with his knuckle before answering. "The trouble is, Danny, I've been treating you for the effects of the bash on your head. I've been trying to help you make sense of the trauma and piece together the fragments of your memory. *If* this dreadful act took place, and *if* you were involved in some way, it happened before your skull fracture."

That wasn't the resounding vote of confidence I wanted to hear from my quack. "So you're saying you don't know if the 'me' before this –" I pointed at my scar – "could have done it or not? But in fact, I might have? Is that what you're saying?"

"I'm not saying that at all. I'm saying I don't know if it would be out of character or not, because I don't know what your character was. What I see today is a personality that may or may not be influenced by a severe brain injury."

There were too many ifs and maybes in this for my liking. "For God's sake, Doc, just tell me what I should do. Where do I go from here? How do I carry this around with me without going nuts?"

"It's such a pity that your man Caldwell is dead. But you've said he was pretty thick with this woman, Kate…" he looked at his pad "…Graveney? Well I'd go back to her and do some more asking, if I were you. See if he mentioned anything else about you. And I'd also see if Mrs Caldwell would talk to you again. Maybe he said more to her than in his report."

His words burrowed away in my head. Mrs Caldwell. Mrs Catriona Caldwell. Mrs *Kate* Caldwell of Chelsea. I dragged myself back to his point.

"Do you think if he'd told Liza Caldwell I was a murderer, she'd have contacted me, far less let me into her home?"

"No, you're right." He flicked through his notes. "But to take it a step further, she mentioned that her husband had said you had mental problems and that you might become a nuisance. Even in these lesser circumstances, it seems strange for her to have let you into her home. Unless it was to head you off by telling you her husband was dead?"

That point had worried me too. This whole thing stank. And the sooner I started acting like a proper detective and got behind all this flimflam, the better. I sat quietly for a minute or two, still facing Thompson. He let me. He could see I needed time to absorb some of the implications of what he'd said. I found I had one last big question to put to him.

"Doc, if someone were to kill in anger or in passion… is it likely… I mean, is it conceivable that they'd kill again?"

He looked wary. "Strictly speaking, a *crime passionnel* of any sort, caused by anger, jealousy, sexual aggression or just to stop someone nagging…" he smiled at that "…is a one-off event. It is a build-up of rage or frustration against one particular person for a particular reason or set of reasons." Straight from the textbook.

"Strictly speaking?"

"It's pretty rare to get a taste for it. Unless there was a deep character flaw that was revealed by the act, such as you might find in a split personality or a psychopath."

"Do I? I mean, do I show signs of being split or a psycho?" I didn't want the answer, but I had to ask it. I wanted him to say don't be ridiculous, of course you're not…

"Frankly, Danny, it's not something we've been looking for with you." He tried to laugh, to make it sound silly. "You've got quite enough recovering to do, without adding to your woes."

In other words, I could be as crazy as a Kamikaze pilot but he couldn't really tell because I had all these other mental health problems. There wasn't much more I wanted to hear from Doctor Thompson. Everything he told me could be interpreted the worst possible way. And in my state of precarious sanity, I could easily convince myself I not only murdered a heroine of the Resistance in a passionate rage, but I could be primed to do it again, given the right circumstances. It was probably just as well that Big Alec had stopped me seeing Sandra again. But I never would have killed her, would I?

FIFTEEN

'd been away two days but it seemed liked a month. With or without being plugged into the mains, it's always a pretty intense experience at the hospital. Partly it's seeing and hearing the *real* nutters around the place: blokes who'd lost it after sitting in a slit trench for ten days while Jerry bombed the shit out of them, or waiting in their tin-can tanks for a Tiger shell to smear them round the inside like jam. But usually I leave in a better mood than I arrived. The Doc gives me hope. This time he hadn't.

This time I was just afraid. I felt there was someone else hiding in my body. I remembered the shock of reading *Dr Jekyll and Mr Hyde* for the first time. It took a concoction to bring out the devil in the good doctor, but I wonder if you get the same effect with a head wound. Two people in one body. The Doc's split personality. I needed an exorcist, not a psychologist.

The bus from Paddington was crawling along Oxford Street and I saw there was still bunting up from new year, or maybe even VE Day. But it couldn't hide the squalor we'd made of our lives. We don't understand how we could have won the war and ended up so destitute. How we could have booted out old Winston after he saw us through the Blitz. How we could have given so much and got so little in return. How we could match the picture now with the one we'd held in our shaky memories as we marched on Berlin.

As I hefted my little case down the stairs of the bus, wincing as the healing ribs tugged at me, I weighed the options. I could give up now and take to the bottle; it would be easy to play the victim. I'd earned that right, hadn't I? Or I could stop belly-aching and go find out the truth no matter how awful.

There was no one waiting for me except the moggy. She – I've no cause to label it a she, but cats always strike me as female – was waiting, hungry and meowing outside my door. It furled itself round and round my legs until I stroked its thin ribs and let it in, then stuck close to me till I'd filled a saucer with milk. I parked my case down and sat on the bed watching her, listening to the rasp of her tongue as she gulped it down. Someone would miss me.

I took off my coat and emptied my case of its dirty shirt, underwear, pyjamas and shaving kit. I made some tea and took it through to my desk. I wanted to plan my next steps; tackle Liza Caldwell first or Kate Graveney; frontal assault or pincer movement.

I drew up my chair and sat down. I stood up and sat down again. Something felt different. I'd sat here a thousand times and my body knew the angles to within half a degree. I looked down at where the desk legs sat on the lino. The dents were a fraction out of line. My desk had been shifted. I looked round the room. There wasn't much to play about with in here. Desk, two chairs, phone, filing cabinet, hat stand and that was it. Had Val been dusting or mopping? Why would you move a desk that weighed a ton?

I walked through to my bedroom and looked around. If the

place had been given a going over it had been done by experts. I went back through to the office and sat down. I opened my drawers. Tumbler still in the usual place, notepad, pencil, pen and ink. No bottle. I thought I had a half-full Red Label, but I guess I'd got through it. I couldn't recall a real session in a while.

I walked over to my filing cabinet to check my client records, such as they were. About twenty of them by now. All neatly ordered alphabetically. A suspicion took me straight to the G section, but Kate Graveney's was there all right, and my few notes were in the correct order. I began sifting through the rest. As far as I could see, they were all there too.

Then it struck me. My clippings were missing. All the newspaper reports of the murders. I checked each of the drawers but there was no doubt. Val? Had she removed it to stop me dwelling on the horrible subject?

Then I heard footsteps. Ones I knew. They were already on the second floor. I found myself gripping the arms of my chair, conscious of trying to control my heart. Wilson hove into sight and stood panting at my door. He was sucking for air but smiling. I couldn't see any marks on his face; I couldn't have hit him hard enough.

"Get out, Wilson. Or rather, don't come in."

He ignored me and slouched in. "Looking for this?" He drew out a folder from under his arm and waved it at me as he approached. He tossed it on my desk and slumped, chest pumping, into my visitor chair. It groaned under him. I wished his heart would pop.

I looked at my clippings file and then at him. There was still some contusion about the left eye, and his mouth looked swollen. Better. I was through playing games. I picked up my smart pen and unscrewed the top. This time I was on my own ground. If he attacked me I'd see how long he could fight with a pen in his fat throat. My voice was cold. "Did you have a warrant?"

He smirked. "By the book."

"Yours, or the police manual?"

"All proper. Of course."

"I'd like to see the section that allows you to steal a man's whisky."

His smile widened. "Thirsty work." Then his face closed. "Why *are* you so interested in these murders, Mr McRae?"

Mister now. What was going on? "I told you before, *Wilson*, I was curious. That's all. Professional curiosity."

He reached out, took the folder and flicked through the clippings. He was obviously intimate with it. He found what he was looking for and laid it out flat on my desk, facing me. It was the one reporting the arrest of the "Ripper". My handwritten *Ha bloody ha!* leapt out from the page.

"Why did you write that?"

"Because I knew you had the wrong man."

"And how did *you* know that? You cleverer than all of us down at the Yard? That it?"

"Looks like it, doesn't it? The man you arrested didn't fit with the picture that was coming through from the newspapers."

"Oh, really. Got that from the papers, did you? Wasn't because you knew who the real murderer was?"

"I don't have to answer any more of these daft questions."

He sighed. "Not here. Not now. But you could, if I was to arrest you."

"What the hell for, Wilson? You're flying a kite."

"For the murder of three women in London. Not to mention the little incident in France."

"That's bullshit! Total shite!" I was furious and terrified at the same time.

"Is it? After our little set-to the other night, I got a warrant, McRae. Saw your personal file at the SOE. Documents missing, weren't there? But there was a note on top. Said you weren't to get any information about events or people in the SOE if you came looking. Made me wonder. Didn't find the missing papers on you when you were arrested for breaking and entering. Had a little hunch. I'm good at hunches. Asked for your old boss's file, Major Caldwell. What did I find?"

I knew what he found. My stomach was knotted with the terror of what he would do with that information.

"Seems you're a handy man with a knife."

"There's no proof!"

"Maybe. But it made me wonder about our little run-in in Soho. Made me wonder what you were doing there. So I got another warrant and found this." He stabbed the clippings with his finger. His nails were shredded and split like a miner's. But they'd seen no such honest work.

"So what? It's no crime to read the newspapers or keep bits of them." Which was true, but I knew how it looked.

"No, but it's adding up. It's all adding up, McRae. Circumstantial to be sure, but it's beginning to come together." He leaned over the desk at me. "You ever pay little visits to Soho, McRae? You know, for fun? Like New Year's Day? If we start showing your photo about the place, would they recognise you?"

This was too close. I panicked. "No more than they'd recognise you, Wilson, if I started asking around."

His face purpled and his mouth worked under his puffy cheeks.

"I think some day soon you'll make the one mistake, McRae, leave the one clue, that ties you to one of these." He pointed at the paper. "And when you do, we'll have you back down the nick and this time you'll stay there. Until, of course…" He mimicked a noose going round my neck and pulling tight.

He tossed the clippings folder on my desk and clumped out the room. I sipped at my cup to stop the shakes. The tea was stone cold, but I drank it anyway. Just when I thought it couldn't get worse, it had. Trouble was, I could see Wilson's point of view. Leaving aside his tendency to punch first and ask questions after, my own police training would have sent me down the same road. I would have made myself a suspect if I'd been in his shoes. And he didn't know about my black-outs, those little gaps in my life that were unaccounted for except for the cryptic – insane? – scribbled residue.

Hell, in the grey world of circumstantial evidence I could make a case for Wilson himself being investigated. God knows what he got up to in Soho with those poor girls Mary said he misused. Did it get out of hand? He certainly had the violent tendencies. Doc Thompson would have him in a straitjacket in a flash.

I've found that when there's so much shit coming your way that you're going to drown in it, the best thing to do is start swimming. It still stinks, but you can take your mind off it by concentrating on staying afloat. That's how I survived when my unit of the Scots Guards was under fire from tanks, machine guns, artillery and Stuka bombers at Salerno.

My leg was broken and bleeding from being blown against one of our Shermans by a near miss. I stopped the bleeding with a tourniquet made from the belt of a man who no longer needed to hold his trousers up. I made a splint from the ribs of the wrecked canopy of a truck. I collected two water bottles and started my hobble towards the rear echelon. Or at least where the rear had been yesterday; we moved a lot. It was a long walk; I had to keep stopping to release the tourniquet before my leg dropped off. The war was going on around me, but all I concentrated on was hobbling along.

It worked. I'm here. It was time to tie on my tourniquet again, set my compass and make a start.

I took my pad out and wrote two names at the top. On the left, the dowdy Mrs Caldwell, on the right, the elegant Kate. Then I started to write what I knew under both of them. Then I wrote down the simple questions I wanted to put to them both.

Kate

Are you also known as Mrs Catriona Caldwell?
What's your real relationship with Tony Caldwell?
What was really wrong with you in the hospital the night of the bomb?
Why hire me to find out if he was dead? You could have done it yourself.

Liza

Are you or are you not married to Tony C?
Why don't you care enough that your husband is dead?
Did he mention the murder to you? What else did he say about me?
Why are you lying to me?

Finally I stared at both columns, trying to plan what action to take. I needed to move fast; Wilson was bearing down on me.

But I also needed to move with circumspection; I didn't think I'd get anywhere by phoning up Kate or Liza and asking if I could pop round for tea and questions. I thought about where they lived, and then the decisions became very easy. Liza's house bordered the heath. It would give me terrain to operate from.

SIXTEEN

The next day, good and early, I got out my sole remaining screwdriver and my hammer. The screwdriver was fine and thin and it didn't take much bashing on the edge of the iron stove to knock up a snake-ended pick. It wasn't the quality of my bike-spoke versions but it would have to do.

I dug out my oldest clothes: a tough jacket of Harris tweed that still smelled of my father, corduroy trousers, boots and a good flat cap. I put them on over vest, shirt and a sleeveless pullover my mother had knitted. When I got out of hospital she'd sent down a cardboard box full of my old stuff, on the mail train that stops at Kilpatrick on its way south from Glasgow.

I inspected myself in my mirror. I looked like a poacher. The pick went into my breast pocket along with a good clasp knife with enough gadgets to earn me a dozen Scout's badges. I washed out a big hip flask and filled it with water, turfed out my gas mask from its canvas shoulder bag and replaced it with the flask. A pack of fags, matches and some Spam sandwiches went in alongside. Lastly I rolled up my plastic mac and stuffed it into the bag. This lot would see me right if I had to hole up for twenty-four hours.

I kept hoping to hear Val's cheery voice before I left. Truth is I'd have liked her blessing. Maybe she'd had second thoughts about me. Or maybe – and I kept wondering this – she was married and couldn't get away. It would explain a lot.

There was one thing I needed but didn't have. I knew where to get it, though: a little army surplus shop at Camberwell Green.

"Bird watching then, guv?"

"Tanks," I replied, twisting the screw on a pair of binoculars and aiming out the dusty window across the road.

"None of my business, I know."

It wasn't. I paid for the bins and found space in my gas mask case, and made for the tube.

If you walk up Hampstead Hill and into the trees on the edge of the Heath, you can circle round and get yourself to a vantage point on the wooded hill above Willow Road. From there to Liza's house was a distance of about four hundred yards. There are enough shrubs and tree trunks, even in their denuded winter state, to provide cover. I found a spot down from the path where I had angled but unobstructed views of the Caldwell house and the whole area either side of her front gate. I didn't need the binoculars to maintain my broad sweep.

The weather was cold and damp, but at least it wasn't snowing. Real winter was forecast, but mainly for Scotland and the north of England. With luck it would steer clear of us. I piled dead leaves under my plastic mac and settled down to wait. I wasn't entirely sure what I was looking for: visitors to Mrs Caldwell? Tony Caldwell himself in some fanciful resurrection? In truth I was following the habits I'd adopted as a private detective: stake out the target and watch, watch and note, wait for them to do something that convicts them. But what could Mrs Caldwell be guilty of?

It was a quiet street, even by the standards of the suburbs. Hardly a soul went by and cars were as rare as a winter tan. I felt the woods gently embrace me. A blackbird echoed through the bare trees and a dog barked from some distance away. The stillness infected me, and reminded me of long walks with my dad in the sounding woods above Dundonald Castle, a bus ride from Kilpatrick. We'd leave my mother laying out the old plaid and setting out the hard-boiled eggs, the meat-paste sandwiches and the vacuum flask with lemonade. And we'd go off into the woods and learn the names of trees and birds.

I raised my glasses and watched a man go by with a dog, talking to it as if he expected an answer. Then a couple who looked like they'd done all their talking years ago; then a weary old woman. I watched their closed faces and wondered about their lives. I trained my sights on the house to see if there was movement behind the net curtains. Nothing. And no smoke from her chimney. Had she gone away for a few days? By mid-afternoon I was stiff and cold and increasingly convinced this bird had flown. Then suddenly her door opened. Liza Caldwell stepped out in coat and hat. She had a little wicker shopping trolley which she carried down the short run of steps. She trundled off down the street.

An hour later she was back, and I could see she really had been shopping. She had to haul her basket up behind her, straining on each step. Soon afterwards lights went on in some windows and finally the street lights did too. I rose, aching and chilled. My ribs felt as though they'd been put through my mother's mangle. I shook my mac and began the trek home, looking forward to warming up in front of a fire with a glass of whisky in my hand.

I repeated the pattern the next day. She was a creature of

habit, our Liza. What did she do all day alone in the house? I would have kept up the vigil for the rest of the week except for the headache that started to come down on me as I travelled back to my flat. Maybe sitting in the cold with my eyes screwed up, peering down at the little house set something off.

I took to bed as the clamps came down. I think I got up a couple of times to be sick. Once I found myself in coat and pyjamas in the entrance hall, not sure if I was just going out or coming in. Sleepwalking of some sort. Then the blackness floored me for a full day and another night. I woke shivering and sick, my bedclothes in a damp tangle.

There were fresh scrawls in my jotter, but they told me nothing new about my condition or where I'd been. I was so sickened by the whole damn business I tore the page out and used it to help start a fire. In the flames I saw old horrors, old beatings in the camp and nearly picked up the phone to see if the Doc would take me back and blast some current through my brain and expunge these sordid memories for good and ever.

I needed another day lying doggo in my flat before I felt fit enough to tackle another watch.

Same routine, same result: nothing. It was on the fourth morning – not counting the two I missed – that my severely tested patience and sore ribs were rewarded. A big car drew up. A Riley. A man was driving. He got out, opened the passenger door and handed a lady out. I would have known that car, that walk, and that turn of a blonde head anywhere. What the hell was Kate Graveney doing visiting her lover's widow? Condolences?

I raised my glasses and trained them on the door as it opened. Liza smiled. I could see a welcome word or two being given and then Kate stepped inside. From their expressions and actions, this wasn't a courtesy call by a woman finally acknowledging her lover's death and come to pay her respects. They'd met before. They might, if you simply read the faces and knew nothing about their relationship, be good friends.

Kate visited for thirty-five minutes. Again, the show at the door was too cosy for the situation. Unless I was hopelessly misjudging their nature. They could have met recently, recognising – in their shared bereavement – a kindred spirit, and become pals in that pragmatic supportive way of women. Somehow I doubted it, and I had to find out what was going on.

Liza's day picked up its usual flow; that is, she disappeared behind her curtains until 3 o'clock. It was a big house, but how much housework could a person get through in a day? I watched her totter off with her wheelie. If she stuck to her routine, I had roughly an hour before she returned from her errands. I flicked off the leaves and dirt and made myself as presentable as I could. This would take strong nerves. I made my way down to East Heath Road and walked back up and into Willow Road.

I strolled smartly in through her gate to the comparative safety of her porch. If anyone had been peeping through the net curtains of the neighbouring houses, they would have seen a man marching straight-backed along the road, open and easy, and then seeking entry at Mrs Caldwell's. Had I met anyone coming along the street I would simply have tipped my cap, said good day and kept walking.

I studied the door. I'd watched her come out, pull the door to, lock the top Yale, and use a bigger key on the simple bolt below. I pulled out my penknife and flicked open the corkscrew gadget. I slotted it into the big bolt keyhole and felt for the single pin. Got it! I twisted and forced it back. I put the knife away and took out my little bent screwdriver and slid it into the Yale.

I began scrubbing. But it wasn't as fine an instrument as my old pick. I felt some of the pins give but I couldn't quite get the driver. I took a deep breath and wiped the sweat off my hands. This was taking longer than I'd hoped. Worse, I could hear the steady sound of a man's footsteps heading my way. I had seconds to open the door and get out of sight, or withdraw now and pretend to have knocked and to be waiting for an answer.

I gave it a little more force and a couple of rubs back and forth and a twist and it gave. I pushed the door open. I just had time – I thought – to slip in and close the door gently behind me before the man could see me. I waited with my heart throbbing, listening for the footsteps to stop and come to the door. People were nosy and protective in the suburbs. If he knew who lived here, he'd want to find out who the strange man was.

The footsteps kept going and I slumped against the door till my racing pulse slowed. I could hear the blood thudding in my ears. It struck me that this breaking and entering was beginning to become a habit. A bit of a career change for a former copper. And if they caught me this time, I was for the high jump.

I edged into the house along the hall. To the right was the best room that I'd been taken into; to the left a smaller room – her day room it looked like – with a scullery leading off. There was a door leading from the scullery into the garden. The grate was warm and the fire had been banked with dross to keep going till she got back. A pile of knitting lay by a footstool in front of a high-backed chair. A similar chair sat opposite. A wireless stood on a display cabinet containing china and glass. I put my hand on the wireless; it was still warm, the dial set for the Home Service. I wondered if she liked Dorsey too. A small dining table with four chairs tucked under it pressed itself against the wall. A carpet covered most of the lino.

The mantelpiece held a baroque clock that ticked too loudly for its size. On either side of it were photos: they showed Liza and an older woman from different periods in their lives. But there was no mistaking their relationship: mother and daughter had the same eyes and nervous smile as though they weren't sure about being seen together or doing something as vain as having their photo taken.

I moved back into the hall. I knew what the best room was like so I took the stairs and found myself on the first landing with three doors leading off. One was the bathroom. The other two were bedrooms each with a single bed. And here was the funny thing. One had the air of disuse; not dirty or thick in dust, just a lack of any daily human presence. Everything was too neat, as though it was waiting for someone to return. On the bedroom table lay a set of hairbrush, comb and hand mirror, all in good tortoise-shell. It was a woman's room but long unused. Her mother's?

The second bedroom was clearly Liza's. It too had a dressing room table and mirror and cupboards. A dressing gown was hung neatly behind the door and a pair of slippers was discarded beneath the bed. Also a single bed. I got down on my knees and examined the carpet. There were no marks of a double bed, a matrimonial bed, or even of a second single. No sign of a man about the house.

I climbed to the top landing. It had the feel of an area long abandoned. The layout was similar to the first. The bathroom was desolate and cold. I shivered and tried the next. It was empty except for a big trunk and some packing cases. The third room was locked. It took me ten seconds to pick it; I was getting my touch back. I opened it, stepped into darkness and switched on the light.

The room was lush velvet and satins, reds and purples. A double bed dominated the space. It was covered by a heavy wine-red counterpane and matching plump pillows. The floor was carpeted wall to wall in a deep soft pile. Heavy curtains to match the bedding blocked the daylight. There was a basin and a sideboard on which tall candles had melted and spilled. In the top drawer of the sideboard, laid out carefully like a trousseau, were layers of fine black silk with red ribbons. For the first time I felt an intruder and wished myself out of there.

I locked the door and crept back downstairs and into the best room. It sat, mausoleum-like, in darkness. I flicked on the light and saw that the chairs and settee had been covered in a white cloth. The table had a leather mat over its surface. The piano too had a white sheet. The curtains would have been drawn to keep the light out and save the carpet. But nothing had fundamentally changed. Then I wondered where the photos were of Tony in uniform and Tony and Liza. They'd both stood on the piano. Maybe Liza put them away to save them from the light? They weren't in any of the other rooms.

I walked over to the chest of drawers and began to pull them out one by one. In the second, on top of a slim photo album, I found the missing pictures. But the black edging had been removed.

I started to flick through the album. There were no wedding photos; perhaps they were bound separately? Then, on a page all by themselves were three photos of Kate Graveney. One was hand-tinted and she smiled out at me in a way I could only dream about. Without thinking what I was doing, I unpicked it from its corners and slipped it into my inside pocket. Every soldier needs a pin-up.

I kept turning the pages and found myself time-travelling. There were no captions, just dates under some of them. Tony and Liza grew steadily younger; they were children and sometimes they were with Liza's mother and twice with a man whom I assumed was the father. But of whom? I'd heard of childhood sweethearts getting married but this was carrying it too far.

I glanced at my watch and saw with a jolt that my hour was almost up. Sometimes she took less. I slammed the album shut and slipped out of the room, casting it back into impenetrable dark. I got as far as the door when I heard the footsteps coming up the path. I froze; my heart stopped. I began stepping backwards away from the door. Footsteps climbed the stairs. I saw the shadow of a head and shoulders through the frosted glass. I would make a run for it out the back. I prayed the scullery door had its key in it.

I'd reached the end of the hall when the letterbox crashed and I heard the sound of envelopes hitting the floor.

I slumped to the floor and waited for the nausea to pass. I wanted a cigarette, badly, and gave myself a shake. There was no time left. I turned over and crawled to the door. I picked up the two letters and saw they were addressed to Caldwell all right: a Miss Caldwell. I dropped them, got to my feet and opened the door. I listened for a second, heard nothing and walked brazenly out, pulling the door behind me. I couldn't afford the time to relock the big bolt; Miss Liza Caldwell would have to believe she forgot to lock it on her way out.

I walked back down Willow Road towards the Heath, in the opposite direction to where she'd be coming from, cut off on to the path and up into the trees, whistling like I'd lost my dog. When I was far enough away I found a log and sat on it and smoked till my hands stopped shaking. I made a very long detour through the woods until I could pick up the High Street.

As the underground rocked me south I sprawled in my seat, emotionally and physically drained. I chain-smoked all the way. I'd gone one step forward and two back. I took out Kate's photo and stared at the daring eyes looking for answers. I rehearsed what I'd found: people wrote to Liza as *Miss*. Widows don't call themselves miss, or if they did, they'd revert to their maiden name.

Tony and Liza had known each other since they were children. They might or might not be married. If they were, it looked like a marriage of convenience to cover up an arrangement between Tony and Kate. But why would they want to hide it? Yet the top floor bedroom – boudoir more like – was furnished for a couple. An intimate couple. Catriona/Kate was named next of kin in Tony's SOE file, and Kate and Liza were much too pally for women who should have been rivals – even if the man was dead.

And that's what I kept coming back to: if nothing else was what it seemed, was Major Tony bloody Caldwell really dead?

I picked up a bottle on my way home. I wondered if Val would come by, and had a bit of bread and jam to see me through for a while. Kate's photo I carefully placed in her file in my drawer.

I turned on the radio and was in time to hear the six o'clock news. I wished I hadn't. The first item was the discovery of a fourth body in Soho. The killing had taken place in the last three days; it was hard for the police to give an exact time and day, as the victim had lived alone after separation from her husband. She'd taken in callers to make ends meet. At first, because she wasn't a known prostitute, the police had discounted the connection. But the method of killing was consistent with the other three murders: bloody, brutal, wounds to head and body.

All during the last three days – when I'd been here, incapacitated, but wandering around in my delirium...

Val found me later with the bottle at my feet. It was as good as empty. She made me stick my fingers down my throat until I brought most of it up in the sink. I felt like death, wanted death. All Wilson's innuendo and Doc Thompson's guarded analysis, all my own visions of hell, added up to one thing: my blackout two days ago had coincided with the murder of this young woman. I wouldn't be the slightest bit surprised to find a pattern of such coincidences stretching back over the three other killings. I was Mr Hyde. Maybe Scotch was my secret potion.

"Why do you do this, Danny?" She pointed at the bottle.

It was a good question. And the usual flip answer "To forget" rang a bit hollow in the circumstances. I had no problems on that score.

"You don't want to know."

"I do. I can take it. Is it about something you've remembered?" Her dark eyes looked huge in the flickering light. She sat in her usual place, hunkered down in front of the flames.

I shook my head. "You know I get these blackouts. I don't know where I go or what I do during them. I thought I just collapsed. Went to bed. Had bad dreams and came out of it feeling like shit. But I think... I think I sometimes go out. And it scares me to death!"

She must have seen the terror in my face for she scuttled

over and knelt at my feet. She gazed up at me. "I've been here once, when, you know, you had a funny turn. And that's all you did; you went to bed. You were tossing and turning and carrying on, but you weren't in any state to be out wandering the streets."

That gave me hope. But I wasn't convinced, no matter how much I wanted to be.

"Val, Valerie. These murders. The ones in the paper. Wilson came round accusing me of them. He raided my office. He found my clippings – the articles in the newspapers – I don't know why I keep them. But he found out about the girl who was murdered in France. And he's putting two and two together. And so am I!"

"But you didn't! You couldn't! You're not like that, Danny!"

"I wish I had your faith! Look, my doctor at the hospital told me that he wasn't sure *who* I was. All he saw was the man with the bashed-in brain and that could be affecting my whole personality, making me different from what I was before. Before France. There's no saying if I had it in me. He said it was possible for someone to…" I didn't want to go on. This was surely losing her. I looked away.

"Possible to what?"

I brought my eyes back round to hers. "Possible to get a taste for it. To do it again, and again. The last killing was a couple of days ago. When I had an episode. It fits, Val. It all fits."

My voice was flat but my head was bursting with the pressure. She said nothing. She searched my eyes like she was looking for signs of the criminal in me. She shoved her hair behind her ears. I wanted to breathe her hair.

"I don't believe it, Danny McRae. That isn't you. Do you hear me? It isn't you."

I cupped my hands and sank my face into them. "But what if it is? What if you're sitting here with a madman who's lost a year of his life? A psychopath who has blackouts and can't remember what he does during them? What *if*, Val?!"

For a moment her eyes flickered then she shook her head. "You didn't do it."

Her certainty steadied me. Amazed me. "How do I prove it?"

"You're the detective, Danny." Her face broke into a grin. "You'll find a way. And I thought you were going to check out Miss Toffee-nose?"

"Kate Graveney? I haven't told you, have I?"

The thought of the tangled little web that Kate, Liza and Tony had spun fired up the professional in me. Even in the darkest times, if I have a plan, an objective, something to drag myself towards, I can carry on. I got up – a bit woozy – and fished in my jacket. I came back and showed Val the photo.

"That's her. That's Miss Toffee-nose."

"Pretty. In an obvious sort of way. And definitely, that nose is made of the finest toffee. How did you get it?" She examined the back.

I told her about my stalking of Liza Caldwell. I hesitated about telling her about breaking into the house, but she seemed ready to take on as much of my mad world as I could give her. I told her about the albums and the photos of Tony and Liza.

"They're related, aren't they?" She was excited, enthralled by the mystery. She was kneeling in front of me, her dark eyes glinting like oil, her thin face lit up.

"That's what I reckon. But there's no resemblance."

"Cousins or something. They've made it up. To keep you away. To stop you finding Tony. He could be alive. Oh, you must find out!" She was bouncing up and down on her knees like a puppy. I wished I had her suppleness.

"Calm down. I will. I'll go see Kate and ask her to her face what's going on. All right?"

She was beaming. She sprang to her feet. "I'll make us a cuppa. Do you know where she lives?"

I thought I knew. Kate hadn't told me where she lived, just her phone number. It was in Chelsea but the operator refused to give me the address behind the number despite my pleas. But assuming Catriona and Kate were one and the same, her address as next of kin was in Tony Caldwell's file. I used to pride myself on my memory, something that really helped when I was in the Force. Even now it could still come up trumps.

SEVENTEEN

Of course, I thought – as I wandered down the elegant Chelsea street the next afternoon – the address could be as fake as the marriage between Tony Caldwell and Liza. But somehow I thought not. Onslow Square was the right sort of stamping ground for a girl like Kate Graveney. I imagined the square was especially beautiful in summer, with the trees shading and defending the central private park, and the tall Georgian house fronts gazing down snootily at plebs like me. Most of the buildings were terraced and single-fronted – a door and one massive bay window. But here and there came a break in the pattern and a house stood clear of its neighbours by taking up twice the width.

Kate's house – the one I thought was hers – was one of those. I walked past, then studied it from behind a parked automobile. There were one or two other cars around, big ones, expensive ones, but no Riley; then I saw the garage doors to the left of the flight of steps going up to the front door. The house was four storeys high and fronted by tall columns. It was painted white and had the girth of a good-sized hotel. It was as far removed from our two-room tenement flat in Kilpatrick as Buckingham Palace itself.

It was growing dark and the street lamps were coming on, shedding pale light over the scene. If I stood around any longer I'd be noticed. The last thing I needed was a local bobby checking me over. Lights began to come on inside, revealing tall ceilings and the occasional figure moving through the rooms. I gathered my jangling nerves and my well-honed inferiority complex, and walked towards the front door.

I stood for a long moment on the top stair, gazing at the heavy brass knocker. Though I'd rehearsed my questions the night before with Val and again today a thousand times, I wasn't certain that I'd be able to get them out. Hell, I might not even get through the door! I sucked in air, lifted up my hand and gave the knocker a good couple of thwacks. My mind was flipping like a jitterbug. Nothing happened for the longest while, then the door opened and a blaze of light blinded me.

"Yes, sir, can I help you?" It was the voice of a young woman, I assumed a maid.

"I'd like to see Miss Graveney. Is she in, please?"

I could now make out the girl's face. She wore a small white cap and a dark outfit and white gloves. She looked scrubbed and clean and saucy, the sort you'd love to meet for a drink on a Saturday night before going dancing. You knew she'd be a great dancer.

"Is Miss Graveney expecting you, sir?"

Bingo! "I wouldn't be surprised." The girl looked puzzled. "Can you just tell her that Daniel McRae is here. She'll know why." She might, but would she see me?

"I'll see if Miss Graveney is taking visitors, sir. It is near supper time. Perhaps you would like to come in and wait?"

"Yes, thank you."

The maid curtsied, not something you see too much of around Castlemilk. "Certainly, sir. Please follow me."

I stepped inside the portico while the maid closed the outer door. She pushed at the internal doors and I followed her into a soaring hallway floored in black and white diamond-shaped tiles. A number of doors were set in the walls. A sweep of banister rose up either side and reappeared as the rail of a long gallery, high overhead. All it lacked was a pulpit. I could see the minstrels playing at Christmas, or a gang of choir boys. Nice, very nice. My office and bedroom could be tucked into a corner of this cathedral and would still leave room for a good-sized congregation.

The maid was prancing neatly across the ballroom floor. I knew she was a dancer. I scampered after her. She opened a door and invited me in. I walked past her while she held the door. It was a library.

"I will inform Miss Graveney and see if she will see you. If you would like to take a seat, sir?"

There was a fair choice. It was like one of the good clubs I'd been scared to go into: a big room filled floor to ceiling with more books, and in much better condition, than the whole of the Kilpatrick public library. I wondered if they were as well read. Half a dozen leather armchairs spread themselves comfortably around three low tables, one with newspapers neatly arranged on it. A log fire sputtered in a fireplace where you could have roasted an ox. Maybe they cooked one at Christmas. The lighting was amber, except where standard lamps cast bright cones to read by. A place to sit and muse and watch the flames eating up the logs, and feel smug about your place in the world.

"Shall I take your hat and coat, sir?"

"It's fine. I'll just park them beside me." I didn't know how long I might be staying but thought it best to have all my kit by me in case of a quick exit.

"Very good, sir."

I folded my coat and laid it on the table nearest the fire. I placed my hat carefully on top of it. I sank into the huge leather arms of a chair next to the hearth and facing the door. I waited. I waited and wondered how folk got to be this rich. Inherited wealth, passed down from some long gone establishment rogue; a sucker-up to the King maybe, or an adventurer with the East India Company carving up continents. Lending money for trade, plundering the new world, setting up factories and screwing the poor. Nobody got this rich by being nice. Was I jealous? Damn right.

I don't know how long my reverie lasted but it stopped when the maid opened the door and let the Queen walk in. I got to my feet. It was the first time I'd seen Kate Graveney without an outdoor coat and hat. She wore a dark blue dress cut to mid-calf. Its soft contours confirmed my febrile imaginings about her figure. A double string of pearls sat easily across her bosom, came to a knot and dropped down to her trim waist. She was all poise and grace and languor. Thoroughly at ease in her natural setting, like a big cat on an African plain.

"Thank you, Millie. Get me two Scotches, will you? Large ones," she said.

Millie the maid, was it? I watched her go to a piece of the bookcase and press a panel. A slice of the bookcase opened up, revealing a drinks cabinet.

"Every home should have one," I said, indicating the hidden drinks unit but possibly covering Millie too.

"I expect you manage, Mr McRae," said Kate dryly.

Millie presented our drinks on a silver tray that I took to be the real thing. Cigarettes were offered from a matching box. After lighting up Kate and me, Millie was dismissed. Kate indicated I should retake my chair and took the one opposite. It looked like she was trying to turn it into a cosy fireside chat. Not if I could help it.

"Bottoms up, McRae." She raised her glass. I did too. We sipped warily. "Now, what can I do for you? I don't owe you any more money, do I?" She was all innocence and condescension.

I felt my resolution and my carefully prepared questions melting in the heat of her gaze. Some women were made to be viewed by firelight. It turned her blonde hair to silver and cast shadows that accentuated her neat nose and strong cheekbones. Her skin was carved marble. I took a bigger swig and felt the whisky bite my throat and burn my insides with resolution.

"I was well paid, Miss Graveney. Maybe too well. I want to know why you've been conducting this charade."

She raised the pale curves of her eyebrows. "Charade?" She took a deep pull on her cigarette.

"The faked death of Major Philip Anthony Caldwell."

She didn't blink. She was good. She knew I knew, and had it all prepared. "Why, Mr McRae, what a lurid imagination you have. But even if it were true, I'm sure you're such a good detective that *you* could tell *me*, mmm?"

Sarcastic bitch. My anger grew at the way these people were making a jackass of me.

"OK, Miss Graveney. Here's what I think. I think Tony Caldwell is alive and that you tried to deceive me about his death. I don't know how you contrived the bombed-out flat; that seems a step too far just to convince me Tony was dead. I do know that Liza Caldwell and Tony are not man and wife, or if they are, it's another charade, possibly protecting you. How am I doing so far?"

She blew out a plume of smoke. "But why on earth would we want to do such a thing? I mean why *bother*?" Her tone made it sound like she meant why would someone like her bother for a worm like me?

"Because I was snooping around, trying to fill in the gaps from this." I indicated my head wound. "And you've got something to hide, *Catriona*."

She snorted and tried to look offended, an easy role for her. But she didn't deny the name. "What could I possibly want to hide from *you*?"

"Your marriage to Caldwell?"

She laughed. It seemed genuine. "Don't be silly."

I was beginning to get really pissed off. "An affair, then?" I accused desperately.

She shook her head. "Mr McRae, I'm sure in your... circle, affairs are simply the stuff of scandal. But with us..." she shrugged and her glance round the sumptuous room couldn't make her superiority any clearer. Her voice dropped to a sarcastic whisper. "And anyway, you can't have a proper affair if you're *not* married."

I wanted to hit her. "Then what's all this about, for God's sake, if it's all so beneath you?"

I had an instant's warning. The creak of a door and a footstep on the wooden floor behind me.

"I'll tell you why, McRae. Or may I still call you Danny?"

That cool voice, that smooth, tough voice that sent me on my way to France, pulled me to my feet in a heartbeat. He ambled into the room from a doorway behind me.

Tony Caldwell hadn't changed much. Still slim, about the same height as me, slicked-back sandy hair and neat moustache. The difference was in the eyes; once calculating they now looked cunning, older and more tired. Too many late nights? I got my bags by lying awake and staring at the ceiling in the hours before dawn. What was keeping him up? He was smiling in that special mocking way of his; he used it to poke fun at me and the other agents during training if we got something wrong.

"You look well for a corpse," I said.

"And you look fine, Danny. Much better than when I last saw you. Thought you mightn't make it, you know. Pretty beat up." He walked over to the drinks cabinet and pulled out the Scotch. "Top up, anyone?"

"*Why*, Tony? Why all this... contrivance? What are you hiding?"

Tony filled his tumbler, walked over and stood behind Kate's chair, an elegant pose for the family album. But whose family?

"*We've* got nothing to hide, old man. It's you we were hiding from." He smiled in what he thought was a sympathetic manner.

"Dear God, Tony, what were you afraid of from me?"

His voice was sweet and sickly. "You're not well, old man. I mean, really not well. Damn shame. I mean, not your fault. But you came back in terrible shape and the quacks who know about such stuff said you were a bit – how shall we put it – barmy."

I'd had enough of this. "That's such shit, Tony! They wouldn't have let me out if I was mad. I've lost some memories, not my marbles!"

He tried to look earnest. It came out patronising. "Danny,

you've seen my reports and the psychiatrist's report. He thought you'd be delusional, paranoiac, wanting to blame someone. The likelihood was that you'd blame me. You were too dangerous. Didn't want you to flare up, don't you know?"

Damn him! It was true enough for whatever case he was making against me. Then a thought struck me. "How did you know I've seen your reports on me?"

"I heard about your little break-in. Went a bit far, that. Afraid it sort of bears out what we're all saying, old chap."

Who told him? Cassells? I was feeling swamped now; a little truth could become a big lie with clever words. I fought back.

"That still isn't grounds for sending me chasing wild geese. All you had to do was meet me and tell me what you knew. That's all. I wanted to find out, Tony. I wasn't blaming you."

"But here you are. Wouldn't let it go, would you? Always saw you as the terrier type. Like the rest of your clan. Get your teeth into something and you'd cling to it till the death. Great spirit. For a war. But not now, do you see? Besides…"

"Besides what?"

"The psychiatrists didn't have *all* the facts, did they?"

I knew what was coming. I felt nausea rise.

"They didn't know about the little problem in France. The little French girl. Did they? And I 'spect if they had, they might have decided to hang on to you for a bit. I couldn't take that chance." He moved out from behind Kate's chair and stepped closer to me. "Couldn't let you near me or mine, d'you see? Done it once and you might do it again, right?"

His concerned eyes searched mine. I could feel the weight of his argument piling on me like a rock fall. Wouldn't I have done the same, in his shoes? I was casting about for a way to fight back. I searched my treacherous memory for the list of questions I'd been planning to pose. I grasped at one. "Do you mean you were so concerned for your safety – and Liza, and your... wife or girlfriend here..." I waved in the direction of Kate who was watching us intently from her chair "... that you blew up the house you were using? And why were you using another house anyway? Doesn't this place have enough hideaways?"

I thought I'd connected for a moment, then his smile flickered back into life.

"Serendipity, old chap. The house belonged to a friend of ours. Used to pop in for drinks and such. But the house was empty when it went up. Our friend spends winter in the South of France. Can't blame him, can you? Must have been a gas leak or something. Gave us the notion of taking me out the picture, d'you see? Very convenient."

"Very." I couldn't hide the sarcasm. "And the shoes, the beautiful blue shoes?" I directed this at her, sitting with a smile on her face, or was it a smirk?

"I quite liked those shoes you know. You should have searched harder, McRae. I'd have liked them *both* back."

I was getting desperate now, angry with them and myself for my inability to break down their smug façade. My questions were coming out more and more shrill. "You turned this into a game, didn't you? It became something to amuse you! What the hell are you doing in this house anyway, Tony? Why is Kate registered as your next of kin? What's going on here?"

His face lost the contrived smile. "Why, nothing, dear chap. Nothing at all. I'm just a house guest, that's all."

They gazed at me, waiting to see if the monkey would jump through another hoop for them. Kate's face had lost its superiority. She suddenly looked puzzled and anxious. Why?

"I don't believe you. I don't know what you're covering up,

here. But none of this adds up. I won't rest till I find out the truth, Tony. For starters, I need to know what happened in France. You owe me that!"

He shook his head. "I owe you nothing, old chap. Can't be responsible for the actions of a madman, can I? I saw you, Danny. I saw you coming out of the house where that girl was murdered. I found her there. I came to confront you in your safe house and you were cleaning up. There was blood on your clothes. You looked wild. I asked you what you'd done. You began screaming at me. Said she was a whore, and she shouldn't have been seeing other men. She was yours, yours alone. Terrible stuff. So sorry, old man. I think the pressure got to you. And you flipped." He shrugged and held my gaze.

Every word drilled into me like a stiletto. I could feel the heat of the fire on my face, could sense the tumbler slipping in my sweat-filled hand. I could see it all now, except her face; I couldn't see her face; just the blood around her head. The tension in my temples was beginning to edge towards one of my turns. I couldn't fall apart here. I had to get out. But I still hadn't heard enough; didn't want to believe what I'd heard. For how can you admit to yourself that you're a monster?

"I don't believe it. There has to be some other reason. I'm not letting this go, Tony. I can't! All these games you're playing. All you had to do was meet me and tell me what you knew. Or turn me in. I'm not leaving till you to tell me what's going on!"

Kate's lips were pinched and she took a hurried swig of her drink. Tony sighed and took two steps towards the fire. He placed his drink carefully on the mantelpiece and turned back to me. For a second I couldn't see what he'd done; he was a dark silhouette against the firelight. Then I saw the glint in his hand. The glint from a big Colt service revolver. A gun that could stop a rhino. If you got close enough. Tony was close enough.

"I was afraid you'd say that. Don't you see? This is exactly what we were afraid of. I know your type, McRae. You go on and on and on, chipping away. We could have got the police involved. But what could we prove? It was wartime, in France. Lot of things happened in the war that are best forgotten. But you won't, will you? You won't let up."

"What are you going to do, Tony? Shoot me?" I began edging back and to the side, so that we were both bathed equally in firelight. I could see past him to Kate. She was hunched in her chair like she was freezing.

"It would be a kindness, McRae. A kindness to us all. Put you out of this pain. Like a mad dog."

"Murder, Tony? You'd kill me and think you'd get away with it? How would you react when they started to question Millie, for example? What would she say?"

He chortled. "She'd say what we tell her to say. It's quite easy, old chap. You forced your way in, became violent, threatened Kate here… self-defence. Inspector Wilson wouldn't take much persuading."

"You bastard! How did Wilson get involved?"

He smirked, and held the gun level with my chest.

I cast my eyes past him, in desperation. "Kate! Kate Graveney. Are you going to sit there and watch a man murdered in cold blood?!"

Kate's eyes were wide. She edged forward in her seat. The leather creaked. It was enough. Tony half turned to see her reaction and I threw my glass of whisky into the fire. The smash of the crystal and the burst of flames made him reel back. The gun lifted and I hit him with everything I had in a desperate shoulder charge. He went over backwards into Kate's lap. The gun exploded in a huge roar that started Kate screaming. The shot hit the ceiling. Before Caldwell could right himself, I had gripped his wrist and was battering it on the tiled hearth.

He was punching at my face with his free left hand but I kept smashing his wrist and knuckles on the stone till the revolver rolled free.

I grabbed it and tumbled clear. I got to my feet shaking with emotion. Caldwell disentangled himself from Kate's legs and they both dragged themselves upright. I had at least wiped the smiles off their faces. Tony nursed his bruised hand. I could feel blood running from an eye. He'd opened up one of Wilson's cuts. But I had the gun.

"I wasn't going to shoot you, Danny. Just hold you till the police got here. You know that."

He kept his face calm but I could hear the pleading note; I liked that.

"Do I? The only thing you're sure of when you're looking down one of these..." I waved the gun "... is that it would make a very big hole in you. Why shouldn't I use it on you, Tony? You tell me I've killed once. It's probably easier the second time, don't you think?" I brought my left hand round to steady the heavy weapon. The thought went through my mind that I *could* do it. It would be easy, and what did it matter anyway?

Some of my thoughts must have registered on my face. Panic flooded his eyes. "For God's sake man! The police are probably already on their way. You wouldn't get a hundred yards. You'd be mad to do this! You'd hang!"

I smiled. "But, Tony, I thought you'd already decided I was mad. Shooting you would be the work of a madman. They'd send me to the hospital, not the gallows."

Kate broke her silence. "Danny, don't. It was all a stupid game. This won't help you. It won't solve anything." Her lovely face was creased in fear. Maybe it was the use of my first name; I stopped enjoying having Caldwell at the end of my gun. She pressed her advantage. "Go now, Danny. Before they catch you. The servants are probably on the phone, right now."

Just as she said this the library door burst open and an anxious face showed round the door.

"Are you all right, ma'am, sir…?"

I cut off any reply. "They're all right. So far! Get in here. Now!"

The servant edged in, face white. He raised his hands. He'd seen too many gangster films.

"Stand over there! And you two." I indicated with my gun that all three should get over behind the table, away from the main door. I held the Colt on them. The firm grip and heavy barrel felt good, familiar. Gave a man confidence. I walked over to the rear door where Tony had entered, locked it and pocketed the key. Then I headed for the main door, grabbing my coat and hat as I went, all the while covering the little group.

I could feel the fury draining from me, along with my energy. The headache was starting. My vision was beginning to go. I fumbled for the key on the main door and walked outside. I closed it and rammed the key home and locked them in. I could hear their voices rushing towards the door. Kate and Tony were furious. Good.

"Is everything all right, sir?" Millie's anxious little face met me halfway across the floor. She shrieked and held her hands to her mouth when she saw the gun in my hand. "You haven't killed them, sir, have you? You didn't…?"

"No, Millie. They're all right. Just get the front door, will you?"

She fled in front of me, darting her eyes round a couple of times in case I was going to shoot her in the back. Her chest was heaving and she was snivelling with fear. I wondered how it had been for the French girl. I shook my bursting head, pulled on my coat and stuffed the revolver into its big pocket. I jammed the hat on and stepped into the night past Millie's terrified face. I paused.

"Show me your hands, Millie."

Her mouth gaped and gulped, but her gloved hands came up in supplication, palms up. The white cotton was immaculate.

I took the gun out of my pocket and laid it across her stiff fingers. She held it like a dead fish.

"Don't pull the trigger, Millie, there's a good girl."

She just nodded, tears streaming down her round face, her round lips pursed with terror. I almost kissed them.

I stumbled down the stairs and off into the night, wondering where I could go and how long before they caught me. For I had no doubt that Caldwell would unleash the hounds on me, and Wilson would be coming after me with glee in his vicious little heart.

EIGHTEEN

I headed north – homing instinct? – home to mother? It was starting to rain, that steady drizzle that soaks right through. Some Ayrshire clouds must have strayed south. I half ran, half stumbled, clinging to the park railings for support as I broke clear of Onslow Gardens, and came to the lit area round the underground at South Kensington. Two policemen were watching the crowds pouring into the station hall. Were they on to me already? I couldn't risk it. I pulled my brim down further and detoured round the corner and away, still heading north. It was getting harder to walk straight; I saw splintered images, fractured lights through the downpour. A car blasted its horn at me.

"You drunken fool!" he shouted.

And that's how it looked; this clown in a drenched coat and hat, crashing off railings and holding on to walls, lurching across roads, one foot forward, two to the side, in a drunken dance. Like the famous parties with the boys back home. Big Tam and Archie and me – fu' as monkeys. The three musketeers. *Here's tae us, wha's like us, damn few, and they're a' deid!*

A' deid. They're a' deid. And I might as well be. Valerie, Valerie, where are you? I need you.

I floundered into another set of railings. They forced me to turn off my course, pushed me to the right. Where was I? The map in my head wasn't working. Then I saw the tall memorial, and the seated man, the golden man, shining in the moonlight. Albert. The love of Vickie's life. It was Hyde Park. The railings were high, and I was dissolving. But I was also desperate. I found the gate which gave me easier footholds and hauled myself up and over, crashing in a heap on the other side.

I smelled grass and horse-shit, and crawled and staggered across the riding track. There were trees and shrubs, blessed camouflage but no place to spend a filthy night. I flopped across the soaking grass like a landed fish. Moonlight on water ahead. The Serpentine. The boathouse. Where Val and I walked the other day, the other life.

I felt my feet hitting boards, and clung to the wooden walls looking for a door or a window. Couldn't be conspicuous. The park police would check later, on their rounds. Had to do it quietly and carefully. Nothing to show. There was a door. With a big padlock and a chain. I didn't have my burglar's kit and even if I did I didn't have fingers that worked any more. I kept searching. Nothing.

I smashed my shins on something, a wood bench. Cursing, I sat down and nursed my pain till it ebbed. I leaned over, feeling sick. When it passed I straightened up and patted the rough slats. At least I was under the shelter of the porch roof. I had no choice. The band was tightening and the bad taste thickened my tongue. I collapsed on the bench, pulled my wet coat around me and sank into hopeless dreams.

I wasn't sure whether it was the cold in my bones, or the daylight or the sound of voices that woke me. I lay under a coarse tarpaulin. I flung it off in panic and peered round in the gloom. I was inside, in a shed of some sort, shivering in a filthy shroud and wanting to be sick. Though I lay on the ground I was surrounded by piles of folded deck chairs. I hadn't been able to set one up and sit in it. I'd become a seaside joke. My coat was still soaking, as was my suit. I could have fallen in the lake and come out drier. On my hands and knees I edged into the farthest recesses, and threw up. Sorry, mate, whoever you are. I don't like your job this morning.

When some strength returned I knew I had to get out of there and dry off. If I didn't, I'd get pneumonia. My head was pounding but I could see again. I'd live. Just. I was desperately tired, as though I'd been on a night march. I rubbed my eyes and longed for a bath. I had a nagging sense of guilt, a sense that there was something important, something I had to remember, but there was no faithless jotter this morning. No revelations of my bloody past to wrestle with, or none I could recall. I shook my head. I had no idea how I'd got here, or where I'd been since collapsing on the boathouse bench. But I didn't have the patience or the courage to sit and sift my dreams.

I wiped down my clothes as best I could, but even in the gloom of the shed I still looked like a tramp. My hands were sticky. I inspected them in the shaft of light. Blood. I looked down and there was blood on my trousers. Christ, what had I been up to? Then a thin memory popped up. I pulled up my left trouser leg and saw the deep cut and remembered whacking the bench last night. Harder than I thought. But at least it was my own blood.

The rain had stopped and some sun was filtering through the sickly clouds. Maybe if I walked fast I'd dry out, then I could brush off the mud. I peered through the crack in the door and saw one or two folk walking past on the opposite shore. To my left about fifty yards away was the boathouse. Some early bird was opening it up. Just in case there were any idiots wanting to sit outside on a deckchair in January, I decided it was time I was gone. I had a thought. I stepped back and picked up the tarpaulin. I folded it carefully, stuck it under my arm and pushed the door open.

Part blinded by the daylight, I walked out fast and away from the shed, expecting any minute to hear cries behind me. Nothing. One piece of luck. Now what? I could hardly go home; the police would be waiting for me. Home to Scotland? The stations would be guarded. I didn't know where Val lived or how to get in touch. My thoughts turned to Liza. Liza Caldwell. Through my headache, nausea and shivering came the distant pulse of anger. I was damned if I'd let Tony Caldwell and his female accomplices do this to me. I was going to find out the truth if it killed me... or them.

I crossed the bridge to the north side of the Serpentine and began hacking my way over the grass towards Bayswater. I checked my funds: I had two pounds three and sixpence on me. It would do for a couple of days. Just over one hundred pounds lay in an account at the Westminster Bank, but my savings book was in my office.

The walk was warming me up and the breeze was drying my clothes. Now I felt hungry. I hadn't eaten since yesterday teatime. Just before I left the park at Marble Arch I found a gents toilet. I cleaned myself up as best I could. My hankie ran red time after time as I dabbed at the trousers and congealed blood on my hands and legs. I combed my hair, but my face looked like I'd drowned in the lake and been brought back to life. Almost. I needed some hot tea and grub.

There were no coppers at the gates. I was surprised, but then

I hardly qualified for a full-blown manhunt, did I? Or if I did, they might well have assumed I was miles away, having got on the underground last night. Abandoning the gun had been the smart thing to do: searching for a man who'd threatened you is one thing; searching for an armed intruder is another.

Paradise! A Lyons corner tea house. I pulled myself as erect as I could, tucked the tarp under my arm as if it were something all normal folk carried, and smiled my way to a corner seat. My clothes steamed gently as I slurped at two pots of tea and a full breakfast, but the girl was too polite to mention it.

Refuelled, I hopped on a bus to Oxford Circus and dived down the tube. A change at Tottenham Court Road and I was on the Northern Line to Hampstead. I was steadily drying out. It was just after nine o'clock, and I was filled with tea, toast and resolve.

Hampstead was its sunny best for me, and I felt the now familiar air of being on holiday, which in the circumstances was pretty daft. As I neared Liza's house, I curbed my instinct to walk up to her door and demand answers. Instead I plunged into the woodland paths I'd grown to know and let the air and sun dry me. I took a circuitous route round to the copse above her street. Just as well; the big grey Riley was parked outside her door. I made a hide behind a tight mass of broom, spread my tarpaulin out on the leaves and grass, and settled down to wait.

I waited throughout the long day, falling in and out of exhausted sleep. I was awake enough to see Liza come and go twice, both times with Kate, arm in arm. It became clear Kate was guarding her. From me. But where was Tony? I slipped down into the village and bought some grub – marge, bread, corned beef – enough for another day. Outside the store was a crate for empty screw-necks. I nicked a couple and filled them with water at the horse trough. I caught sight of myself in a shop window. My growing dishevelment was making me stand out in this otherwise genteel corner of London. In the city proper, men like me – unshaven and unkempt – were commonplace, jettisoned by the war's end on to the streets, wandering around in army greatcoats begging for help from the people they fought for, and not always getting it.

I returned to my hide, in time to see a police car draw up and figures get out. I wished I'd had my binocs with me but they weren't needed to identify Wilson's black bulk. Liza let him in and he was there for some time. When he came out, he stopped before getting into the car and spoke to a uniformed policeman. Then Wilson's eyes swept the street and up into the woods; I froze, feeling his gaze brush over me like a searchlight. He got in the car and it eased off in a cloud of smoke, leaving the copper on guard. I had no doubt that all this was my doing.

It was a rough, cold night. I slept fitfully, continually pulling the tarpaulin tight round me to try to trap body heat. I shivered and tossed till dawn, then got up, ate some bread and tinned corned beef and went for a walk to warm up. I used the bushes like an animal, and with my roughening face and leaf-encrusted clothes I began to feel like one of Pan's mates.

Occasionally, through the trees or when I stumbled on a path, I'd see other people: men with dogs, or taking shortcuts or simply out for a walk. I fled from them, like a squirrel. But I thanked the gods for the temperate weather; I'd heard Glasgow was under six inches of snow two days ago. The lucky south of England was basking in temperatures well above freezing. It still wasn't balmy enough to be sleeping in the woods without a tent or fire. I'd have given anything for a hot fish supper.

I returned to my vigil, determined that this was my last day. If I couldn't break through to get some answers from Liza I'd have to rethink my plans entirely. Maybe go west down to Devon, and lie low for a couple of weeks. But the money was running out; dared I sneak back to my office for my savings book?

I found myself shivering even in the watery sun that filtered through the naked trees. This wasn't good. The soaking I'd got the other night, the continuing lack of sleep and accumulation of cold and pressure were taking their toll. The Riley was there again today, and the copper still stood sentry. This was beginning to make little sense, and was getting to the point where I couldn't think straight. Though my body felt cold my head felt feverish. Not good. I needed to get warm. I needed hot food and shelter.

I kept slipping in and out of sleep throughout the day, not sure if I was dreaming and not sure where I was when I woke up. What a stubborn spark flickers inside us, insisting that our petty lives are worth fighting for. At times I thought I was back in the camp, cold and hurting and wishing for death. Whatever I'd remembered two days ago in my fugue was fighting to surface. But I had no notes to trigger the memories. Neither did I want to. I was especially scared of this one for some reason.

As the evening drew in, I dragged myself upright, ate the last of the bread and the canned meat, vowing, if I survived, that I'd never eat the damned stuff again. Then I stumbled into the village.

It felt like I was coming down with flu. I spotted a pharmacy and got some Beechams powders. I was in time to get some hot tea and a scone at the café on the high street. I swilled the powder down with the tea. I got pitying looks from the waitress and scowls from the supervisor, so I didn't stay long. But it gave me a little new energy and my head was clearing. I was good for an hour or two, but where could I lay my shattered body out of the cold? I walked on down the hill; walking up was too much effort. Then I saw it.

The Rosslyn Hill Chapel sits back from the street in its own grounds. Its squat arches look welcoming enough, even to a non-believer. Amid the red brick of the surrounding tall terraces the grey-white stone made the Chapel an invader, a missionary among heathens. The sign said it was built in 1691: before Scotland lost its independence.

I pushed open the door and walked into a warmly lit hall with a great wooden-arched ceiling. Above the entrance floated an organ gallery with tall pipes glittering under the hall lights. Stretching away from me were the pews leading to the altar and pulpit.

It seemed empty but expectant. Candles had been lit and subdued electric lights illumined the stained-glass panels on all sides and behind the altar. It was prettier by far than the dour Presbyterian Kirk of St Mungo's in Kilpatrick, but then so was a Nissen hut. This Chapel felt snug and safe, and I took a seat in the back row under the organ. I laid my head down on my arms and rested on the wooden shelf jutting from the pew in front. I must have nodded off; I jerked awake to the sound of music playing above me. My neck felt broken.

There seemed to be no one else in the church except me and the unseen organist, so I settled back down. The eyes of saints and Mary Magdalene and a tortured Jesus inspected me. I wondered what sort of man they saw. I couldn't tell them. The last time I was in church was for my dad's funeral. I'd vowed never to go in one again.

I'd forgotten the power of the sanctified space and its battalions of ghost congregations. I could hear old hymns rising and falling, lauding their god with martial words. Slow marching down the aisle in my Boys' Brigade uniform, the tall flag held at an angle and straining at my arm. The minister's cadences echoing through shards of sunlight on a summer day. Only the hard pew keeping me awake through the droning and the exhortations to be good, to be better, to lead us from temptation and to forgive our trespasses. Sitting rigid between my parents as the velvet collection bag clunked round and our envelopes went in.

It was so soothing – the warmth and the music – that I stretched out on the pew. My head felt thick and hot, and black dreams began to crowd in on me, to drag me to my confessional.

I am in her bedroom. Standing over her. She is lying on her bed naked from the waist down. Her thighs are parted and blooded. Between them lies the hilt of a bayonet.

I lean over and take hold of the slippery grip. I clasp it firmly and tug. It gives, and jolts her limbs. It releases a fresh gout of blood. There is a foul smell. I pull out the long blade. I push Lili's thighs together and flip the corner of the bedspread over her. I walk over to the sink and drop the bayonet in it, and begin running cold water. My bloodied hands are sticky and I have to scrub at them to get them clean.

That's how they find me. The cries in German echo through the house and their boots rush through the hall and on to the stairs. I turn and wait for them.

I woke sobbing in the darkened church. The organist had long gone and moonlight spilled through the stained-glass panels. Mary Magdalene looked down on me, her face blank and piti-less. Jesus strained at his nails and called for release. None came. None ever comes. I let the tears flow down my face until I could weep no more. Lili... the girl had a name. The girl whose body I assaulted was called Lili. I got up and stumbled down the centre aisle and up on to the dais where the altar stood.

There was a big bible resting open on the lectern. It was too dark to make out all the words. But I didn't need much light. It was the Beatitudes, Matthew Chapter 5. I had to learn the whole text by heart to earn my badge for bible studies. The familiar litany sprang up: *Blessed are the meek: for they shall inherit the earth.* Thanks, Lord. I'll take comfort from that next time Wilson beats me up.

Blessed are ye, when men shall revile you and persecute you and shall say all manner of evil against you falsely…

And there standing in that holy place, facing the congregation of St Mungo's Kirk, with my father and mother in the front row proud to burst, I laughed out loud. I laughed until it choked me and sent me back down on my knees in the moonlight. A good joke, God. Now you can stop. Now you can fuck off and wreck someone else's life. I get the message. You're the boss. I'm sorry about playing three-card brag in the Kirk at the school assembly; I'm sorry about kissing that Catholic lassie… Well, you know what I have to be sorry about, Lord. Just let's call it quits now, OK?

Blessed are the merciful: for they shall obtain mercy. Killing myself would be exactly what Caldwell wanted. "A kindness," he'd said. "Put you out of this pain. Like a mad dog." I let his words roll through me, eating me. I punched the tiles till my fist hurt.

But then I held my breath. He said he saw me coming out of Lili's home. That he confronted me back at my safe house. His SOE report talked about me being shopped by the Maquis *after* they found out about the killing. That wasn't my dream. The Germans found me. Did it matter? It was only variations in horror. Either way, I murdered her. Yet the last dogged, pig-headed bit of me demanded the final truth. Like arguing over whether the *Titanic* hit an iceberg or a rock. Yet I clung to this discrepancy like a Sanskrit scholar gnawing away at an eroded inscription. Either I was mad or he was lying. Where there was ambiguity, there was work for an obsessive private eye. Marlowe never gave up. I crawled to my feet.

There was a big clock above the altar. It was just after three. Behind the altar was a door which led to some back rooms. I found a toilet and a kitchen, and made myself some tea. In another room was a couch and chairs. I bedded down on the couch but lay sleepless – I thought – till the dawn, pushing the memories around, trying to lift the haze that surrounded the time before the killing. Trying to see if there was a reason for what I'd done.

I must have slept, for I woke stiff and full of dread, but not immediately knowing why. Then it flooded back to me. But was it a dream or a memory? It was back to the big question: what was truth and what was false?

I gazed at my reflection in the mirror in the toilet and wished I could find a razor. A three-day stubble on a redhead looks plain dirty. I found a small knife for peeling potatoes in one drawer and tested it on my skin. It might as well have been a spoon. I pocketed it anyway. At least I could wash my face and comb my hair. I rinsed my mouth as best I could.

With my hat pulled down and my coat collar up I was Cagney on the run. I lit my first cigarette of the day, coughed like a TB victim, and left the church by a side door. It was driz-zling again. The easy thing would be to aim for the tube station and vanish into the city. So I took the next turning and headed towards Willow Road. It was time to confront Liza Caldwell.

NINETEEN

Willow Road was empty of police, grey Rileys and passers-by. It was now or never. A down-at-heel character like me couldn't hang around for very long before someone started phoning the police. I had no idea if she was home. All I could do was try a frontal assault.

I walked determinedly from my cover among the trees, along the street and straight up her front path. I stood on her top step, knocked and waited. A voice called out from within.

"Who is it?"

"Police, madam. Just a quick word, if you please." I tried to hide my Scots accent; it came out more Welsh than English, but it seemed to work. I listened to her heels on the tiled floor and turned my back on her just as the door opened.

"Yes, officer?"

I turned swiftly and before she could call out I pushed past her, slammed the door and slapped my hand over her mouth.

"Promise me you won't scream and I won't hurt you. Nod if you agree." I felt her head tilt twice. I let her mouth go, but my grip slipped to her throat.

"Now, Liza. We're going into the kitchen and we're going to chat about you and Tony Caldwell. OK?" She nodded again. I

181

pushed her through in front of me. I made her sit in a chair and dragged a stool over beside her. Fear had paralysed her; she gripped the arms of the chair as if she'd fall off. Her legs were twisted round each other. Her eyes said I was about to stab her to death. Which I guess was exactly what she thought if she believed Caldwell.

"I just want some information. I told you, I'm not going to hurt you."

She found a voice. A shrill one. "The same way you didn't hurt all those poor women! What you *did* to them!"

"Liza, I'm not going to be able to convince you one way or the other about that. All I want is to find out the truth. I need some answers. No matter how unwelcome."

She looked completely unconvinced. "What do you want?"

"What's Tony Caldwell's relationship to you?"

She studied me for a while, like I was a bug under a microscope. "He's my brother."

"Why don't you look like each other?" Seeing her like this, close up, was to confirm the complete lack of family resemblance.

A strange look came over her face, as though she was holding back a sneer. I suddenly caught the likeness. "We're only half-related. We had the same mother but different fathers."

Of course. "But why does he use the name Caldwell? Was that your father's name?"

She nodded. "He was brought up by my dad. Here in this house. His real father wouldn't let him use his name."

Always half-answers. One question leading to another. But before I could ask it, she exploded.

"What does this matter? Why are you doing this? What's the point?"

"Same as before, Liza. When I first came here. I'm trying to get to the truth about me and a missing period in my life."

"You know the truth! You killed that poor girl in France and all these other girls. And now you're going to kill me!"

An illogical response struck me. "The London girls were prostitutes. Why – if I *was* the killer – would I bother with you?"

"You're sick, you know that. That's what you are." She was crying and angry at the same time. I thought she might throw herself on me. "Tony was right!"

I let her sobs continue until her chest steadied. Her face settled and then changed. Terror was replaced with cunning.

"Why don't you give yourself up before you hurt anyone else? The doctors will look after you. You won't hang. They'll help."

"Look, if I'm mad you might as well humour me, right? So let me ask you about Tony and Kate Graveney."

She looked wary suddenly. "What?"

"Are they married?"

"Of course not! Why on earth…?"

"It's in his file. His army records. She's next of kin. Mrs Catriona Caldwell."

Her face melted. I don't think I'd ever seen a look so despairing.

"Oh Tony, Tony," she said to herself. She looked up at me. "They're not married."

"Then why did he falsify his records? What's going on, Liza?"

She was shaking her head. "What does it matter? Why should you care?"

"Because you need all the pieces to finish a jigsaw." The next question would take me a long way. "Who was Tony's father?"

She snorted and shook her head. I was getting fed up with her stonewalling. The police could reappear any time. I had to force the pace. I got up, fast. I moved behind her and dragged her back into her seat. I pulled out the knife I'd nicked from the kirk and pressed it into her neck. The blade was dull but the point pricked her skin.

"Don't move," I warned her. Her skin was roughened where her collar rubbed. She smelt of talcum powder. She was trembling like a hare among hounds. I didn't like this. I didn't like me. Which was a good sign, right?

"No more games, Liza. I want answers. Are we clear?" I felt a bastard, but I had to do this. I had to know.

She was sobbing quietly. "Don't kill me, please don't kill me. Please don't." Her shoulders were shaking so much I pulled the knife back in case I cut her by accident.

"What's the problem, Liza? It's a simple question. Who was Tony's real father?"

"It doesn't matter." She dissolved again.

"Tell me!" I snarled in her ear. The more she hedged, the more important it seemed. I pressed the blade down.

"Philip Graveney, *Sir* Philip bloody Graveney. There! Are you satisfied now?"

I walked round in front of her, trying to gather my scattered wits. "So he's a half-brother to you and to Kate? A bit confusing, I agree. But what's wrong with that, for God's sake?"

She gave me a look that suggested I was stupid to even ask that question. I pressed on. I never minded asking the obvious questions. I suddenly missed my police notepad; this scene had exactly that sort of feeling.

"What's wrong with that, Liza?"

She sniffed and dried her eyes with a handkerchief. "You

know. I don't want to say it."

I thought of the pair of them so comfortable together in the Chelsea library.

"They're lovers too, aren't they?"

She didn't reply.

"Aren't they?"

Her face twisted from fear to anger. "And they will go to hell and damnation!"

"I expect so. I don't know all the rules on incest, but this doesn't look good."

She gave me a pitying look but said nothing.

"When did it start?"

She shrugged. "He was just a boy. My dad – Tony's step-dad – worked at the Graveneys'. So did my mum. We all lived in the servant quarters there. We'd play in the kitchen. Tony was three years younger than me. Always wanting to see what the master and mistress were doing. Fascinated by the big house and the rooms we used to sneak into when the master and mistress were away. And I suppose he was jealous."

Liza seemed to be unloosening, almost as though she wanted to get it off her chest. "Did you see much of Kate?"

"Catriona. Oh, yes. Little madam. Had Tony round her little finger even though she was a year younger than him. We used to play together. They didn't mind that when we were little. But it stopped when Tony began showing an interest in her. She was a pretty little thing. And knew it. You can't blame him!"

"I'm not."

"He used to tell me how he loved her and how he'd take her away some day and marry her. Poor Tony."

"Did *you* know?"

"Of course not! Not then. Not till Tony did."

"When did he find out?"

She thought for a bit. "He was thirteen, going on fourteen. I was seventeen when *my* dad died. Cancer. He said on his death bed that Tony needed to know. Mother told us after."

I kept my voice soft. "How did you both take it?"

"I wasn't surprised. There was always something different about the way Dad treated Tony…"

She stalled.

"Like what?"

She took a deep shuddering sigh. "He used to beat him. For the slightest thing. I thought it was because he was the boy, and boys needed more discipline. It wasn't, was it?"

"How did Tony take it? When he found out?"

"Bad. Very bad. He howled for days. Wouldn't eat. Called Mum a whore and dad a dirty liar. We had to send him away for a bit till he calmed down."

"Where?"

"Mum said a place in the country. I never really wanted to know."

"How long?"

"About six months or so. When he came back he was quieter, lots quieter. And he'd changed – not that the others saw it – I did."

"How?"

"Deceitful. Got up to things around the house. Made mischief, but never got caught. He gave Mum a hard time, though. Couldn't forgive her."

"When did Kate find out? I mean, about Tony and her father?"

For the first time since I forced my way in to her home, Liza Caldwell smiled. "Why, Mr McRae, you're not as clever as I thought."

I sat stunned. "No one's told her?"

"Who? Her own father died a few years after mine. Left us this place in his will. Conscience money. My mother died without telling anyone in the big house. Only Tony and I know."

"And why haven't you told her? For God's sake, woman, you let her commit a cardinal sin!"

"Is it? Why is it, Mr McRae? Tony was denied his birthright, now he's getting it. Sort of. He's my brother."

"But he's Kate's brother too!"

"Only half."

"Dear God. So this is why you wanted to make me think he was dead? Why you played along with them?"

"Can you blame us?"

Us? What was Kate's motivation if she didn't know? But in a way I couldn't blame Liza, or even – in a moment of rare generosity of spirit – Tony. The scandal would have destroyed everyone. I was the loser so far. And so was Kate Graveney – if she ever got to learn about it.

Before I could ask her more – like who used the boudoir upstairs – I became dimly aware of the very familiar sound of a police bell. So familiar that I didn't immediately pick up on the notion that it was coming this way. The Flying Squad. For me. I heard tyres squeal outside. I jumped past Liza and into the kitchen, bashed open the back door and nearly took a nose-dive down the steps into the garden. I raced over the grass and through the canes holding up last year's dead plants.

Before the first cries followed me I was over the high wall at the back and in the back garden of the house in the next street. I looked wildly about, but couldn't see a gap. Then I did, but it was a dozen houses away. I began hauling myself over walls and crashing through privets until I found a gap of daylight. Along the way I lost my hat. I wrenched it from the hedge, sprinted for the side of the house and was through and into the street, fleck and shrubbery flying from me like a runaway horse at Aintree.

Way behind me I could hear the clanging start up as the chase began again. A car was heading towards me. I leaped out and flagged it down. It screeched to a halt. The woman driver rolled down her window.

"You idiot! I could have killed you!"

I wrenched open the door and pulled her out. The engine was still running and I whacked the car in gear, leaving the poor woman shrieking and wailing in the middle of the road. I had about a minute to get round the corner and into the High Street. I flung the wheel round and round and took corners in a screech of rubber. I broke on to the High Street and abandoned the car by the roadside.

I turned my collar down, removed the dents and debris from my hat, and began walking slowly and calmly to the underground entrance. Police were checking faces at the station; I did an about turn and walked back down the road. A bus was stopping up ahead. I ran after it as it began chugging away, leapt and caught the bar. The conductor grabbed my arm.

"Only just, mate! Only just!"

I managed to pant out, "Where are you going?"

"Cor, mate! You nearly kills yoursel' an' you don't know where you're going? Marble Arch, mate, that's where. An' that'll be threepence, if you don't mind."

I didn't mind. I didn't care. So long as I had some breathing space to get my thoughts straight and plan my next moves. One way or another I was going to get some answers.

TWENTY

The chase across the gardens and the sprint for the bus left me with jelly legs. I hadn't eaten or slept properly for days and was fighting flu and a flood of bad memories. I must have looked a nightmare to the other worthy citizens on the bus. I stank to high heaven too. A couple of old women tut-tutted me. I couldn't blame them. As my heart slowed to around two hundred, I tried to think, tried to draw on my SOE training. It was simple: I needed a safe house. I changed buses three times and kept away from empty streets or boys in blue as best I could until I got to my goal.

I kept telling myself Soho was the last place they'd be looking for me. But I had my hat wedged down over my face just the same. It was lunchtime – no time to be entering a whorehouse, though there were a few half-hearted blandishments from girls on corners or their pimps. My big worry was the reception I'd get. But I was at the end of my strength. I was dizzy with fatigue. If I wasn't welcome here, I might as well phone Wilson and tell him to come and get me. I turned into Rupert Street and stood leaning against the doorjamb and knocked.

Mary opened the door with a smile, then the smile evaporated. "You in big trouble Danny! Your picture in papers. They say you a big-time no-good murderer. I no want trouble here."

"What? What are you talking about, Mary? Trust me. Please let me in."

She heard the desperation in my voice and by rights should have slammed the door on this filthy tramp – newspapers or no newspapers. Instead she took a quick look round the street and dragged me into the hall. She pressed me against the wall.

"You stay here. No move."

I stood shoulders drooping while she scampered into her parlour and came out clutching a *Daily Sketch*.

"You see. You see. You front page." She shoved it at me. I took it and slid down the wall till I was sitting on the floor. I gazed at the photo and the screaming front page headlines: RIPPER ON THE LOOSE! The photo was of me. In my sergeant's uniform. They must have got it from Army files. I looked much younger than the image I'd stared at this morning. But it still looked like me. I looked up in bewilderment. Mary was standing over me, her arms folded and her eyes slitted. I read on:

The Ripper strikes again! But this time police have a lead suspect from evidence found at the scene. A manhunt is under way to find former Sergeant Daniel McRae..."

Police Inspector Herbert Wilson told reporters that "Every murderer finally makes the mistake that catches them out. A gun was found at the scene of this latest vicious crime, covered in the murderer's fingerprints. We believe the weapon – a service revolver – was dropped when the murderer was disturbed. Thanks to diligent police work, we are able to match the fingerprints from the gun with those of a known criminal, Daniel McRae..."

God hadn't finished with me yet. Caldwell and Wilson were his avenging angels. I laughed, but was near my wit's end. This fifth girl had died two nights ago, when I was lying half-demented in the shed by the Serpentine. When I woke in a strange place with blood on my hands. As I read and reread the words, my flabby grip on sanity began to slip again. I thought I'd given the gun to Millie. What was it doing by the body?

I looked up at Mary. "I don't understand. I don't… I didn't…" But I hadn't a clue what I had or hadn't done. I must have looked pathetic and not much of a threat, for she grabbed the paper from me.

"On feet, Danny. Stop messing my hall. Customers no like."

I struggled up and she walked off and stood by her parlour door. She pointed in. I took the hint. I shambled past her into her room. Her dazzling room. Nothing prepares the eye for this much red. Crimson dragons, scarlet cushions, cherry curtains, carmine couch, coral chairs. A room to please a vampire.

"You stink, Danny! Don't you sit on my best sofa." She picked up a paper from the huge pile behind the door and spread it out on her couch and then indicated I could take a seat.

I took my coat and hat off and slung them on the floor. I sat down and saw her face crease in pity for me. Was I in such a mess?

"Second thoughts. No sit. Stand and take off all clothes. You need bath! I got a business to run and don' need stinky men about place."

Her tone brooked no opposition but I wasn't sure I had the strength to stand up and struggle out of my clothes. Mary had ducked into the hall and was shouting up the stairs.

"Colette, get you lazy fat ass down here! We got smelly customer need bath!"

She turned back to me and saw me struggling. "OK, big baby. You need mama take your clothes off." She didn't wait to discuss it, just started in on me with expert fingers. "What you worried 'bout, big baby? You think I no seen bare man before? I seen plenty bare man." She pushed me back on the paper and wrenched my trousers, socks and pants off and threw them in a heap along with suit jacket, shirt and vest.

She left me sitting, too drained to be embarrassed by my nudity, while she rummaged in a cupboard. "Put on." She flung me a huge dressing gown in ruby-red satin.

"Was he a sumo wrestler, Mary?" The dressing gown reached to the floor when I had it on.

"Just big man, Danny. Very big!" Her little face crinkled and she guffawed at a memory I was glad not to share. "Now, first you have bath and shave, then food, then you talk. What you say?"

I say thank you, thank you, let me light some incense in homage to your gods, Mary, because mine doesn't listen. Or if he does, he's a bloody sadist.

Mary and Colette made me sit in the steaming tin bath while they added kettle after kettle of hot water. They fed me rice and sweet chicken and tea. Mary shaved me while Colette soaped me down. Bliss. I felt better than in weeks. Colette left us and I lay back, wanting desperately to sleep and let the world go to hang.

"Now, Danny. You talk."

She slopped water on my face. I talked. I told her everything and she interrupted for more details of how I turned the tables at Kate's house and how I got away from the police. Mary kept darting to her feet and bringing out old newspapers from the bundle by the door to check what I was saying against the public comments. The pile of soggy newsprint grew. It was a long and complicated story. I wasn't sure it made complete sense, or that she was taking it all in. I was wrong.

"You sure you gave gun back?"

"I don't know. Nothing seems real. Maybe I did keep it and used it to threaten that girl. Then I killed her."

The jumble in my head could be read any way you like. I tried to think of myself in the witness box defending myself. It wasn't a pretty thought: I think so, your honour, I'm not sure, your honour, I can't remember, your honour, and so on until the jury was so convinced I was lying that they'd hardly have time for their first cup of tea before they were back with a guilty verdict.

"I no think that."

"Why?"

"You no killer. I seen plenty killers. Can tell a man by how he is with girl. My girls say you kind. They want mummy you."

No rosettes for my tigerish bedroom performance then. But I could have reached out and kissed Mary for that vote of confidence. I splashed water on my face to mask the tears that had sprung up.

She was shaking her head. "But big mistake, big mistake give gun back."

"I should have wiped it at least."

She nodded. She knew the trade. I forced my addled brain to think. A strand of excitement floated up from the murk. It grew as I worked through the implications of the newspaper report. This could be the first real mistake by the killer. If I *had* given the gun back at Kate's place, it meant that it was *planted* next to the last girl's body. Planted either by the murderer himself or by someone who knew him.

"The question is, how did the gun get to the murder site?"

Mary was nodding furiously. She was way ahead of me. "Caldwell he give big fat bastard gun. He plant gun."

"Possible. But how does Caldwell know Wilson? And then there's the question of timing. When did the gun get planted? At the time of the murder or after?"

"Could be strange man around. Doing all killing. And big fat bastard want you to swing."

I fingered my neck. "The coincidences are piling up, Mary. Especially this last one: I ditch a gun with my prints on it the same night a woman is murdered. And the gun is magically whisked from Caldwell's hands to Wilson's and into the murder scene? No. I think I've already met the killer."

"I think too. Sounds like you know three men who might got blood on their hands." She raised her tiny hand and stuck three fingers in the air.

"Who's the first Mary?"

"Why, you, Danny." She pulled down one finger.

"I thought you said…"

"I no think that. But maybe you have a devil inside that come out some time."

I stared at her for a while, and believed in devils for a moment. "Maybe, Mary. Maybe. OK, who's next?"

She lowered the next finger. "Mr big fat bastard…"

She was right. I'd half-jokingly thought Wilson had all the attributes of a murderer. He was vicious, violent and liked hurting good-time girls who could hardly turn to the police for protection. Was that why he wanted me off the scene? The last thing he'd need was a freelancer blundering around. No one inside the force would ever suspect that the DI in charge of the hunt was the killer. He was a suspect. But not my prime one. The one I could scarcely believe. Rule out nothing, suspect everyone, check everything until you have hard proof. Those were my rules.

"He could be, Mary. Caldwell gives him the gun, Wilson kills another girl and leaves the gun with my prints on it. But if Wilson was the killer, how would Caldwell know that? And why would Wilson risk him knowing that?"

"So it Caldwell." She dropped the last finger.

"That's my hunch. Caldwell planted the gun with my prints on it at the site of the last murder. Caldwell is the killer."

The detective in me – and Val's and now Mary's faith in me – made me cling to Wilson or Caldwell being the killer. Maybe in cahoots with each other. Tony Caldwell's final betrayal of me. Maybe – despite my dream - *he'd* killed Lili in France; he'd known I was due to see her and set the Gestapo on me. Maybe he'd framed me by planting the incriminating gun on the latest victim.

What was I to believe? And who would other people believe? A CID Inspector and a decorated Army Major, or a man with a hole in his head? I could feel the noose tightening already. My brain seemed to have become paralysed.

"You get dry. Get sleep. We talk later."

I did as I was told. At least, I lay on the tiny bed she gave me in a spare room and stared at the ceiling. So many fragments swirling around. It reminded me of the time I got so drunk that I had vertigo lying down. Yet in the debris of my life at this moment, a little Chinese woman had given me hope, just by believing in me.

Maybe that slender lifeline opened a channel in my brain,

for I began to wake in the morning grasping desperately at the tendrils of a dream. The familiar one, but this time there was more. I squeezed my eyes closed and tried to project it on to my lids. I got a purchase on it and hauled it in, reel by reel, to inspect it with my conscious mind. I lay as still as a corpse. It wasn't a dream. It was a memory of that night in Avignon. A complete memory.

The clock is striking eight and I'm walking fast down the back lanes towards the safe house. I feel the familiar knot of fear and excitement in my stomach as I choose streets which I hope aren't being patrolled. I have good papers on me and my French will stand up to simple interrogation from the Germans, though not from a Vichy militia-man.

We have a drop coming in tonight and I need to make sure everything has been set up for it. The last load was blown completely off course and landed in the town. It was a race across the back yards of the suburbs in the dark; we lost, and twenty Sten guns and ammo ended up in the arsenal of the Gestapo. I am determined not to lose this consignment. We have a better system of flares and I've doubled the number of Maquis ready to pounce on the crates.

We've mustered nearly thirty bicycles and one truck – Gregor's. Perhaps more importantly, the weather is with us; a soft spring evening, a gentle breeze and clear skies. Perfect. And it has to be; I'm determined to impress Major Tony Caldwell who was dropped in by Lysander a week ago on an inspection tour of all the agents in the south west.

My boots sound loud on the cobbles and the smell of wood fires salts the air. I feel good, alive, as though every part of me has been freshly oiled and polished. And I'm seeing Lili.

On business. As quartermaster for the town's Resistance forces Lili has no time for romantic liaisons even if she did fancy me. We're finalising the plans for tonight's drop. She took her nom de guerre from the song we're all humming or hearing – Nazis or Allies – on the radio stations. A funny business at times, war.

I cross the last street and head down a little alley. A path leads off it to the right. The path twists and turns at the foot of the back gardens of the neat row of houses. A fence follows the path. About halfway along is the garden door into the safe house. I turn one last corner and am almost at the door when I glimpse a figure moving away from me. The retreating walk seems familiar, a loping stride, but I can't place it.

I walk fast past the back door; it's slightly ajar. I quicken my pace to a jog, but when next I have a clear view, the figure has gone. Up ahead I can hear running footsteps heading away from me.

I stop, turn back and go through the gate. It's a short garden leading to the kitchen door. There don't seem to be any lights on. Perhaps Lili's being over-cautious. I get to the door and I'm about to knock when I notice it's open a fraction. I push and go into the dark kitchen. There's a smell of soup from a big pot on the range. Lili promised me dinner. I sniff the air and think it's caught. I turn the gas off.

I let my eyes adjust until I can see where the hall is. I walk on into the hall and there for the first time, call out softly for Lili. There's no reply. I call again. Nothing.

I find the light switch in the hall. I walk into the tiny sitting room and see a table laid for a meal; fresh bread and two places: me and Lili. I back out of the room feeling something is wrong, very wrong. The floorboards groan as I slowly take the stairs. I call her name again as I round the corner and emerge on the landing.

There are two bedrooms. I try one and find it empty. I enter the next. I can't see much; the curtains have been drawn and I can't find the light switch. As my eyes adjust I see the rounded contours of a body on the bed. I walk over, dread filling me. As I get close I see that it is a woman, naked from the waist down. I lean over and touch her shoulder and say her name.

My hand touches stickiness. I find the bedside light and my shaking hand switches it on. Lili is face down in the pillow. Her hair and the shoulders of her blouse are soaked dark red. The pillow and the bedspread are saturated. My eyes are drawn down. The cleft below her spine is oozing blood. Her white limbs are parted and blooded. Between them, lies the hilt of a bayonet.

I am paralysed with horror and grief. I don't know what to do. I want to run. I want to hold her, give her succour. She is beyond hurting, but the bayonet goes on desecrating her. I want to remove this filthy intrusion. I lean over and gently take hold of the slippery hilt. I grip it firmly and tug. It gives, and jolts her poor limbs. It releases a fresh gout of blood. There is a foul smell from her ravished body. I pull out the vile weapon. I push her thighs together and flip the corner of the bedspread over her. I walk over to the sink and drop the bayonet in it, and begin running cold water. My bloodied hands are sticky and I have to scrub at them to get them clean.

That's how they find me. Even as the cries in German echo through the house and their boots rush through the hall and on to the stairs, I know I've been set up. I turn and wait for them.

In the Kirk I wept for me. Here in this whores' palace, I lay grieving for her. Eventually I eased myself up and got my feet on the floor. I wiped my face and looked around. It was a little bare room with cheap Chinese prints on the wall and some red satin throws on the bed and over the one chair.

I felt drugged and stiff, like I'd swum the Channel then got roaring drunk. Or vice versa. But I couldn't think of anything I'd done that was so meritorious. My watch said three-fifteen and I assumed that was a.m. But it was too light. I peeked out the one curtain to check; full daylight ransacked the room. I got here about four p.m. Had I slept for nearly twenty-four hours?

The door creaked. I looked up and saw Mary's dark fringe peeping round. I was naked but too tired to pull the covers round me. Besides, she and Colette had handled every inch of me in the bath. I don't recall any erotic charge out of the event, just the soothing balm of warm water and gentle hands, like a child again. I wonder if I hurt Colette's feelings?

"So you not dead, Danny." Mary came fully into the room.

"Unless this is heaven, Mary."

She laughed. "Just back room. You sleep whole day. Now, you put clothes on and come eat. Plan next things." She pointed at my suit and shirt hanging in smooth clean drapes on a hanger behind the door. I did as I was told. The clothes were fresh and perfectly pressed. Chinese laundry. I found my way through the labyrinth to Mary's front room.

While Mary made more tea I kept going over my new recollection. It felt true. If only I could prove it. I stared at the mountain of newsprint she'd dragged out yesterday to check my tale. Headlines shrieked of murder most foul, starting just after I left the hospital and arrived back in London. But then a thought struck me. I cursed myself for not thinking of this sooner.

"Mary! Have you got a piece of paper and a pencil?"

I explained, and we began scrabbling among the papers until I could get the dates straight for all five murders. I knew that at least some of my fugues corresponded with a killing. Though in truth, my episodes had been so frequent it was hard not to. I jotted down the figures. Once a month I did have an alibi, and a prominent psychiatrist who would confirm where I was on each occasion. The trouble was the dates varied; they were roughly around the middle of the month but it depended on Doc Thompson's schedule and what they wanted to inflict on me. The normal visit – talks and examination – took two days. Electrocution took a week out of my life.

I didn't have my diary with me, but I had an idea. It was a long shot and it might prove nothing. But it was a worth a phone call to Thompson's secretary. My one big risk was if the national press had picked up my photo and the accusations in the London papers. It was four-thirty and I might just catch her before she clocked off. I used Mary's phone in the hall. I could hear the two operators trying to put me through.

"Good afternoon. Doctor Thompson's office. How can I help you?"

"Elspeth? This is Danny McRae. I have a query about my appointments." Mary was eavesdropping so close I could smell her sweet breath; she was always dipping into a little bowl and chewing some cumin seeds.

No hesitation. "Hello, Mr McRae. I thought we'd confirmed next month's?"

"It's not about the next one, Elspeth. It's about the earlier ones. I'm trying to check some dates. It's to help with my memory. A little exercise for the Doctor."

"What exactly do you want to know?"

"It's a pain, I know, but could you give me the dates of my appointments since…" I looked down at my pencil jottings "…August last year?"

"Hmm. Can I call you back with this, Mr McRae? I need to check through the diary and I'm rather busy at present." She didn't like being rushed. Elspeth had her methods and her routine.

I looked at Mary. She raised her already elevated eyebrows. "Yes, please, Elspeth. I'm sorry to trouble you but this is fairly important. So if you could call me today? My number is…" I inspected the phone base "…Westminster 5191."

"I'll see what I can do. Good afternoon, Mr McRae."

All I could do was sit down and wait. And hope Elspeth didn't call the police.

She didn't call that evening and I was beginning to think the worst, waiting for the door to crash down and Wilson to steam-roller through. It was a rotten night's sleep, what with the worry and the noises through the paper-thin walls. Those girls worked for their money. I was down in Mary's parlour by seven-thirty.

"Mary, I won't ever be able to thank you for what you're doing. You could be in big trouble for looking after me."

She giggled. "I know. You gonna have to use my girls lots in future." I doubted that. Having listened through the paper walls to the fake sounds of pleasure, I'd probably never use room service here again.

"Why are you doing this, Mary?" It wasn't as if I was her best customer.

She studied me for a moment. "You no such bad man. You help me before. Now you ask for help, I give it. Bring me luck. Some day you give it back. That how life work."

The phone rang in the hall. It was nine o'clock. We looked at each other. We dived through the door. She picked it up.

"Yes? Just minute." She put her hand over the mouthpiece. "It for you." She handed me the phone.

"Mr McRae? Who was that person?"

"We share a phone in our building, Elspeth. First one there picks it up."

"Hmm, right. I have your dates for you. Do you have a pencil and paper?"

"Yes, yes. Fire away. Thank you." Mary handed me the implements.

Elspeth rattled off the dates: when I arrived, when I left. Some were two days, some were six. I thanked her profusely and then sat back afraid to take the next step. Mary didn't move, just sat with her hands folded in her lap waiting for me to pluck up the courage. Finally I reached over for the list we'd made last night, the list of dates of the murders.

Tick, tick. Nothing, nothing. Yes! Dear God in heaven, a match. In November, while someone – *someone else* – was slaughtering a young woman, I was safely tucked up in the hospital. I ringed and ringed the date with my pencil till the relief started to ebb away. I stood up and grabbed Mary and lifted her up in the air and hugged her. She squealed in merriment like a young girl. I put her down.

"Thank you, Mary. Thank you."

"See. I tell you, you a good man."

"No, Mary. You said I wasn't such a bad man."

She shrugged. "All men got bad in them. Some more than others. So now only two men might got blood on hands."

She was right. It still hadn't quite got me off the hook; there was still doubt about Lili's murder. But I'd have to leave that for the moment. I had Caldwell and Wilson to tackle. If either one was the killer I had to find a way of pinning it on him. I didn't think dreams would be admissible in evidence.

Both men were dangerous to go after. Caldwell probably had a personal armoury and a strong motivation for seeing me dead. Wilson would tear my head off and ask questions after. And he was surrounded by the system; who would I make an accusation to? For the same reasons I didn't feel inclined to surrender and ask him to check my alibi. It would prove he'd either planted evidence in a conspiracy with the real murderer or done it himself.

Mary had piled my little set of belongings from my suit and coat on her table. It amounted to some loose change, my office and flat keys, and the list of questions I had for Kate and Liza. I picked up the crumpled list, smoothed it out on the little table and examined it.

Kate:
Are you also known as Mrs Catriona Caldwell?
What's your real relationship with Tony Caldwell?
What was really wrong with you in the hospital the night of the bomb?
Why hire me to find out if he was dead? You could have done it yourself.

Liza:
Are you or are you not married to Tony C?
Why don't you care enough that your husband is dead?
Did he mention the murder to you? What else did he say about me?
Why are you lying to me?

I could cross through most, now I had the answer to the one question I hadn't posed: Tony Caldwell, alive or dead? He was very much alive, and Kate and Liza were his half-sisters and protecting him. But I still didn't know why Kate had gone into hospital on November thirtieth. Was it important? Had she faked an injury just to make sure she had an alibi if I checked? Or had something happened to her – coincidentally – at the time of the bomb? It niggled me and I kept coming back to one of my tenets in a murder enquiry: there are no coincidences. I turned to Mary.

"Mary, do you know anyone who can make me a business card?"

TWENTY-ONE

I swung through the doors of St Thomas's hospital as if I owned the place. Self-belief was everything in what I was about to try to pull off. My confidence was increased by what Mary had managed to do. She'd found me a pair of specs with clear glass in them from a relative of hers in Lisle Street. The thick frames partly hid the scarring round my eyes. Together with the battered briefcase forgotten by a customer in his post-coital bliss or funk, they gave me the studious air I needed.

My plan would be scuppered if I found the same girl manning the reception desk from my first visit and she remembered me. But behind the desk was a large woman with a big laugh. She looked mid-thirties, and was talking and having fun with one of the nurses. I took a deep breath and marched up to her.

"Good morning, young lady. I'm Doctor Ferguson and I'm here to collect the notes on one of my patients."

"Oh, right, sir. See you later, Alice." The nurse left, smiling at me as she went.

I slammed my briefcase on the counter, reached into my jacket pocket and pulled out a set of cards. I made a show of picking one out – they were all blank except one – and handed it over.

She took it and I knew that she was seeing:

Doctor James Ferguson, MD, MSc Edin,
Consultant
105 Harley Street
London

Telephone: Marylebone 2131

"Yes, Doctor. And what was it you wanted again?" She handed me back my card.

"I can see that you don't recognise my name. Were you on duty yesterday?"

"No. This is the start of my shift this week."

"That would explain it. I phoned up yesterday and asked for the notes on one of my patients. I needed them rather urgently and wanted to speak to the doctor who attended her."

"I'm so sorry, Doctor. There doesn't seem to be a message here. What was the name of the patient?"

I put on my exasperated air. I was a busy man and here specially to deal with an urgent matter. "Miss Kate Graveney. She was brought into the hospital on the thirtieth of November last year. This is too bad. I don't have a lot of time." I glanced at my watch.

The woman's chubby face was beginning to take on a flustered glow. "Just a minute sir; perhaps if I looked in our records?"

"Please do. As quick as you like. Thank you." I smiled encouragingly at her. I watched her begin to pull out drawers and check the files. Sweat was starting to pour down my back. All it would take was a real doctor to pitch up and start asking questions and I was done for.

"Here we are," she said triumphantly. "Miss Kate Graveney. Address…"

"Onslow Square… yes, yes, I know."

"Here you are sir." She handed me a thin brown folder with Kate's name on the edge, sideways. I flicked it open and had a quick glance, but I wasn't taking anything in. I just wanted out of there.

"Which doctor was it you wanted to see, sir? I'll see if he's around."

My eyes dropped to the foot of the page of notes. "Doctor Cunningham. Is he on duty?" I prayed and prayed Cunningham was on holiday, on nights or had broken his damn leg.

"I'll just see." She turned to her desk and flicked through a clipboard list. "Thank goodness, yes. Doctor Cunningham is on duty. He'll be on his ward rounds now, but he won't be long. If you'd like to take a seat, Doctor, I'll send someone to find him."

I glanced again at my watch, and closed the file. "I don't have time. Look, keep my card. It's got my phone number on it. Could you ask Doctor Cunningham to phone me as soon as he can?" As I was saying this I was stuffing Kate's notes into my briefcase. The receptionist was looking a little panicky about it but I was gambling on her not gainsaying a doctor.

"Well, yes. I can quite see. I'm sorry things weren't arranged as you asked, Doctor. I'll get Doctor Cunningham to call as soon as possible." She clutched my card like a talisman.

"Please see that you do. What was your name again, young lady? I want to mention it to the doctor when he calls. You've been very helpful."

That did it. She was purring as I walked quickly but calmly out of the waiting hall. I kept walking like a robot across Westminster Bridge, up Whitehall and on through Leicester Square. I didn't stop till I was knocking on Mary's door. I collapsed on her sofa. Mary was grinning like a marmoset at the success of my mission.

"You nice in glasses. Like teacher. Or lawyer."

"Or conman? Shall we see what we've got?"

I opened the case and pulled out the folder. There was a covering note giving details of admission time and date and personal details of the patient such as date of birth and home address. I almost missed it. The date of admission wasn't the thirtieth of November but the twenty-third. The house blew up a week later. It *was* a coincidence. And Kate and her brother had thought to use the two events to fool me. If – as happened – I went checking hospitals, they were counting on putting the discrepancy in the dates down to a simple clerical error.

But it was the second sheet that gripped me. It was the write-up by the good Doctor Cunningham – who even now would be harassing the phone operator to get through to the non-existent Doctor Ferguson. Or maybe he was beyond that stage and was ranting at the poor receptionist for being duped. I felt bad about that.

The note was brief but unequivocal :

The patient was admitted with severe internal injuries causing bleeding from the vagina. Inspection showed damage to the lining of the womb consistent with a termination. Scarring has become infected and ruptured. Bleeding was staunched and area disinfected.

*Prognosis: patient was advised that damage to womb is
extensive. Further surgery may be necessary (D&C or full
hysterectomy) to ensure seat of infection removed. Review
in 1 month.*

Poor Kate. I read and re-read the note and handed it to
Mary. She donned a little pince-nez and squinted at the page.

"No more babies, now. Right?"

"You read English very well, Mary. All those newspapers of
yours. What I don't understand is why she went to the
hospital? Wouldn't she go back to where she had the abortion?"

Mary was shaking her head. "Abortion not legal. Risky business. But if you got problems after, you can go real hospital and
get fixed. I seen it. Happen all time here."

"But why would a woman like Kate Graveney go to a back-
street abortionist, Mary? People like that have access to
private clinics. They can pay for the best."

"Depend who father is." She gave me a knowing look.

I was slow at times. She must have got pregnant by Tony.
Her half-brother Tony. No wonder she wanted to keep it quiet.
But Liza told me that Kate didn't know Tony was related to
her. Had she found out? Either way, the Graveney family physi-
cian probably wasn't the type to put his gilded stethoscope on
the block for something like this.

"But surely you don't have to track down an old woman with
a rusty knitting needle. There must be some trained folk that
are prepared to do this?"

"Sure. Halley Street!"

"Harley Street? But they're not back-street butchers."

"But need middleman to get right man. Right man like little
money on side." She rubbed her fingertips together. "We use all

time. Halley Street just round corner. That's why girls in trouble come Soho."

It was true. I could walk to the centre of the best private medical system in the country in ten minutes. "Are you saying that Kate Graveney might have come to Soho to find someone to do this?"

"Sure, Danny. We got lots of middleman. We got everything here," she giggled.

There was a certain irony in that. No wonder the church wanted Soho razed to the ground and salted. I felt I had to follow this lead through, find out if Kate did pass through here, and if so, where she went next. It wasn't clear why it seemed important; it just did. It didn't begin to explain why Caldwell might have murdered several women, but it was the only thread I had. I had to reel it in. As to how to follow Kate's tracks, I had an idea, but it was a long shot.

"Mary, if I had a photo of Kate Graveney, would you be able to take it around Soho? See if anyone recognised her?"

"Cost you money, Danny. Not for me. People want money for information. That's how Soho work."

"Mary, will you help me a little more? I've got a bank book and a photo of Kate in my office. I daren't go there, but maybe one of the girls?"

"This make big fat bastard unhappy?"

"Pig sick, Mary, with any luck."

"Then, shoo thing, Danny!"

Colette grumbled about losing her siesta but I promised her ten bob if she could get hold of my savings book – assuming the coppers hadn't cleared out my whole flat and office. I told her to look out for a skinny girl with long hair, and if she saw a cat and it looked hungry, there was a can of Carnation in a cupboard.

She returned triumphant three hours later, waving my pass book and Kate's file with the photo in it. There was no sign of Valerie. Or a note. Or anything untoward. Colette said if the place had been ransacked, they'd put it all back together very neatly. She'd seen nothing except a very peeved cat, who'd gone daft at the sound of the can of milk being punctured.

Valerie, Valerie, where are you? If only you'd given me an address.

I sneaked out – wearing the glasses again – to my Westminster branch at Elephant and Castle. I didn't breathe much during the transaction in case a stop had been placed on my account or a note left to call the police if I showed. I tried not to grab the fifty pounds in fives and ones as the girl counted it out twice in front of me.

I hopped on a bus going back up to Piccadilly with a light heart and an even lighter bank book. But I swear the weather had turned while I was inside the bank. There was a lightness in the air, a sense of change, a feeling of hope. Or maybe it just felt good to have money in my pocket and a game plan unfolding. When I'm stuck or trapped and can't see my way forward, I fret and droop. When I'm on the move with an objective and a plan, cares fall away. Even if I'm heading in the wrong direction, it's better than standing still waiting for life to turn out right for you. It doesn't.

I was almost whistling when I got back to Mary's but I wasn't so carefree that I didn't zigzag my way to Rupert Street taking sharp turns and crossing roads whenever I saw a blue uniform. I carefully recce'd the street before approaching her door. I couldn't spot anyone hanging around looking as if they weren't looking. In I went. I paid Colette and she hinted I might get one for free if I asked nicely and Mary wasn't counting. That would have been stupid; Mary was being kindness herself, and she was always counting. Besides, I was feeling part of the family now, not a customer.

I showed Mary the photo.

She whistled. "She pretty girl. Any time she want work, I get her plenty customer."

I enjoyed the thought. "I don't think that's her style."

"All women the same. Only price different," she said, as if it were a universal truth.

"What happens now, Mary?"

"I take photo big timers round here. You go any bar and ask who top men are. They tell you Maggie Tait, Jonny Crane…"

Crane? That rang a bell. "Who did you just say?"

"Jonny Crane?"

"You've mentioned him before?"

"He got lot of businesses here." She tapped the bridge of her flat nose. "Drugs, money, contacts, girls."

Girls. Now I had it. "It was his girls got murdered, wasn't it?"

Mary nodded, her eyes searching my face.

"This is getting interesting, Mary. Very interesting."

Threads spinning and twisting together. Gather enough threads together and you have a tapestry.

TWENTY-TWO

I t may be some men's idea of heaven to live in a whorehouse, but if you're a non-participant and all you can do is listen to the radio or do some handiwork around the place, it gets wearying. The perfume clings, making it difficult to venture out in case you got mistaken for a nancy boy. The hunt for me was still on but the initial frenzy had gone out of it. It was only once mentioned on the news; I just hoped my mother wasn't listening. Occasionally I'd hear the clamour of the cars of the Flying Squad and wonder if they were heading this way. Police patrols had doubled, according to Mary, and certainly there were more uniforms on the streets than I could recall. All bad for business, said Mary.

So when the call – summons more like – came through to meet Jonny Crane I was on my way like a greyhound out his trap. But Mary's advice rang in my ears.

"Jonny nasty piece. You keep back to wall and hand here." She grabbed her crotch. "And no mention you was bobby!"

I mulled over the image of a girlie gangster as I started down the steep flight of stairs to one of Jonny's hangouts in Wardour Street. I gave my name through the hatch and it was clear they were expecting me. The door was opened by a gorilla in a midget's suit. He had mean eyes, maybe from having his nose broken so often. He pushed my face against the wall and smoothed his great mitts over me and grunted – with disappointment, I think – at finding no weapons on me.

It had been getting dark outside, but it was darker down here until we came to another door. The gorilla pushed me ahead of him and I stumbled into a wide, well-lit drinking den. It was too early for customers but a barman ground away at a glass with a dish towel, clearly not worried if I had a drink or a coronary.

At a table on the left sat two men: one young and chewing gum and sitting back on two legs of a chair which could go over any minute; the other small, with glasses, his chin resting on clasped hands. He could be the young guy's accountant. On the table in front of them – breaking the barman's heart – were tea cups and a pot. A photo and an ashtray with a cigarette-holder lay between them. I walked over. The gorilla stuck to my tail. What did he think I'd do? Chuck tea over them?

The young guy wore kohl round his eyes and his lips were red and wet. He shifted his gum to one side of his mouth and spoke. His voice was high and piping. I didn't laugh.

"Mr Crane wants to know who you are and why you're asking about this doll."

Doll? Where did this jessie think he was, Chicago? "Can't Mr Crane ask me himself?"

The accountant eased back and sat upright. Now I could see the heavy rings on both hands. He was much older than I first thought; his lined face was filled in with powder and rouge. His eyes bulged behind his glasses as he sized me up, maybe wondering how much concrete it would take round my feet to sink me.

"I'm asking. Who are you and why are you sending the word out on this bint?" His voice had all the depth and weight that his pretty friend lacked. He sounded like a sixty-a-day Capstan Full Strength man.

I'd thought about how to answer this if the time came. Suddenly I didn't feel so confident about my story. But it was too late now. "I'm David Campbell. I'm a private detective. Hired by her husband. He's been getting curious about how she spends her time."

"You're a Jock," said Crane.

"That a crime?"

"Not necessarily." The implication was that it depended which side of the bed he'd got out of that day. And who with. I hoped today was a love-your-fellow-man day regardless of predilection.

"Have you seen the lady?" I asked.

"Lady, is it? Sit down," said Crane, sucking on his cigarette then stubbing it out. He handed the holder to the boy, who refilled it, lit it and handed it back to him.

I sat. The boy rocked forward on to four legs and the gorilla scraped a chair up behind me. Now we were all cosy. Would they offer me tea?

I asked my question again.

"Depends," he said.

I raised my eyebrows.

"On what you're going to do with the information."

"Do you care?" I asked.

His lengthened lashes blinked behind the glasses. "Let's say, if I knew this bint, and if I'd done something for her, that would make her a customer of mine. I look after my customers. If they look after me." He sounded less like an accountant and more like a priest: one of the hard-boiled variety who taught the boys Latin and buggery.

"It's not my business what my clients do with the information I provide," I replied.

"I like that. I like compartments. Keeps things simple. In a complicated world, know what I mean?"

I shrugged. Spare me from amateur philosophers. "Mr Crane, this isn't essential information to my enquiry. Just corroboration. I have enough to make my report, but this would... help. So I'm prepared to pay a fiver for answers to some simple questions."

Crane turned to his companion and laughed. The boy broke into a high piping giggle. The gorilla spluttered behind me. Crane turned back to me.

"Campbell, I spend five quid on a round here. Is that all you've got?"

"It's all it's worth." I could feel the sweat breaking out in the small of my back. I hoped it wasn't showing on my forehead.

Crane sobered up. "I was forgetting; you're Scotch." His eyelids closed slowly for a moment as he thought; it was like a reptile blinking. He refocused. "Make it twenty and I'll give you some answers."

Twenty was a fortnight's wages. "Ten is the limit."

He shrugged. I reached into my pocket, pulled out my little wad and counted out ten ones on Crane's table. He reached to take them and I slapped my hand down on the money. The boy was on his feet in a second, a knife glinting in his hand. Behind me the chair grated on the floor and I steeled myself for the blow.

"Easy, Sammy." Crane's command brought the boy to heel.

He waved at the gorilla behind me and I felt the heavy breathing recede.

"You get three questions. Make 'em count," said Crane.

I thought for a minute. "OK. Did you help the lady in that photo?" I pointed at the table.

"Yes. One."

Shit. I already knew he did. Think harder. "What sort of help did you give her?"

The corners of his mouth lifted. "I gave her some contacts. Two."

The bastard was playing with me. He was smiling. So was pretty boy. I wanted to hit him. I took a gamble.

"Did she come to you for an abortion?"

He looked at me for long second. "No. Three." He reached out and took the money. "We're done. Now bugger off back to Glasgow, Campbell, or whatever your name is."

Sod. If you could believe a grade-one crook like Crane, my theory was out the window. I got up to go but couldn't resist a shot in the dark. "Sorry about your girls, Jonny."

The room went still. Even the barman stopped rubbing his glass. "What do you know about my girls, Jock?" he growled.

"Word on the street. Seems the Ripper was picking on you."

"Is that so, Mister private dick? Is that so? S'none of your fuckin' business, all right?"

"No offence, Jonny. I was just wondering if you'd been grilled by the lovely Inspector Wilson, that's all."

"Sit."

I sat.

"You and him close, are you?" he asked.

"Let's say my head and his fists got too close for my liking. An experience I won't forget in a hurry."

Crane's hand stroked his red mouth. He had his cigarette holder replenished again. "Who are you, Campbell? Why you really here?"

I weighed up the odds. They weren't good. If I told him the truth, it might put me on the same side of the law as him. But I never, ever, got taken in by that lie about honour among thieves. Crane was more than likely to turn me over to Wilson's tender care. That would earn him brownie points, a favour to be called in. I'm sure Jonny Crane needed all the favours he could get from the law. Homos had a tough time of it in the nick. On the other hand, Crane and I might find common cause; my enemy's enemy is my friend. But it would be like siding with a rattlesnake against a scorpion.

"My name's McRae. Danny McRae."

Crane's brows furrowed behind his glasses. "Fuck's sake! The one the law's after? You the Ripper?" He peered at me as if it were unlikely. Then his thoughts gelled. "If you done in my girls, you effing toerag...!" His words had the boy moving forward with his knife aimed at my eyeballs.

"No, Jonny, no! I'm the one they're after, but I'm *not* the Ripper. Would I be sitting here telling you this if I were?" They settled back in their chairs and I swallowed hard. He was all ears now.

"I have an idea who is, though," I said.

"You know who killed my girls? Cos when I find out..." His face was dark, and I didn't know if it was his pocket or his pride that had been hurt. I didn't for a moment think it could be his humanity.

My hook was in his mouth. "I know someone planted the gun beside the last victim. So Wilson must have been in the loop – maybe even did the planting. There's even a wild possibility that Wilson is directly involved."

Crane jerked forward over the table with both his hands pointing at me like pistols. The rings glittered and flashed. "Wilson done them in? You're fucking joking, right? This ain't a joking matter, Jock."

"Jonny, would I be that stupid? I'm being fingered for something I didn't do. Why would I wind you up?" That got a grudging nod.

A high-pitched voice cut in. "He's got something there, Jonny. You know what that fucker Wilson's like with the birds. Roughs 'em up and never bleeding pays."

"Price of doing business, Sammy," said Crane. "Look, McRae, if you have a name for me, you'd better share it. Right now. Do you want money?"

"I'll tell you in forty-eight hours. I've got a couple of things to check through first and if they pan out, I'll phone you with the name. I don't want money, Jonny, though I'll take back my tenner, if that's all right?"

He looked at me like I'd asked his mother to go to bed with me. Then he slowly pushed the pound notes across the table to me. "What do you want?"

"I need to know what the woman in the photo was doing with you."

He took a deep breath. "If you're pulling my wire, Jock, you'll never see the bonnie banks again, right?" I nodded. "The *lady* got given my name. She wanted a flat and some clients. I arranged it."

I sat and stared at him. "Sorry, Jonny. There's some mistake, surely. Are you saying this woman worked for you? On the streets?"

He laughed. "Not on the streets, exactly. I found her a nice little pad and sent her some business. I took my twenty per cent."

I couldn't take this in. Kate Graveney working as a prostitute? The perfect lady, doing it for money? Impossible. "Can you tell me a bit more? What she was like? Her name? I need to be sure, Jonny."

He was smiling. "You think an upper-class tart like her wouldn't get her knickers down for money? Think again, chum. I don't know if she needed the money – and she made good money, let me tell you – or if she did it for fun. I've seen it all, chum. They're all the same."

Mary's words rolled round my head as Jonny's world-weary air began to convince me. "When was this?"

"September last year, she comes to me. I remember. She kind of stands out, don't she? That hair. It was a hot day. She kept her sun specs on."

I pictured Kate down here in the gloom, anxious behind her glasses, but shining like a diamond in shit. And then coming out with her request. Did Caldwell know about this?

"Was there a man around? Working for her? With her?"

He shook his head. "Nah. I got a list of top clients who like something special." He tapped the place where his heart should have been. If he had an address book in there it would be worth the gorilla's weight in gold. "Once madam was settled and she'd turned a few tricks I had my phone ringing off the hook. Nice little earner, Sheila was," he said wistfully.

"Sheila?" I asked incredulously.

"Her stage name, shall we say. Never gave me her real moniker."

A worse thought occurred to me. "These clients... was one of them our friend Wilson, by any chance?"

"Let's put it this way: if he was, he didn't pay for it."

My mind was reeling but there was a question still unresolved. "The lady – Sheila – ended up in hospital in November, Jonny. Know anything about that?"

He smirked. "You thought it was a bit of family planning gone wrong, didn't you? Not that simple, chum. Not that simple. Seems our Sheila liked it a bit rough. I don't know exactly what she was getting up to – I don't interfere with the details of my girls, you know – but I hear it got a bit out of hand."

I couldn't take any more in. I needed air, and time to rethink. "Jonny, thanks. That's all I wanted to know." More than I wanted, in truth. "I need to digest this." But this was as digestible as raw liver.

"'Spect you do, chum. But don't take long. I still need that name. You owe me now. I don't know how it's connected to the lovely Sheila, but I want that name. We'll take it from there."

I didn't know how it connected either, *chum*, but I was sure it did. "I'll call you in forty-eight hours, Jonny."

"Be sure you do. If you don't, Sammy here will find you. You do know that, don't you?" The boy smiled and licked the blade of his knife with a tongue like a lizard.

I emerged into the last of the daylight. It was a mellow London evening, the type you get sometimes even in mid-winter; a false spring. In Glasgow it would rain or freeze or snow from November to March before you felt any forgiveness. Here in the south the weather was like a clever mistress: treated you well enough to keep you interested and optimistic, but never too much to make you blasé.

As I sidled through the streets I wrestled with the new thoughts and the images they conjured. I felt sick to my core. That first night she came to my office I fell a little in love with a dream. She was everything better than me, everything I couldn't have. Or so I thought. It never occurred to me that I could have paid for it. If I could afford it.

I shook myself. I was lucky to get out of that cellar with my head on, and here I was with another bit of the puzzle in place. But the overall pattern had slipped out of focus. I had to find the remaining pieces. All I knew – thought I knew – was that I'd been set up by Caldwell to keep me away from some squalid secret surrounding his sister. Had it been enough to cause the death of five young women? And how was Wilson involved?

My head was running through the choices I'd just made. I could have given Caldwell's name to Jonny Crane, and let nature take its course; Sammy was malice in make-up, and his gorilla was an unstoppable force of nature. But two things had stopped me: first, I suppose, my days wearing a blue uniform had left a vestigial preference to work through the law rather than via the likes of Crane. Second, and more important, I wanted this for myself. I wasn't sure quite how to arrange it, but there needed to be a face-to-face showdown between me, Caldwell and his lovely whore of a sister. Wilson too. They owed me that.

TWENTY-THREE

I woke next morning in Mary's cathouse wondering what to do first. I had to move fast. I was on a countdown with Jonny Crane. He might look like a nancy accountant – some gravy with these casseroled books, sir? – but I'd found from my Glasgow days that they could be the worst. All that inner turmoil.

I'd have liked to question Liza Caldwell some more, find out if she knew about Kate's bad habits. Our last little chat had been interrupted. I lay thinking how I could get to her. I'd chanced my arm too often stalking her in Hampstead. Could I lure her away somewhere?

But Kate was the real target. I couldn't make a return visit to Onslow Square; I'd be shot on sight. Could I tail her? Get her in her car and spirit her off somewhere? More than ever now I couldn't rely on the rozzers to help me. It was all down to me.

It was seven a.m. but it still seemed very dark despite my curtains being a fraction ajar. I got up and peered out at a real London pea-souper. Spring *had* come too early. The weather matched my thoughts. I couldn't think clearly. Maybe I should abandon the trail and make a run for it; get across the

Channel. Europe was still in such a mess that one more piece of flotsam would go unnoticed.

There was a knock on my door and it was opened before I could say yea or nay. Mary sailed in. I suppose she was within her rights; it was her house. And she was carrying the right passport: two cups of tea. She put one down by my bedside table and sat on my bed, delicately holding the other. Mary had no social conversation; she came straight out with whatever was on her whirring little mind. I liked that. Usually.

"Time you go, Danny. Too many police after you. Too much trouble for me."

I slurped my tea alongside her. "I know, Mary. You've been great, so you have. And I've overstayed my welcome."

"You need money? I lend you money. Good interest."

I bet. "Thanks, Mary, but I'm OK for a while. I've got enough to get me out of here, out of London, maybe out of England."

She banged her cup into her saucer, and put it on the table. "You give up? After all you do? Why you give up?" She crossed her little arms with an operatic gesture of anger.

"Because the folk I'm up against don't play by any rules I know. Because they have money and power; I have bugger all. Because even the law is bent. Correction: it's broken. I don't stand a chance."

"Huh. You face Jonny Crane. That brave. You can do next step."

"Mary, I need to question Kate Graveney or Liza Caldwell – both, preferably – and see where that takes me. But they'll have protection round them that's as tight as the King's corset."

"Huh." She slurped some tea and studied me, as if the answer was on my forehead but needed interpretation. "So – Kate come here."

"Why in God's name would she come here, Mary?"

"Cos your pal Jonny ask her." She smiled at me to show how clever she was.

"I think I might be pushing my luck with Jonny Crane, you know. And, anyway, he doesn't know her real name, far less her address."

Mary shook her head in pity. "Thought you smart. Not so sure."

She wasn't going to help me any further, so I sipped at my tea for inspiration. I got it, finally.

"OK. So someone phones her from here, saying they're calling on Jonny Crane's behalf. We tell her Jonny needs to speak to her. But why? What would make Kate come over? What hold would he have?"

"You think of something."

Nothing came. I drank some more tea and continued, "And, anyway, what are we going to do when she's here? Kidnap her? Mary, I thought I'd been enough trouble already?"

"I know other place. You fix."

She described the empty flat she had access to; I didn't ask how. Mary waited. I sat reading my tealeaves. In their depths a plan began to form: a daft plan, wild, high risk and bloody dangerous. Maybe I should stick to coffee.

I *could* think of a way of getting Kate to come over to Soho, but once here I needed some way of getting her to admit to some pretty unpleasant truths. I needed a lever. I knew a lever, a big one...

Mary left me to get washed and dressed. I came down to her room and walked her through the idea. When I was finished she looked hard at me.

"You madman, you know?"

"I know. But will you help? Just one last time?"

"You get lot of luck for helping madman. What you want? You want gun, I get you gun."

It was tempting. An elephant gun preferably. "Not this time, Mary. Thanks. I just want you or one of the girls to make that call for me."

We let Colette sleep till nine before waking her up. She came into Mary's room blowsy and grumpy. It took two cigarettes and a pot of tea before she stopped grousing and began to take in what we were asking. Then her sunny nature began to show through and she entered the spirit of things. It was all part of the human drama that Colette lived for every day.

I gave her the little script I'd prepared and we crowded round the pay phone in Mary's hall. We were praying Kate was at home. It wasn't the sort of message you could leave with Millie. Colette put her twopence in and got the operator. Colette gave her the Chelsea number and it began to ring. She pressed button A.

"Good morning, Graveney residence. Who is calling please?" It sounded like the butler that I'd brandished the gun at. He was back to his pompous self.

Colette's rough accent jarred against the posh tones. "I wanna speak to Kate Graveney, please."

I could picture him holding the phone well away from his cultured ear. "I'm sorry, Miss Graveney is not down yet. May I ask who is calling? Perhaps Miss Graveney can call you back?"

"Listen, you old fart, I want to speak to Kate, now! You hear? Tell her it's about Sheila. She'll know what I mean."

"I need to know your name, please." There was a bit of panic and anger creeping into his voice; no wonder, with Colette

blasting his ear. He wasn't used to having guns pointed at him
or whores being rude to him first thing in the morning.

Colette upped the volume; I had to step back a pace.

"Look, mate, Kate is going to be really pissed off with you if
you don't fucking get her on the phone pronto. All right? Tell
her it's about Sheila. You think you can handle that?"

I don't know if it was the scorn or the oath that did it, but
butler boy beat a retreat to find his mistress. It took a couple
of the longest minutes in the world, but then we heard the
phone being picked up and that familiar cool voice came
through. I stopped breathing.

"Kate Graveney here. Who is this?"

"Never mind, Katy dear, or should I call you Sheila?"

I signalled frantically at Colette who was clearly getting
carried away with it all. She had to tone it down, or we'd lose
her. Whatever Kate was she had mettle and getting her angry
would just lose her.

"Unless you tell me who you are, I'm hanging up and calling
the police."

"I don't think you want to do that, do you, Sheila?"

"Stop calling me that!"

"Don't you like your old street name?" I winced. Colette was
way off the script.

Kate had the cool tone back. "Is this blackmail? I won't
stand for it, you know."

"Blackmail? No. Not yet. Jonny wants a word with you."

"Jonny who?"

"Why, Sheila, you know Jonny. Jonny Crane. Soho Jonny.
Your old boss."

The line went quiet. I pressed closer. I thought Kate had
gone. Then there was a sigh. "What about?" So it was true then.

Right up to that point I realised I hadn't quite believed it. I was surprised at how disappointed I felt. Like finding out about Santa.

"Money, what else. He says you owe him. He wants to see you."

"I owe him nothing! Why should I talk to him?"

"Sheila, I'm only the messenger, deary. He just wants a little word. Today. I know Jonny. If he says he wants something, he usually gets it. It would be easier for you. Otherwise he might come knocking."

That made her think. "How did you get this number?"

"Jonny has contacts."

The line went quiet again, but I thought I could hear her breathing. It certainly wasn't mine. I hadn't taken a breath in ten minutes.

"Where?"

Colette recited the address. "Two o'clock."

"Tell him he gets five minutes. And tell him I owe him nothing."

"Two o'clock. Don't be late, Sheila." Ouch. Colette couldn't resist the last kick, could she? I suppose she thought of herself as the honest whore of the two. But at least the first part of the plan was under way. Now there was another call to make: one that should be easier, now I had the bait.

Mary took me round to the flat, her tiny figure nipping ahead of me like a sprite in the swirling fog. It was real Jack the Ripper weather. I only hoped the pair I'd summoned would be able to find their way through. Mary darted down the narrow street, her little clogs sounding on the cobbles. Brick house fronts sagged and curved, and the windows were tiny and multi-paned, like an Elstree film-set for *Great Expectations*. She stopped at a door, opened it and led me up the stairs.

The house had been broken into four bedsitters. Number three had its own door. We went in and I found the usual dreary one room with a single bed and basic cooking facilities. The floor was bare boards. A scrap of mangy carpet lay in front of the bed. A one-bar electric fire sat dormant in the hearth. Like my own flat, there was a second door in one of the walls. Mary unlocked it and I walked into number two. We tested it. Mary stayed in three and closed the connecting door. Then she spoke. She didn't have to shout:

"You hear OK, Danny?"

"Loud and clear, Mary." The walls were as thick as the skin on a rice pudding. You'd have to hope your neighbour didn't snore. Or given its likely purpose, that they weren't screamers. But it was perfect for my purposes. It was a quarter to two. Mary left me in number two and gave me the key to the connecting door. I locked it. I also had the key to number three, which Mary left on the latch.

I pulled up the room's only chair and lit a fag to calm my frayed nerves. Whatever happened next door was going to be interesting. I waited.

I was on my third smoke. She was the first to arrive. The sound of those footsteps echoed in my heart. I wanted to rush through the door and shake her. I heard her pause, then push on the door of number three. She waited to see if she was alone, then walked carefully in. She stopped in the middle of the floor. I could see her eyeing the place up. There was a click: she'd switched on the fire. Then a scrape as she pulled up the chair. I heard her lighter flick and a deep suck and blow as she pulled on her cigarette. I followed suit, but quietly. We both waited, hunched on our chairs, with a wall between us.

We heard his steps, heavy and slow. He was wary or tired. Her heart would be racing. I wanted to shield her, and suddenly regretted not taking a gun from Mary. He paused at the top then came forward to stand outside her door. I could hear his laboured breathing, like a man with emphysema.

There was a huge crash. He'd kicked the door open. I was on my feet. She must have been too. This was a mistake. His violence was uncontrollable. Stillness fell.

"Well, well, well. What a pleasant surprise. Have you been waiting for me?" Wilson's coarse voice carried loud and clear through the wall. She must have been terrified.

And yet she managed, "What are *you* doing here?" with a steely hauteur that told me she *did* know him, and that she placed him somewhere near the earthworm on the evolutionary scale.

"I think I'm the one that usually asks questions. Are you really saying you weren't expecting me? That you didn't want to see me again?"

I imagined him licking his already wet lips.

"You pig! I never wanted to see you as long as I lived!" Her chair scraped and the angle of her voice altered, higher up. I knew she was now on her feet.

"That's funny. My message from Jonny said there was a new girl here. That I should try her out. You're not new. And I've tried you. But I don't mind another go." The door slammed. She was trapped in the room. "See, you've even put the fire on for us. We can get comfortable." I heard the sound of a coat being tugged off and thrown to the floor.

"I'd rather die, you swine! I'm out of all that business!"

"Oh, I don't think so. It's the sort of business you don't ever really get out of. It leaves a mark. For life. You're as bent as your boyfriend."

"What are you talking about?"

"Who do you think told me about you the last time? Who put me on to your dirty ways?"

"I don't believe you, you bastard!" she screamed. "He wouldn't do that!"

"Sweetheart, I've seen every filthy, twisted thing in the book. More than even you could think of. Or any of your fast set. I'm no longer amazed at what people get up to. How they get their fun. And here you are, back for more."

Kate's voice was tearful now. "Don't. Please don't. Can't you see this is a set-up? Why are we both here? Think, damn you!" she cried desperately.

It seemed to stop him. I could almost hear his brain cogs meshing. "All right, let's you and me sit and have a little think, shall we. Then we can get back to business. I'll sit here." I heard the bed creaking and straining. "You sit there. Now then, why are you here if it's not to turn some tricks?"

She was desperate. "I got a message. From Jonny Crane."

"Jonny himself?"

"No. Some little tramp. But she must have been from Jonny. She called me... she called me Sheila. The name I used."

"I know the name. I remember the name. But so would a lot of men... *Sheila*. It needn't have been Jonny."

"Oh, Christ! This is too, too horrible. I can't stand it!" I heard her feet making for the door, but Wilson's size was deceptive, as I knew only too well. He slammed into the door before she'd half opened it.

"Let's sit down, shall we?" It was an order. I heard the first sob, and hated myself for doing this to her. No good saying she asked for it.

"Shut up. How did you get this message?"

She sniffed. "Phone. This morning."

"Did Jonny have your address? Your real address?"

"No, of course not." She blew her nose. She had guts.

"So who else would know you were coming here? Think, woman. Tony? Once more for luck, eh?"

"No!" Her voice dropped. "Nobody knew. Besides, he's been out all day."

"Doing what?"

"He's out stalking that crazy man, McRae."

"Tony's a busy boy. When you see him, tell him ta."

"For what?"

"The tip-off."

"About what?"

"He said McRae phoned him to boast about the latest killing. After your little drinks party with him. And that's where we found the gun with his prints. Lovely. Didn't Tony mention it?"

"Yes. Yes, of course."

"There's a thought. Could McRae have set this up?"

"How could *he* know... about this... and Jonny and... things? It's impossible."

"He's a tenacious little bastard. Devious..." His voice trailed away. Then I heard him move. I had just a fraction of a second to jump back and sent my chair clattering to the floor.

Then Wilson smashed through the connecting door.

He sailed on past me, bellowing and tripping over the chair and crashing down in a flurry of flailing limbs and splintering wood. Olé! His head hit the boards and the noise seemed to go on echoing for ever. Then I realised Kate was screaming.

"Belt up!" I shouted.

She stopped and stood facing me through the wreckage, her beautiful hands clasping her face. We gazed down on the heap between us. Wilson wasn't moving. I hoped he was dead. No such luck. The great bulk began stirring and a groan escaped. Kate and I were transfixed, waiting to see what he'd do. I took a step forward ready with my skilful boot.

He began to pull himself on to his knees, but his trunk and head stayed on the floor. I was about to kick him, but a great moan shook him and he fell slowly on to his side. He was clutching his stomach. Then I saw why. A spar of wood – part of a broken chair leg – stood out from between his hands. Blood was already flowing round his fingers and staining his shirt. His face was scratched and ashen. He looked like death. It suited him.

I stepped past him. I'm not sure he saw me. If he did, he didn't recognise me. I walked up to Kate. She was wide-eyed and open-mouthed, breathing quickly.

"Oh, God. Oh, God. What have we done?" Her voice carried notes of hysteria.

I took her shoulders with both hands and shook her roughly. "*We* haven't done anything. He did it to himself."

"What are we going to do? We have to get out of here."

I thought fast. It was tempting – very tempting – to leave him here to die like a stuck pig. The world would be a better place for his departure. But I wouldn't let a dog die like that. And more important, it would be trouble for Mary. The biggest trouble there was.

"Kate, Kate! Listen to me!" Her eyes were in shock. I wasn't sure I was getting through. I slapped her. She blinked.

"Kate, we're walking out of here, now. I'm taking you some-where safe. I'm going to call an ambulance for him. OK?"

She nodded. I took her under one arm and hauled her out of the flat and down the stairs. We emerged into the murk and plunged off in the direction I thought was Mary's. In the fog I missed the turning twice, but on the way blundered into a telephone box. I pushed Kate in with me while I called 999. She was unresisting and stood looking dumbly at me as I gave the address to the operator. I could do nothing more for Herbert Wilson. Even though I now knew he wasn't the killer, he certainly wouldn't get my prayers.

TWENTY-FOUR

"Tea, Mary, please. And brandy. Make that two."

I made Kate sit down in Mary's parlour. She began to shake, and I sat staring at her perfect face, blotched and stained with running eye make-up. The mark I'd made on her cheek was a livid pink. Her shoulders convulsed as quiet sobs hit her. She tore off her hat and bent her head into her hands. The cap of hair gleamed in the tarty room like a platinum ball in a toy shop. I wanted to go over and put my arms round her but at the same time wanted her to suffer for a while. I felt a cold anger at what she'd done to herself. And me.

Mary came back with steaming cups and balloon glasses swirling with dark pools. She sat beside Kate and touched her. Kate jumped and sat up, panic and wretchedness all over her face. She looked a beautiful, ravished mess.

"You drink. Brandy first, then tea."

Kate took the glass and sniffed it suspiciously. Then she took a great gulp. She coughed and retched and finally fell back on her chair. She glared at me.

"Where is this? Who is this person?"

"I'm surprised you don't recognise it. You're in a whorehouse. This is the madam. Mama Mary. Be nice to her, Kate. She's being nice to you."

"Is this your idea of a sick joke? What are we doing here?"

"This is a sanctuary. For one thing, you were in shock. For another, I have questions I need answers to."

"I can't take any more, McRae. I just want this all over."

My voice got harder. "So do I, Miss Graveney, so do I. You started it, remember." She looked fearful again, as though I was going to leap over and hit her. I took advantage.

"Why did you do this, Kate? Why did you get involved with Jonny Crane?"

She looked at me from a long way off. I wasn't sure if she'd ever come back. "You wouldn't understand."

"Because I'm lower class? Because it's only something rich folk would get up to? Bored with cocaine, Kate?"

She took another big gulp of brandy. This time it went down easily. She took a deep breath and rested her head back on the chair. Her throat was exposed, thin and vulnerable.

She spoke to the ceiling. "It was a game. It started as a game. Tony and me."

"A game? You mean like cowboys and Indians? Or maybe doctors and nurses?"

"Stop it! You make it sound so cheap."

"Chess then?"

She shook her head at my sarcasm. She wasn't ready to tell me.

"All right, when? When did it start?"

"Oh, ages ago." Her words were already slurring, what with the shock and the booze. "We were children. He was showing off, trying to impress me. God, the things we did."

I could imagine. I could see the pair of them, her with all

her privileges and him desperate to stay up with her and keep her interested. "When did you become lovers?"

She lifted her head and stared defiantly at me. "Why, Mr McRae, I do believe you're jealous."

"Why should I be? When I could have bought you?" The words came out without thinking. She looked lashed. Tears formed in her eyes again.

"Good hit, McRae. Good hit." She took a handkerchief out of her bag and dried her eyes. She sipped at some tea, ignoring Mary sitting beside her. Mary was giving me daggers.

"Well, if you must know, we're not. Tony has never slept with me." She said it with so little emotion that I knew it was true. Bizarrely – in the circumstances – I felt a surge of pity for the young Tony Caldwell. Faced with this glorious, tantalising young woman, teasing him, leading him on all those years. And always being rejected. Always on a piece of string, always trying to impress, just in case she relented. And when he found out she was his half-sister, had that finally turned his mind?

I weighed up the next question. What she'd just told me made it easier. But did I need to ask it? Was I just twisting the blade? Or was it time that she knew?

"Did you know he was your half-brother?"

She gave me the look she reserved for shit on her shoe. "Don't be stupid, McRae! What a perfectly stupid, stupid, cruel thing to say."

"Mary, could we make a phone call?"

"Sure, Danny." She got up, walked into the hall and picked up the handset. "Where you wanna call?"

"Hampstead 4032."

"That's Liza's number! What are you playing at, you bastard?"

"When you get through, Mary, hand the phone to the lady here. And then she can ask the question herself."

"Wait, wait!" Kate looked befuddled, as though she couldn't take any more in. She pushed her hair back and tried to think. Mary stood waiting for my word. I got up and pulled Kate to her feet and into the hall. I took the phone from Mary. The operator connected us. Liza answered.

"Liza, don't hang up. I have Kate here. She wants to talk to you."

I gave her no chance to think. I stuck the phone in Kate's hand.

Kate said carefully, "Liza? Hello, dear. Yes, I'm all right. No I'm not being harmed. No! Don't call the police. Not yet. Liza, I have a question for you. It's too silly for words."

"McRae here tells me that Tony is... well, related to me. I know it's perfectly silly and..."

She went quiet. If it was possible for her to become paler she did.

"No, no... But how...? When...?"

Then her voice went cool. "How long have you known, Liza?"

And now frosty. "Why didn't you tell me?"

I couldn't make out Liza's words. All I could hear was the steadily rising sound of a woman losing control. Liza sounded angry. As though it was all pouring out of her. Both ends of the conversation went quiet. Then Liza asked something.

"No, I'm all right. I'll call you later. Bye, Liza." She handed me the phone and looked at me with despair and grief.

"What a mess we've made of it all, McRae. What a goddamn bloody mess. All those years..."

I said nothing. I let her blow her nose and gather herself.

"Cigarette?"

She nodded. I gave her one and lit it. She sat up and inspected my face as though guessing how I was taking all this.

"You asked me when Tony and I became lovers. *We* didn't." She took a long pull and blew the smoke out at me. "But did you ask Liza the same question?"

The idea hung in the air like dirty linen. Yet suddenly it made sense. Sort of. In this nightmare of twisted relationships, it made sense. It explained why Liza was willing to go out on a limb for Tony, why she would lie, why she would pretend to be his wife. Maybe that's what she'd have liked. It explained the harem-like bedroom in Liza's house, God help her. And there was Tony in the middle, manipulative Tony, spurned by Kate, taking cold comfort with Liza. Both women lying to each other for his sake.

I asked softly, "How did Wilson get involved?"

She shook her head.

"Tell me."

She rubbed her streaked face. How had I found it beautiful?

"It was all supposed to be controlled by Jonny. He was supposed to..."

"... vet your clients?"

She nodded.

I pressed on. "But Wilson got past the vetting." It wasn't kind. "I heard him, Kate. I heard him blame Tony."

Her face crumpled. She burst into tears as though her body would explode. I let her sob and weep until there was nothing left in her.

"I thought it was Jonny. That Jonny was using me to buy him off. It was horrible, just horrible. Wilson..." Her chest was heaving, she couldn't get the words out. "He... hit me. He knew who I was. He enjoyed it. He hit me..."

I couldn't resist the shot. "I thought you liked it rough?"

She started to wail. "Noooo. Oh, no. It was all a game…"

The game again. I kept on at her, wanting to hurt her. "Wilson didn't play by the rules, did he?"

"He was filthy, a pig. He forced me. He used his handcuffs!" She was outraged, close to hysteria, gripping her wrists and shaking. "Then he hit me with his belt. He kept hitting me! Is this what you want? Are you enjoying this, McRae? Like hearing dirty stories? Because it gets dirtier! He gagged me. And he stuck things in me. Because *he* couldn't! He stuck… he stuck… oh, Christ!"

I felt pity, then shame for forcing this out of her. I thought of Wilson lying impaled on the shaft of wood. I wondered which of them had been more violated.

I said softly, "Enough, Kate. Enough. I'm nearly done. Tell me about the gun. The gun I left with Millie."

She peered at me through glassy eyes. "Tony took it. He went out. I assume he gave it to Wilson. Wilson did the rest."

"That's not what Wilson said. He said Tony had tipped him off. That I'd phoned Tony to boast about another killing."

She looked hunted. "I don't know anything. Nothing. Tony didn't mention it."

"You don't know me too well, Kate, but does it strike you that I would have called Tony up with that news?"

She just stared at me sullenly.

"Well, let me tell you that I didn't, and I didn't kill the girl. And if I didn't, who did? Who killed her, Kate? And all the others?"

She shook her head. She wouldn't look at me. "I don't know!"

"I think you do. When did they start? Why did he do it?"

She shook her head again. "I can't say any more. I just can't!"

"You might as well get used to it, Kate. Because the police and the judge will be asking you the same questions. They hang accessories to murder."

Her eyes widened, but she sat back with her arms folded as though hell would freeze over before she'd say another word. Mary, who'd sat uncharacteristically quietly all this while – scowling at me – took the cold tea cups and empty glass away. She came back and touched Kate on her shoulder. Kate raised her stricken face to Mary's.

"You come with me, lady. Fix your face."

Kate looked uncertain. I shrugged. I knew when an interrogation was going nowhere. Besides, I was sure of my man now. All I'd have to do was prove it. Or get him to admit it.

"Come, lady."

Kate rose to her feet, towering above Mary's tiny frame. Mary took her hand and led Kate, unresisting, out the door and down the corridor to the bathroom.

I sat back and sipped my own drink. I felt empty. All a game, she said. Five dead women was a high forfeit. I wondered if Wilson was alive. I didn't much care. I thought about Tony Caldwell, somewhere out there, hunting me. I had to act first. Was it time to set Jonny's hounds on him? Perhaps. But I needed to see him first. Needed to have him tell me his side. If there was a side.

Doc Thompson used to say that you could be affected for life by what happens to you when you're young. Freud and Jung and others all seemed to hand out excuse notes for any evil act. It cut no ice with me. You're not telling me that every single guard in every one of the hundreds of concentration camps across Europe had their toys taken from them as kids? Or if they did, it was any sort of half-arsed excuse for the pain they inflicted?

We have choices. Some of us more than others. Colette told me she chose her profession; it was easy money and she didn't find it so hard. The men were usually pretty grateful. I know I was. But she also recognised she didn't have much choice; she had no skills, could barely read, and needed money to pay the rent.

Kate had every choice. She was rich, beautiful and smart. Maybe too smart. An intelligence that was looking for something to engage it, stave off the boredom of the cocktail circuit. Don't tell me she had an unhappy childhood. Not by the standards of ninety-nine per cent of the world. The old Scottish phrase came back to me: *Ye've made your bed, now lie in it*. No excuses, no blaming somebody else; you caused this, take responsibility for what you did and get on with it. It was a tough creed and seemed uncaring, but it worked, mostly.

Mary came back into the room leading Kate. Kate looked better. The streaks were gone, she had on fresh make-up and her hair was brushed and gleaming. But there was no hiding the puffiness round the eyes. Or the haunted look in them.

Kate sat down. "Thank you, Mary. You've been very kind." She turned to me. "Mr McRae, I want to go home now. I think you've got what you wanted, don't you?" Her tone wasn't humble, but neither was it haughty.

"Danny will do. I think we're past the formal stage."

She weighed me up and shrugged. "Very well, *Danny* – what next? What about the police and Jonny Crane and...?"

"Tony? First off, I don't know if Wilson is alive or dead. And if he's alive, how long he'll take to come after me. He may not remember much of what happened back there." I smiled. "I think you're off the hook, though. I don't think he'll bother you, not with what I can say about him and what he's been up to.

As for Jonny Crane, he doesn't know anything about today or your part in it, remember? I arranged for you to come to the flat this afternoon. Crane thinks of you only in the past tense." I couldn't help adding, "I'm sorry for what I put you through."

She studied me as if she were seeing me for the first time. She nodded. "Thank you, Danny. What are you going to do about Tony? You know he's looking for you? He's got a gun. Another one. Our house is full of guns."

"I'm going to help him find me. With your help, Kate. One phone call is all it will take."

TWENTY-FIVE

The fog was clearing as I walked down through Soho. Clumps still shredded themselves on St Martin's spire and menaced the alleyway between the Strand and the river. As I crossed the Hungerford footbridge, a train gasped past me into Charing Cross, leaving chunks of smoke clinging to the girders. Mist lay along the river like a dirty yellow blanket.

Kate had made the call, telling Caldwell what had happened this afternoon and that Wilson might be dead. Her voice was strained and clipped when she told him that Liza had revealed their three-sided relationship. Her anger fuelled two patches of red in her cheeks. I could hear Caldwell's voice rising and accelerating as he begged for understanding. Kate cut off his bluster as though reprimanding a careless servant. She told him I wanted to meet him, just the two of us, and settle this thing. She didn't tell him – because she didn't know – that if I didn't come back from the meeting, Mary had instructions to give his name to Jonny Crane. Tony seemed to have responded with alacrity. And now we were converging on the meeting ground. I'd chosen somewhere open but quiet, and with a queer resonance for this whole damned business.

I picked up a bus outside Waterloo station. We chugged

through the patchy smog to Camberwell Green, past my office. I didn't want to meet there; too cramped, too many police watching. I got off and made my way up Denmark Hill past the hospital. I seemed to be climbing out of the murk. The sign for Ruskin Park beckoned.

I climbed over the fence and started down towards the pond. From there I'd be able to see people entering the park but it was far enough away to be private. Fog billowed through the trees, making it hard to follow the path. But the smell of decay led me easily to the stagnant water. I stood gazing into the mist, wondering if I could pull this off without getting shot. I went over my questions again and again, which was why I didn't hear her coming.

"Hello, Danny."

I spun round. My heart lifted. Valerie was walking towards me. She was wearing a long coat against the night, just like the first time.

"Hey, it's great to see you, Val! I've missed you! Where have you been?"

"Where have *I* been? You've got half the police in the country looking for you and you ask me where *I've* been?" she laughed.

"It's a long story, but it's coming to an end. Tony Caldwell is the killer. He killed the girl in France and he killed the prostitutes here."

She seemed a long way from being surprised. "See. I knew it wasn't you, Danny."

"But, Val, what are you doing here? How did you find me?"

"I'm here when you need me."

"But you can't stay here, Val. It's too dangerous. Caldwell is coming to meet me. You mustn't hang around. I don't want you hurt."

"Silly. I'll be OK. I'll give you moral support."

Through the sound-dampening fog I heard the noise of a car wheezing up the hill and slowing. Then I saw the twin beams of light cutting through the heavy air, as the big Riley rolled to a stop by the park gates.

"It's him, Val! You've got to go! I'll be fine. I've got a gun, you see?" I dug into my pocket and pulled out the small-calibre weapon Mary had given me. It was barely more than a starting pistol, but it would do the job. I hoped I wasn't going to need it.

Val searched my face as though it was the last she'd see of it. She smiled sweetly then backed away into the mist.

I could see the car clearly. There were two people in it. Kate was at the wheel. She was staring straight ahead, her eyes unseeing. Caldwell was alongside her. She killed the engine and silence fell. She cut the beams of light and the car was left silhouetted by the masked glow from a street lamp. High above me, the clouds cleared and the stars began to stutter into being. But down here wraiths still swirled and danced through the trees and across the pool.

Caldwell opened his door and got out. Kate stayed hunched over the wheel. I wondered what their conversation had been like. What excuses had he produced? Had he denied it? What did she believe now?

He straddled the fence and began walking towards me, a long stride, heels hitting hard on the path like he was pacing out a cricket square. And suddenly I knew that gait. I'd seen it loping away from me. Down a back alley in Avignon.

This time he was wearing a thick coat and hat against the clinging air. His hands were in his pockets. As he got closer I could see that whatever he'd done wasn't getting to him. A bit red and strained round the eyes, but none of that bulging, berserker look the public expects in the insane. Take it from me, and I've seen plenty, some of the craziest guys in the world look perfectly normal until you engage them in conversation and find they can only talk about rats or the colour red.

Caldwell stopped ten feet from me. How was I going to knock that smile off?

"Well, McRae. You've saved me a lot of trouble. I've been hunting high and low for you."

"You have it wrong, Caldwell. I've been hunting *you*. Didn't Kate tell you the cavalry won't be coming to save your neck?"

"You mean Wilson? An oaf. He got what was coming to him."

"I thought you were buddies?"

"A common cause."

"When did you point him my way?"

He laughed. "Remember that first visit he made to your office? You don't think that was an accident, do you?"

No, I didn't. Too many coincidences. "Did you know him before?"

He shook his head. "He likes giving interviews. I saw his name."

"After the first murder?"

He said nothing. I changed key. It was too soon to go down that road. "Your sister has been very helpful. I mean, the Graveney one."

He frowned. "You shouldn't have told her that. She didn't need to know."

"Because it spoiled your games? What were these games, Caldwell? They sound fun."

The frown vanished from his face. He grinned, like a dog grins just before it takes a piece out of your leg. He considered the question for a while.

"We had a dare. A double dare. Truth, dare, kiss or promise."

"The kids' game?" I asked with wonder. We used to play it in Hayward Park. A gang of us, girls and boys, average age ten, looking for excuses to cop a feel or allow a secret passion to be dragged from us in front of our object of desire. We'd spin a bottle and the loser had to call out his or her choice: tell the truth, take a dare, kiss a girl, or make a promise. The loser had the right to pronounce on the action.

I remember Lizzie Kirkland getting a double dare to put her hand up my short trousers. I think she was disappointed. It seemed a big deal at the time. But it wasn't very brave or inventive alongside what Caldwell was telling me...

"Not kids!" he exploded. "At first, yes. But it was more important than that. Kate liked it. It was our thing. The thing only *we* knew about. No one else would have understood. The game went on for a long time. Years. Higher risks, more excitement. Our game." His face had changed. It was as though he was describing a religion. Perhaps he was.

"But you didn't let Liza play?"

He snorted. "She was never in our league. It was just Kate and me. Just the two of us. Since I first saw her."

"So you went on playing the game, hoping it would lead to what? Fucking your sister Kate?"

His face twisted. "Shut your filthy mouth! You don't understand. I didn't *know*. I didn't know who I was until it was too late! I wanted her. Thought I could have her. Only Liza knew." He fought for control. He wiped both sides of his moustache with his left hand. His right stayed in his pocket.

"And you bought Liza off with sex."

"It wasn't like that! It made her happy."

I laughed. "Charitable of you. And it let you go on playing

the game. Then you got to the big ones. Life and death. You started murdering people because she dared you?" I wanted to hear this story and I was gambling that he wanted to tell it. Murderers always want to justify themselves.

"*She* never thought I'd do it. It was the ultimate dare. The one she thought I'd stop at. I came back from France and told her. Told her what I'd done. She should have…"

"Should have let you fuck her, Tony? Liza wasn't enough for you? Was that the deal?"

"Stop it, stop it, you bastard! Don't talk of her like that! You don't know what it was like! She was so lovely, so beautiful. I worshipped her. I almost had her."

The control was slipping. His face was the face of a man whose dreams had been shot to pieces. All those years, keeping him dangling, teasing, leading him on. Pretending he was married to her. What a bitch. Enough to drive anyone out of his mind. For a moment I almost felt sorry for him. Then I remembered how he'd used Liza, the surrogate. And how he'd slaughtered the others.

"And Kate became a whore in return?" That really got home. He blinked and his jaw hardened. I drove it home. "You dared her to become a prostitute?"

His face was twisting, shifting from distress to anger. He stepped closer. His eyes were bleak.

"It didn't matter by then. She hated me. She hated herself. For making me kill the French girl. The game was all we had left."

"What exactly was Kate's dare? Twenty men? A hundred? Six months? A thousand pounds?" He flinched at every cut.

"I thought she wouldn't do it. But she did. Like me. I thought it would teach her, but she said… she said…"

The man was crying. The poor sod was crying. Tears dribbled down his red face. He looked pathetic. But I was convinced he had a gun in his right pocket. Sad or mad, he could put a bullet in me. So why was I still needling him? Because I felt the disgust in my mouth, like vomit.

"She liked it? And you couldn't stand that, could you? She did it for others, for strangers, for money. But she wouldn't do it for you. So you wanted to hurt her."

"I *couldn't* hurt her, don't you see?" Pain was wrenching his features out of shape. "Don't you see?!" He pulled his hand out of his pocket. It held the gun I was expecting. It was almost a relief to see it. Almost. It looked like a cannon alongside what I was holding. He levelled it at me and for a second I thought he was going to pull the trigger. I shouted at him to keep up the flow.

"Is that why you killed all these poor creatures, Tony? Five of them, after the French girl." I gentled my voice, coaxing, encouraging him to let it all come out. "If you couldn't hurt Kate, you could hurt her kind?"

"It showed her." His eyes were wide. He was twisting his moustache with his free hand as though he'd rip it off. I'd seen other faces like his, other eyes. Not in the mirror. At the hospital.

I was nearly whispering. "Showed her what, Tony? What did it show her?"

"That she could be next. She should have been afraid. She just laughed."

"So you sent for Wilson?"

He nodded his head. He was snivelling like a child but the gun was still wavering at my chest. I carefully cocked my own wee pistol in my pocket. I wasn't going to do anything heroic like try to outdraw him. I'd just shoot him through my coat. It could be mended. I couldn't.

"It was to teach her. He wasn't meant to hurt her. I loved her. I love her…"

I should have shut up there. I had to stop needling him before I took a .45. But I plunged on, reckless with revulsion at the pair of them.

"So you killed for *love*? Those poor lassies? I think you enjoyed it, Tony. I think you got a thrill out of it. You got the taste for it in France and began to kill for kicks."

His eyes were agony. He was rolling his head from side to side. "She could have stopped it, you know. She should have loved me. That's all. It's her fault." He stopped and drew himself up and took a deep breath. He wiped his face on his sleeve.

"But it doesn't matter, McRae. She's too involved. She can't leave me. Not now. And we can get away with it. Scot free, McRae, as it were." He grimaced and placed his left hand round his gun hand to steady it. I clasped my pistol and pointed it at his chest. Then I realised he was staring behind me. I thought it was a trick but he kept on staring.

I half turned. I saw a face in the fog. It looked like Val's.

"No, Val! Go back! Don't come near." I moved a little to one side and turned half to her so I could see them both. Caldwell looked terror-stricken.

"What are you doing here?" he shrieked.

Val stepped closer. She had a wild look on her face. I scarcely recognised her. She seemed to have lost her coat. It was too cold to be here in just a blouse and skirt.

"Stop! Stop or I fire!" Caldwell was pointing the gun at her, away from me.

"Valerie, get down!"

She came on. We formed a triangle, with six feet between us. Mist drifted and coated us, one after the other. Valerie said nothing. Her long dark hair was pulled forward over her shoulder. She did a slow pirouette, so that her back was to us. The neck and top of her blouse were soaked dark. The dark hair above was matted and glistening. In the back of her head, just where the skull joins the neck, was an entry wound. I knew her now.

She turned round to face him. There was blood on her skirt and running down her thin legs. She stepped closer to him.

"Stop or I fire!" Caldwell was demented.

She didn't stop. He fired once and must have missed. He fired again. And still she came on. I heard a car door slamming and running feet. A cry went up. "No, Tony, no!"

Caldwell dropped to one knee, then the other. He was sobbing. Sobbing and firing. The gunshots echoed round and round in this limbo we'd created.

Valerie stood in front of him, an arm's length away, a thin smile on her lips. She leaned forward and carefully touched the barrel of the gun. Slowly she tilted it up. The gun barrel rested under his chin. His sobbing stopped. He looked straight into her remorseless eyes. And pulled the trigger one last time.

I walked slowly over to him and knelt by his side. Blood was pooling round his skull. His legs and body twitched, then stilled. His chest fell, but his eyes stared up in endless horror.

"Oh, no. Oh, no." Kate skidded to her knees and touched his hand. It still held the gun.

"Don't touch it. The police will want to see what happened. Though God knows what we'll tell them." I turned to look for Valerie but she'd vanished into the mist. I wasn't surprised.

"What did you see, Kate?"

She looked up at me, shocked but dry-eyed. She had no tears left. "I thought he was going to kill you. He shot at you and kept missing. Then he shot himself. What did you say to him, to do this?"

I gazed down at his lifeless body, then up at her lifeless face. "I dared him, Kate. I double-dared him."

TWENTY-SIX

I've always liked trains and boats. My dad took me by train to Ardrossan on the Ayrshire coast one day. He let me stick my head out the window. I got off with my face speckled with black measles and my nostrils filled with the smell of the steam. As if that hadn't been the best trip of my young life, I nearly exploded with excitement when we walked on board the *Glen Sannox*, a great white paddle-steamer. I ran up and down every ladder on the boat, as tireless as a yo-yo. We sailed down the Clyde estuary like kings, the wind whipping my face and the sun burning my bare arms and legs. A cloud of greedy gulls hovered over our wake, raucous courtiers to our royal passage.

Today the Channel winds tossed spume against my face as I stood on the prow. And later I sat sedately in my window seat as we chugged through the French countryside towards Paris. I changed at Gare du Nord and found I'd forgotten all my French; either that or everyone was talking faster here in the capital. I resisted the temptation to become a tourist in Paris, even though the April weather tried to woo me; a day like this in Glasgow would be counted as a heatwave.

I had a funny moment at the south-bound Gare d'Austerlitz. It was the noise and the steam and the whistles of the guards sending trains off into the southern sunshine. The queuing people sprang yellow diamonds on their chests and arms, and the porters and guards took on grey coats and rifles. For a daft moment I thought they were going to herd me back into the cattle truck. I stopped and smoked a fag till the panic attack was over. Doc Thompson said there could be more to come.

I'd seen him twice since Caldwell's death. I was still getting the headaches, but they weren't lasting as long or coming as often. Resolution he called it. And the memories that I was left with after each episode seemed to be infilling rather than pivotal. Like discovering an old reel of film and playing it and finding holes in it, but not enough to obscure the story.

The Doc had all sorts of explanations for what had happened but I know what I saw. Though I'm not sure what Caldwell saw. After only three months, the fog of that night was beginning to blur the memory of it.

I bought a paper at Austerlitz and waited till we were chugging out of Paris before opening it. I could understand the written word better than the jabbering back at the station. It seemed they were facing the same aftermath as us: lack of food, coal and work. But from what I could see, Paris had hardly lost a chimney pot during the war. And there was no sign of gratitude from De Gaulle for what we'd done for them.

I thought of the papers at home, in the week after that night. I went from villain to hero in five days. Despite what they found on the bomb site – Caldwell's hand was stiff round his gun by the time they arrived – and despite Kate supporting my version of events, I was hauled off as the Ripper and the attempted murderer of a brave policeman, injured in the line of duty. It was my second time in the cells in a month. This time they treated me with kid gloves.

Wilson, the said brave policeman – damn his black heart, I *should* have let him bleed to death – survived his encounter with the chair leg, though minus a kidney. But to show his spleen was still in good order, he accused me from his hospital bed of trying to kill him. Fortunately he was too ill to come and beat a confession out of me, and gradually something of the true picture began to emerge as Kate, Liza and I stuck to our story. Of course, we didn't tell the boys in blue everything. Who needed to know about Kate's little stint as a Soho tart, for example? Or the first murder in France? And I decided not to reveal her knowledge of the London murders. What was the point? To see her pretty neck stretched on the gallows? Though in truth, with what I saw in her eyes, hanging might have been a mercy.

I'd left Kate in her car while I walked off to find a phone box and call the police. They took a while, long enough for us to hammer out our script. Eventually, even the papers managed to get a fairly consistent version of the same tale we'd spun. That war hero Caldwell had come back changed from his harrowing experiences working with the Resistance. That he'd begun killing while the state of his mind was unbalanced. That he'd tried to blame it on me, his old comrade-in-arms, until in a showdown he'd admitted his guilt and had taken his own life in remorse for his terrible deeds.

Though Kate still didn't understand exactly what had happened to Tony at the end, our views were close enough, she and I agreed. Especially when she confessed over a shared cigarette while we waited for the police that she'd set Tony up.

"I didn't want this to happen, you know."

"But you set me loose, Kate. In my office, that first night."

"You knew?"

"Your show of concern was unconvincing. And when I told you Tony was dead, you didn't even pretend to be sorry. You meant me to come after him."

Her bleak eyes searched some inner distance. She nodded, reluctantly. "I didn't know how to stop the game. You did."

"You must have known something like this would happen?"

"But not to end like…" She shivered and waved her hand at her brother's body lying on the cold ground.

Wilson backed off, though I heard he was still angry at me, despite saving his worthless life. Seems the lack of a kidney had put an end to his drinking. But as his booze-soaked brain began to dry out, he began to see it was in his own interests to run with my version of events. Especially as it kept his own rancid involvement with Caldwell out of it.

Doc Thompson was asked to add his pennyworth to the profile the police had of me. I doubt if it was very flattering but at least it didn't condemn me. When I caught up with him, he was even more excited than usual about my case. It was as though he couldn't wait to write up the paper on me for the *Psychologists Monthly* or whatever these characters read for fun.

"It was a cathartic experience, Danny. Like the equivalent of a bloodletting for you."

"That's not a helpful image Doc, if you don't mind."

He seemed pretty pleased with his idea. "No, no, you see, your brain has been healing from the physical trauma for a year now. Maybe assisted by the EST. The severed synapses will have been trying to re-lay themselves. Like roads washed away in a flood. All the memories you had were still there. But cut off. Now they're reconnecting."

"You're saying the brain re-grows?"

"We're not sure, to be honest. But it seems remarkably resilient. Even if there's no new growth, it seems capable of some re-routing."

"So. I'm back to normal, am I, Doc?"

I wished he hadn't hesitated. "As normal as me. Hah, hah, hah."

There was no real answer to that. I raised the big question. "What about Valerie? How do you account for that?"

"Tell me, Danny, on all the occasions you think you saw Valerie, can you recall anyone else seeing her talking to you?

"Why sure. The first night we were in a pub celebrating New Year's Eve. There were masses of folk around us..." My voice trailed away. Did the two of us have a conversation with anyone? I thought of our day out in the park; people were looking at us, amused at the sight of lovers, weren't they? Maybe all they saw was a demented man talking to himself, sucking his own fingers and drinking two cups of tea.

"Did you ever touch her? Kiss her?"

"She was shy, going through a tough time with a bloke. It wasn't that sort of relationship." I shrugged helplessly.

He waved his hand and went all hearty on me, so I knew he was making it up. "Very normal, Danny. The mind tries to deal with something shocking and finds a way of rationalising it. Children often have imaginary friends. Particularly if they are imaginative and lack real friends."

So he saw me as a lonely kid. Terrific. He went on hurriedly.

"But in adults, we see the same symptoms and call it schizophrenia. In your case, while you are evincing all the classical signs of schizoid delusions, I think they have been caused by actual physical damage to the brain. Which is remarkable. It confirms the growing view that brain chemistry and make-up are the defining factors in perception. Rather than some non-physical mental flaws."

"Should I feel better or worse at that?"

"Oh, better! Your delusion has gone now the threat has gone."

"So what did Caldwell see?"

He laughed. He was very bad at it. He needed more practice.

"Fascinating, simply fascinating. You've said it was a foggy night. So that gives us the starting point if you like."

"It wasn't fog. Valerie wasn't fog."

"No, no, quite," he said trying to humour me. "This is a well-recognised syndrome. Remember Macbeth? The ghost of Banquo? What Caldwell saw was his own guilt, if you like. It was clearly eating away at him. You forced him to confront it and it overwhelmed him. He 'saw' a manifestation of his guilt, in the form of one of the women he murdered."

It sounded plausible. If you hadn't been there.

I fell asleep in the wagon-lit rocked by the steady click-clack and swaying of the train.

Hard light filtered through the blinds and warmed my sheets. I peeped out. The flat landscape of north France had been replaced by green hills and woods. Vineyards sprawled across the slopes. Rows of short black stubs were already filling out with new leaves, like markers on pauper's graves. It was such a thrilling contrast to the war-damaged streets of London that if the train had stopped or even slowed down enough I might have run off into the rolling hills and never gone home.

I washed and got dressed in time for the chug into Lyon. Another change of train took me onward into the south and to Avignon. But now the thought of the reception I might get was beginning to weigh on me. Major Cassells had become wonderfully pally once matters had been cleared up. He'd been in touch with the Resistance fighters in Avignon, he said. Telegrams had been flying and the old radio sets had been wheeled back out to give me safe passage. But they were a tough bunch, unforgiving, suspicious, and as likely to fight each other as the Germans. So it was anyone's guess how I'd be received.

It was mid-afternoon when I stood down from the train and stretched my limbs. My gammy leg was aching and swollen from so little exercise. I looked round the station. It was a different place from the one I left so unceremoniously, so recently. Yet it was hauntingly familiar. I was in fairly bad shape the last time I came through; only one eye working and strung between two German soldiers. The memory was lopsided and splintered, but I remembered the big clock with its gilded cherubim. And back then it was freezing. Or maybe I was. Today it was so warm that I took off my jacket and slung it over my arm.

"Captain McRae?"

I turned and peered into the sun, using my hat as a shield. The squat little figure was unmistakable especially in silhouette.

"Gregor? Is it you?"

He came closer and moved so the sun was on his side. I made out the huge black moustache that had always seemed too big for his moon face, but compensated for his sparse hair. He was grinning as though a giant wedge of Gouda had got stuck in his mouth.

"Hello, Daniel."

I dropped my jacket and suitcase and we embraced. As usual, he reeked of tobacco and sweat, but to me, today, it was Chanel No 5.

"You got the telegrams, Gregor?"

"Yes, Daniel. We got them. It settled a lot of things here, I can tell you. I never doubted you." He held my gaze and I believed him.

"I wouldn't have blamed you, Gregor. For a while there I even doubted myself."

He grinned and then he reached out and touched the scar. "Does it hurt?"

I shook my head. "Not any more. Not much."

"Bastards." Suddenly he was all action. He grabbed my case with one hand and my arm with the other. "Come, my friend, there are people waiting for you."

I hoped it wasn't a firing squad. Outside, in the station courtyard was a familiar sight.

"Still got the truck, Gregor. She looks magnificent!" And she did. The battered old vehicle gleamed in its newly painted coat of green. We hadn't cared much what she looked like on those midnight runs to collect a weapons drop.

Gregor swelled with pride. He'd coaxed it like a lover to perform even in the harshest conditions, trundling across muddy fields and down farm tracks where trees lashed the windscreen and the sides like flails. It fired first time – always a matter of honour to Gregor – and we revved off into the town.

I recognised the café in the centre, but I kept expecting German soldiers to be strolling past, flirting with the girls and humbling the men. Instead there were market stalls spilling over with early-season greens and people back at their sniffing of vegetables and haggling over prices and quality.

They were waiting for me inside. The sound of Gregor's truck is recognisable for miles. I counted six of them, before they hit me.

They hit me with hugs and kisses and a fuselage of warm words. I found I could tune in better to their more nasal, earthy French than their Parisian brethren, and once the first passions had died they spoke slowly enough for me to stay with it. The wine seemed to help, or maybe I stopped caring.

We talked long into the evening and drank too much and ate too much. They told me how they'd exploded in rebellion when the Normandy landings had begun, and how at first it had seemed they'd been too soon; the Germans had driven them into the hills. But there had been no reprisals this time, and soon a great Nazi convoy had formed and set off north to join up with their beleaguered battalions defending against the Allies.

That's when the plans we'd laid came into their own. The Maquis had hit them from every side. They'd blown up bridges and railway lines in front of their advance, eating up precious days. It was a well-known story now, but these men relived it for me over the wine and the cognac as though they'd just walked in from the last raid.

I wish I'd been there to lead them. I waited till the last of them had embraced me and gone off into the now quiet streets before sitting down over a cigarette and a coffee with Gregor. I was drunk but not so drunk that I couldn't make out the pain and bitterness in his eyes when I asked about Lili.

"She was a fine woman, Daniel."

"A fine soldier, you mean."

"That too."

We toasted her memory and I went to bed.

The morning was still warm but clouds scudded across the blue backcloth heralding rain. Gregor came for me at a decent hour after breakfast. I had him stop once in the market on our way. We drove up to the gates on the edge of town. Long lines of poplars swayed behind the low walls. We pushed the gates open and walked down the gravel path past the great slabs and the stone angels.

It was in a quiet corner of the grounds. The grass was neatly trimmed and a few more stones had been placed next to hers, with newer dates. Gregor left me alone and walked away and lit a cigarette.

I stood, trying to remember her as she was before I found her. Tried to find a way of seeing her smile. Tried to wipe the last image of horror from her young face.

I laid the flowers on her grave. Brave yellow daffodils. I stood and read the inscription.

To "Lili"
A soldier of France
Who died for her country
In memory of
Valerie le Brun
1920 – 1944

Rest in peace, Val. Rest in peace.